SHIVERED

Shivered

CAROL A CAMPBELL

~ 1 ~

J.H. PITT STOP

It was five o'clock in the evening, and a thin layer of snow covered the ground as Kyle Parks drove through Chattanooga, Tennessee, on his way to his next job in Atlanta, Georgia. Donald and Catrina McSpadden expected him to arrive today so that they could return home to Louisiana.

Donald's eighty-year-old mother could no longer live alone, so they hired Kyle to avoid placing her in a nursing home. They liked the fact that Kyle has thirty years of experience as a home care nurse.

Kyle would have been in Georgia four days earlier if Jennifer, his ex-wife, hadn't interfered. He left his last job in Vidor, Texas, and Kyle had no choice but to go to her house in Louisville, Kentucky. Jennifer knew how Kyle earned his living, which she took advantage of by extorting him every time he completed a job. This time, it cost him over two hundred thousand dollars. It was less than three weeks until Christmas, and she demanded that he deliver her share in person before the holidays.

The news predicted a heavy snowstorm for the area that evening that was threatening to delay Kyle even further, so he drove faster than usual and made very few stops so he could stay ahead of the storm. He changed his arrival date once before because of Jennifer, and he worried that the McSpaddens might find a replacement if he moved the date again. Kyle needed that job and felt confident he could complete it within a year. Kyle could always con a woman more easily than a man because the women always trusted and relied on him. He would flatter them and charm his way right into their hearts.

Kyle looked into the rearview mirror and smiled. "You may be fifty, but you've still got it," he stated with his southern twang as he ran his fingers through his dyed, thin, chocolate-brown hair from one side and combed it over the bald spot on the top of his head. "Kyle, you handsome old devil, look at those crystal blue eyes. That's why no woman can resist you." He winked and blew a kiss at himself in the mirror. "You sexy thing." He continued to gaze at himself when he noticed a new branching wrinkle in the outer corner of his eye. "That's impossible," Kyle said, rubbing his finger over the thin line. "I'm getting rid of you, you little devil, as soon as I get to Georgia."

A loud horn startled Kyle, and he quickly looked away from the mirror. His heart raced when he saw a blue eighteen-wheeler directly in front of him. He jerked the steering wheel towards the right and swerved back into his lane. His red Corvette slid side to side across the slick pavement until he finally regained control. The driver of the eighteen-wheeler blasted the horn as he drove past.

"Asshole!" Kyle angrily shouted. "It took two long years with that man to get this car. All the crap that I endured, I deserved everything that I got. Ain't that right, sweetie pie," he lovingly rubbed the top of the dashboard as he looked across the guardrail and down the mountainside's steep slope. Suddenly, the temperature plummeted, and the snow fell heavily. "Where in the hell am I?"

A sudden gust of wind caused the car to swerve out of the lane. He gripped the steering wheel tightly and reduced his speed to a crawl. "This can't be happening?" Kyle panicked as he stared out of the foggy windshield at the narrow road ahead that twisted up the mountain. An icy shiver ran down his spine. "Damn, it's freezing in here." He turned up the heat and nervously smacked his gum loudly. The heavy snow quickly blanketed the ground. Then, in the distance, a bright glow captured his attention. "Please, let that be a gas station." He muttered as he slowly drove towards it. Large, bold red letters appeared on the lighted sign: J.H. Pitt Stop. "What a stroke of luck," Kyle breathed a sigh of relief and quickly pulled up to the gas pumps. He hurriedly checked himself in the rearview mirror before getting out of the car. As Kyle rushed to the front door, he slipped on the icy sidewalk and scrambled to regain his footing. "What the hell!" He shouted as he combed his hair through his fingers back across his head.

Kyle opened the door, and a loud doorbell chimed to announce his arrival. The moment he walked in, he spotted two attractive young women behind the counter with big smiles on their faces. Kyle could tell by their expressions that they must have been watching him when he slid on the sidewalk. The burgundy-haired girl looked at him and whispered something to the blonde. Kyle grinned and self-consciously tugged at his oversized black Gucci hooded sweatshirt.

"Well, hello there, gorgeous ladies." Kyle smiled so big that his gum fell out of his mouth. His face turned bright red from embarrassment as he swiftly picked up the massive wad of gum off the floor and shoved it inside the large pocket of his hoodie. "I hope your day is going better than mine."

The two ladies roared with laughter and watched Kyle as he walked towards the back of the store. "Man, Kyle, you made an old fool of yourself." He muttered and shook his head. Metallic blue garland intertwined with twinkling white lights lined the cooler doors. "Bah, Humbug!" He flicked the decoration away from the door handle and got a frappuccino out of the cooler. As he headed back to the front, he grabbed a bag of almonds and stopped for a second to admire the silver-tinsel Christmas tree decorated in blue that stood at the end of the aisle. It reminded him of his childhood, and it looked exactly like the tree that his Mom would set up every year.

Kyle nervously cleared his throat as he approached the counter. "Well, dolls, let us try this again." Kyle embarrassedly chuckled. "Good evening, lovely ladies." He pointed at the two overstuffed stockings on the wall behind the cash register. "Someone must have been extra good this year." He raised his eyebrows as he read the blonde-haired lady's name tag. "Jamie Huse, so you're the owner?"

Jamie rolled her eyes and pointed towards the tag. "Well, that's what it says below my name, so I guess that makes me the owner." She elbowed the other lady, and they laughed.

Kyle's face once again turned red. "Yes, I can see that," he snapped and sat the two items on top of the counter. "What I meant to say is that I wasn't expecting someone as beautiful to own or to be working in this place as you two ladies are." He took a deep breath and anxiously tugged at his watch.

"So, what were you expecting? Maybe a dirty old man with a long, shaggy beard playing the banjo?" Jamie laughed.

"That would have been better," Kyle mumbled under his breath as he nervously rubbed his chin and lowered his head.

"Are you okay?" The burgundy-haired girl asked.

Kyle quickly looked up and read her name tag. "Sesailee Morris, no, I'm not." He frowned. "It's just that I had a dreadful week, and today is rapidly going downhill too. Then, to top it off, someone is expecting me, and I'm running late." Suddenly, a big, silly grin filled his face as he awkwardly winked. "But doll, it ain't over."

As Sesailee mimicked Kyle's grin, she turned towards Jamie and winked. Jamie giggled and winked back.

"I know that you're not from around here, with your fake orange tan," Jamie mumbled as she leaned across the counter and inspected him from head to toe. "What brought you to Tennessee?"

"I'm just passing through," Kyle anxiously said, looking at his watch again.

Jamie watched Kyle's odd behavior and became curious. "Why do you keep looking at your watch?"

"I guess it's a nervous habit," Kyle grumbled. "As I said before, it has been a horrible week, and this day is rapidly turning into a nightmare. I'm just very frustrated." Kyle quickly pulled the cuff of his shirt over the Rolex. "Plus, I had to run halfway across the United States because of a certain person. On top of that, I have another job waiting for me, and I'm late, very late."

"Well, I didn't ask you for your life's story," Jamie chuckled. "Judging by the way that you keep looking at your watch, it must be an important job," Jamie smirked.

"Oh, believe me, doll, it is," Kyle quickly remarked. "I'm sorry about rattling off about my troubles. I'm sure you two dolls have better things to do than listen to me."

Jamie looked through the window at the red Corvette. "Well, as you said before, doll," she replied, glancing at Kyle with a big, silly grin and winking. "Charlie, it ain't over."

"Charlie," Kyle shrieked. "Why did you call me Charlie?"

"Well, according to your Texas license plate, that's your name," Jamie stated smugly.

"What? No, my name is Kyle." He quickly glanced out of the window towards his car. "I forgot about that damn plate," he nervously muttered under his breath and looked back at Jamie. "Charlie is the guy I bought the car from."

Sesailee scanned the two items on the counter. "So, Kyle or Charlie, whatever your name is, what else can I get you today?"

"I need twenty dollars in gas." Kyle pulled his Gucci crocodile wallet from the back pocket of his skinny jeans and handed Sesailee a credit card.

"You must like name-brand products." Sesailee chuckled.

"Oh, gosh, yes. If it's not, I'm not wearing it." He smirked as he tapped his wallet on top of the counter. Then, out of the corner of his eye, he noticed Jamie as she leaned against the counter and stared at him. "Maybe you can help me, Jamie." Kyle's voice quivered as he looked into her deep blue eyes.

"Maybe," Jamie hissed, raising an eyebrow and looking at him suspiciously.

"I thought you said that your name is Kyle?" Sesailee held the card in front of his face. "Who is Charlie Hanks?"

Kyle quickly grabbed the card from Sesailee's hand and handed her a different one.

"Old Charlie must be a generous man to sell you a car and to give you his credit card." Jamie took the card from

Sesailee and looked at the name. "Kyle Parks, if that's really your name."

"Yes, that's me," Kyle nervously laughed. "Well, Charlie's my friend."

"An overly generous friend," retorted Jamie. "Maybe someone needs to give your friend Charlie a call." She watched for Kyle's reaction.

"You can call him if you want." Kyle smiled and remained calm.

Jamie seemed satisfied with Kyle's response and hesitantly nodded her head for Sesailee to proceed with the transaction as she handed the card back to her. "So, what did you need my help with?"

"Just outside of Chattanooga, I was traveling on the highway heading towards Atlanta. I took my eyes off the road for a minute, and the next thing I knew, I was on this two-lane road, twisting around this godforsaken mountain. Where in the hell am I?"

Jamie and Sesailee laughed.

"What's so funny?"

"I don't know what highway you were on, but you had to have your eyes off the road a lot longer than a minute to end up here." Jamie laughed.

"You are almost an hour away from any major highway." Sesailee placed the items in a white plastic bag and pushed it across the counter towards him.

"That's impossible," Kyle shrieked. "I swear, I just glanced in the rearview mirror for a second. Where am I?"

"You're in Shivered, Tennessee. Chattanooga is seventy miles away." Sesailee handed the card back to Kyle.

"What? How is that possible?" Kyle grabbed the card and nervously searched his hoodie pocket for his phone. "Oh, where did I leave the stupid thing?"

"It's impossible," Jamie firmly stated. "What are you looking for?"

"My phone. I must have left it in the car." He smiled and looked back at Jamie. "Do you have a phone that I can use? I need to call the couple in Atlanta, Donald and Catrina, and let them know that I'm going to be late."

Jamie and Sesailee roared with laughter once again.

"Yes, extremely late. You might be in Atlanta tomorrow night, but I doubt it." Jamie chuckled.

"What?" Kyle placed the credit card inside the wallet and quickly tucked it back into his pocket. He then reached into his hoodie and pulled out a red gumball. He picked up the bag and popped the gumball into his mouth. "Why would you say that?"

"Well, I would let you use my phone, but neither my landline nor my cell phone work. Every time there is a storm here, the service always goes out, so I could not contact Charlie, and, believe me, I wanted to. Furthermore, the weather is deteriorating, so it is unlikely that you will be able to proceed far, especially driving that." Jamie pointed towards Kyle's Corvette. "The good news is that if you continue on this road for about fifty miles, it will eventually lead you back to the highway. In the meantime, you should find a place to stay and get off the road. Approximately two miles from here is a newly renovated country inn where you are welcome to stay. The owner's name is Steve." She grabbed a business card from the side of the register and handed it to Kyle. "Strittmatter Inn is the name of the place. It is reasonably priced, and the food is excellent. My favorite author, Carol A. Campbell, is staying there."

"Oh, I heard of her. Isn't she the one who writes all those twisted ghost stories?" Kyle blew and popped a bubble.

"Yes, Jamie and I both enjoy all of her books." Sesailee smiled. "Kyle, don't worry. Jamie is just messing with you. The storm should only last through the night, and it will only take you three hours to be in Atlanta. So, you will be there tomorrow night."

"Oh, thank gosh." Kyle smacked his gum loudly and grabbed the card. "At least it's only for one night."

"One more thing, Kyle. There is a fork in the road about one mile away, and you need to be sure you stay to the right. Otherwise, you'll go farther up the mountain and not down." Sesailee smiled as she placed a green elf hat on top of her head that matched the color of her eyes.

"I'll definitely stay to the right." Kyle grinned as he leaned forward, resting his elbows on top of the counter while bracing his chin with his right hand. "I have a question, dolls. Seriously, how did you two good-looking babes ever end up in a place like this? This place is in the middle of nowhere."

"Just lucky, I guess." Sesailee turned towards Jamie and rolled her eyes.

"Well, you must be from a tiny town because I don't think I would consider being here as lucky." Kyle chuckled and felt irritated that they did not flirt back. "But to each their own."

"I wouldn't consider Houston as small," Jamie snapped. "You're lucky that we are here, so that makes you the lucky one. Otherwise, you would be lost somewhere up on the mountain."

"Whatever," Kyle stood back up and looked outside. "Jamie, you're right. The weather is deteriorating, and it is getting darker, so I should make my way to the Inn as soon as possible."

"Yes, you better," Jamie smirked. "I hope everything works out for you, Manther."

Kyle glared at Jamie and gave her a dirty look as he walked out the door. "A manther." Kyle turned around and looked toward the store when he got back to his car. "What the hell is a manther? Is that like a cougar? So, they think that I'm an old man who likes young girls." Jamie and Sesailee laughed while they stood behind the counter and stared at him through the window. "Well, I have news for those two. I have better things to do than chase after them." He lifted the nozzle from the gas pump and began pumping the gas. "Besides, I like my women old, with one foot in the grave, and rich, very rich." He opened the door and tossed the bag and the card into the car as he smugly looked at them. Jamie and Sesailee continued staring out the window and laughing, so he turned and faced the other way.

A red Lexus pulled up to the other side of the gas pumps. The driver's door flew open, and a gorgeous Black lady got out. She smiled at Kyle as she briskly walked by him and headed toward the store. "Well, hello, beautiful," Kyle muttered as he turned and watched her strut across the parking lot. She wore a red leather fitted jacket and had her black jeans tucked inside a pair of red knee-high boots that accented her curvy figure. He continued to stare at her as she went inside and walked up to the counter. The lady laughed and talked to Jamie and Sesailee for a few minutes before heading back to her car.

Kyle quickly moved to the other side of the pump. "Hey, beautiful, let me get that for you." He winked at her as he lifted the handle.

"Oh, okay," She said with a smile.

"What is a sexy woman like you doing in a place like this?" Kyle asked as he leaned against the car, admiring the large diamond necklace around the lady's neck.

"Just traveling through," the lady replied, blushing and giggling.

"Oh, doll. How rude." Kyle chuckled. "Let me introduce myself." He held his hand out in front of her. "My name is Kyle Parks."

"Brenda Menifee." She smiled as she shook Kyle's hand.

"You have a beautiful smile."

"Thank you."

"You said you were traveling, so where are you from?" Kyle heard a loud knocking noise in the distance and looked towards the store. Jamie and Sesailee had their lips pressed against the glass.

"I'm from Houston, Texas. I bought the land next to this gas station, and I'm opening up a restaurant." Brenda looked toward the store and laughed. "The restaurant's name will be Brenda's Red Rock Café."

"Oh, you're from Houston, too." Kyle's face turned red as Jamie and Sesailee continued to knock on the glass and blow kisses through the window. Finally, he rolled his eyes at them and turned back towards Brenda. "Do you know Jamie and Sesailee?"

"Yes. I've known Jamie since she was seven years old." Brenda grinned. "Jamie is the one that told me about this place."

"Do you think that this is a good place for a restaurant?" Kyle glanced at the massive twenty-foot-tall red rock along the roadside in front of the clearing next door.

"Oh, God, yes. A new Inn is right up the road, and his business is thriving. The construction of a new movie theater, five new retail stores, and many new homes has begun. We even have a sheriff, RD Blevins."

"I didn't know that," Kyle pointed towards the store. "I thought I was in the middle of nowhere by the way that Jamie and Sesailee talked."

"It does look like that here, but it quickly changes a mile down the road." Brenda giggled. "Five years ago, there was nothing here, no houses, no stores, only that big red boulder." Brenda pointed towards the rock and noticed Jamie and Sesailee at the window. "Those girls are so silly." She looked at Kyle and grinned. "You must be lost."

"Yes, very lost," Kyle grumbled. "I have a job waiting for me in Atlanta, and I hope I can make it in time."

"I'm going to Atlanta, too," Brenda replied enthusiastically. "We should be there by tomorrow night. This storm is only supposed to last until midnight. I plan on leaving Shivered around noon tomorrow, but you need to get off the road for the night because you will not make it far in that Corvette. Did Jamie and Sesailee tell you about Strittmatter Inn?"

"Yes, they did." Kyle smiled.

"That's where I'm going."

"Oh, really." Kyle's face lit up as he reattached the nozzle to the pump. "Me too, honey."

"Good." Brenda smiled. "See, our paths crossed for a reason."

"I believe that." Kyle chuckled. "I would love to visit you more and get to know you." Kyle grinned. "I love a smart, beautiful woman."

"I would love that." Brenda opened her car door and got inside. "Did they tell you about the fork in the road about a mile ahead?" She started the car and turned the heat on high. She rubbed her hands briskly together in front of the vent.

"Yes." Kyle rested his hand on top of the car door as he leaned inside. "Sesailee said to stay to the right because the left will take you farther up the mountain. Have you ever taken a left at the fork to see what's up there?"

"Oh, no," Brenda shrieked and grabbed Kyle's arm. "Don't go that way. Stay to the right."

"Don't worry, doll," Kyle replied, looking puzzled and curious by Brenda's reaction. "I'm definitely going right because I don't need any more surprises. They didn't make it seem that big of a deal, and I thought you might have been up there since you have been here before. But, judging by your reaction, I can tell that you haven't. Is there a reason that you reacted that way?"

Brenda released Kyle's arm, and a solemn look came over her face as she looked into his eyes. "I heard stories in town about people that went left at the fork and were never heard from again."

"What?" Kyle shrieked.

"It seems like someone turns up missing every year around the Christmas season. Just the thought of it gives me goosebumps." Brenda quickly crossed her arms in front of her.

"Really?" Kyle gasped. "Were they ever found?"

"No, they just disappeared. The roads are very twisted and dangerous. Most likely, the missing people perished after falling down the mountain's edge. That is one of the rumors. The other story is too ridiculous to repeat. The road is supposed to be closed off, but they move like turtles around here." Brenda shook her finger at Kyle. "So, you better stay to the right."

"Honey, don't worry about that," Kyle quickly agreed.

"We better leave because the weather is worsening," Brenda smiled. "I will be waiting for you at the Inn."

"Okay, doll, I'm looking forward to it." He waved at Brenda as she drove away. "I knew that my day was going to get better."

Kyle went to the other side of the gas pump and removed the nozzle from his car. He placed it back into the holder and glanced towards the store as he tightened the fuel cap, but no one was there. A bitter cold gust of wind pierced his body and chilled him to the bone. Kyle hurried to get his leather jacket from the back of the car. "Oh, come on," He angrily shouted, pushing the button repeatedly until the trunk popped open.

"What the hell is that?" A large cardboard box sat next to his suitcases. "This wasn't back here before." He pulled the box towards him and opened it. Wrapped in black tissue paper were over a dozen dolls. Their bodies were made of straw and colored burlap with a ribbon of a different color tied tightly around their waists. The same colored feathers as the burlap framed their clay-masked face. The red and black doll immediately caught his eye. As he held the doll in front of him, he noticed Charlie's name embroidered in large, red, bold letters across the doll's chest. Suddenly, excruciating pain filled his body. He looked away, and it stopped. Kyle immediately thought of Charlie's wife, Deniese. She had an entire wall of bookshelves inside her bedroom, full of scary-looking dolls from all over the world. Charlie always told him they were all evil and cursed.

"Oh, hell, no!" He threw the doll back inside the box and jerked it out of the trunk. He sat the box on top of the garbage can by the fuel pumps. "Well, hell, Deniese," Kyle chuckled. "Old Charlie boy, it looks like I'm not the only one who couldn't get along with you." Kyle grabbed his leather jacket from the trunk and quickly put it on. He glanced at the store and noticed that Jamie and Sesailee were back at the window. "Nosy," Kyle muttered, got into his car, and turned on the headlights. He pulled in front of the window, honked the horn, and blew a kiss at them. Jamie and Sesailee laughed. "Silly girls," Kyle chuckled. "Now, you can call me a manther."

~ 2 ~

CASSANDRA'S COUNTRY INN

Kyle thought about his last day with the Hanks as he pulled out of the driveway and drove past the massive rock. He spent most of the day fighting with Charlie. Deniese stayed in the kitchen and tried to avoid the bickering between the two. Kyle liked Deniese and got along with her because they shared similar likes and dislikes, but he had nothing in common with Charlie. The only time that Kyle and Charlie didn't argue was during movie time. At eight o'clock, Charlie and Deniese would watch a movie every night, and Kyle would make hot chocolate for them. It was always the same routine, and Kyle looked forward to his favorite time of the day. Kyle enjoyed some much-needed alone time and remained in the kitchen while Charlie draped a blue and white striped blanket across his legs in his favorite recliner, and Deniese rested on the couch with her head propped up on the feather pillow. They would watch the movie and eventually drift off to sleep. They looked peaceful and content that night when Kyle walked out of the door.

"I can't believe that I wasted two years of my life catering to you, Charlie. You always argued with me and put me down. Nothing was good enough or done right. Charlie's way is the right way. Otherwise, it is wrong," Kyle babbled as he searched for his phone. "Charlie, I have done a lot for you, but I don't think you appreciated anything I did."

Kyle finally found his phone buried under the passenger seat. He tried to call Donald and Catrina, but there was no signal. Looking through his text messages, he saw that Catrina had sent him one an hour ago. It read; *we will expect you to be here at six. Please do not be late, or you will give us no choice but to find someone else!*

"Damn it!" Kyle tossed the phone angrily onto the passenger seat. "Thank you, Jennifer. Because of you, I probably lost that job." Immediately, he picked up his phone once again and texted Catrina. *I'm stuck overnight in a town called Shivered, somewhere around the Georgia and Tennessee state line, because of a dreadful snowstorm. I promise I will be there tomorrow night. Please do not look for someone to replace me. I really need this job.* "Hopefully, she'll get my text when the service comes back on," Kyle huffed as he shoved the cell phone inside the front pocket of his hoodie.

The wind and snow intensified, and Kyle struggled to keep his car on the road. "Okay, the divide that Sesailee and Brenda told me about should be around here somewhere." A loud horn blasted behind him, and Kyle quickly looked in his rearview mirror. The bright lights blinded him at first, and then he realized it was the same blue eighteen-wheeler as earlier. "Where did he come from?" Kyle speeded up and tried to determine the driver's details, but the truck stayed right on his bumper. His car slid to the right, and he quickly slowed down to regain control. The truck's thunderous horn blasted again. "Okay, asshole," Kyle rolled down his window and motioned for the driver to go around, but the eighteen-wheeler continued to tailgate. "What the hell is wrong with him!" Kyle looked ahead and did not see any oncoming vehicles, so he slowly swerved his car toward the left into the other lane. The giant eighteen-wheeler drove up to the side of Kyle's car and stayed even with him, almost like he was trying to taunt him. "Is this guy crazy or what?" Kyle laid on his horn and reduced his speed even further.

The truck slowed down and stayed by the red Corvette's side. Then, suddenly, a large white Styrofoam cup flew out of the truck driver's side window and crashed against Kyle's windshield. When the cup broke, the liquid inside quickly transformed into an icy slush as it spread across the glass. Kyle turned the wipers at high speed and furiously laid on the horn. The driver of the truck honked back and speeded off.

"Damn, idiot! Wait until I get my hands on you!" Kyle got back into the right lane and chased after him.

The snow fell more heavily and made the driving conditions even more treacherous. The red Corvette began to fishtail across the road, causing Kyle to reduce his speed significantly. He watched the truck's taillights until they faded out of sight.

"Well, you got lucky, asshole," He shouted.

The windshield suddenly iced up and made it impossible to see the road. "What the hell?" Kyle stopped the car and turned up the defrost. He waited for a few seconds before he placed his hand over the vent. "Oh, that's just great. It's not working." He griped as he pushed the button off and on. "Piece of crap!" Kyle remembered the ice scraper he had bought in Kentucky in his trunk. When Kyle got out of his car, he noticed that a large tree blocked the road and hesitantly walked in front of his vehicle. "That wasn't there a second ago," He stood in the glare of his car's headlights and examined the snow for the eighteen-wheeler's tire tracks but could not find any. It was like the massive truck disappeared into thin air.

"That's impossible," he muttered, walking closer to the snow-covered tree. "I watched him go this way." Thick underbrush covered the ground that led to the forest on the other side of the fallen tree. "What the hell? Okay, I've had enough of this ghastly mountain." Kyle panicked and quickly headed towards his car. He decided he would go back to the store and stay there until morning. "Jamie, Sesailee, your dreams are coming true, girls. Your manther is coming back." He shivered as the icy wind cut right through his leather jacket. "At least it's a safe place, and it's obvious there's no Strittmatter Inn."

As he stood at the back of the car and opened the trunk, he noticed an old, post-mounted mailbox next to him. The rusted-out post leaned to the side next to a long tree-lined driveway. In the distance, he could see the welcoming glow of Christmas lights. "Maybe that's the place that the ladies talked about." He grabbed the ice scraper, closed the trunk, and walked quickly to the front of the car. "What in the hell happened to the ice?" Kyle shrieked. "How can it just disappear?" Kyle eagerly got into his car and felt the heat as it blew through the vents. "Oh, thank goodness! At least that can be explained, unlike that demonic eighteen-wheeler," Kyle mumbled as he tossed the scraper on the passenger floorboard and began to drive up the driveway.

A decorative post with a large white oval sign with *Cassandra's Country Inn* in purple letters protruded from the snow. "This isn't the place that they told me about." He muttered as a deep sense of uneasiness swept over him. But, as he approached the clearing from the thickly wooded tree-lined driveway, his concern quickly dissipated as he saw the beautiful old Victorian Inn.

Two large cedar trees with twinkling-colored lights, approximately thirty feet tall, stood on either side of the sidewalk. The white vintage Christmas lights draped around the windows, door, and roof illuminated the intricate white wood carvings that adorned the porch and windows of the three-story house. The Inn's beveled glass door emanated a warm glow and provided a sense of welcome. It reminded Kyle of a charming storybook house straight out of a fairy tale book.

"What a beautiful place," Kyle breathed a sigh of relief as he stopped the car and observed the snow-covered property. "Maybe getting lost wasn't such a bad thing, and I found a hidden gem."

A dense forest surrounded the entire clearing and secluded the magnificent Inn. Kyle noticed a small log cabin next to a pond by the edge of the woods. A bright light glowed through the frosted glass window. "That's an odd place for a building," Kyle muttered as he watched for any movement. Suddenly, a strange, eerie sensation of being watched came over him. He glanced towards the Inn but did not see anyone. "Get a grip on yourself, man," he nervously chuckled. Kyle looked back toward the log cabin, and his eyes widened with fear. A shadow of a person with an ax appeared in the frosted glass window.

Kyle's heart raced as he watched in horror as the ax swung up and down. The color quickly drained from his face when something splattered across the window. "What the hell is he doing?" Kyle nervously smacked his gum. "What is that? Is that blood?" He jumped when something abruptly hit the back of his car. He glanced in the rearview mirror, but again, he did not see anyone. Kyle quickly looked back at the log cabin, and the light was off. He stared anxiously into the window as he attempted to make sense of what he had just seen. "What is happening to me? There has to be a logical reason for all of this." Kyle took a deep breath as he continued to stare at the log cabin. After a few minutes, he looked at himself in the rearview mirror. "First, you don't know how you ended up here. Second, a psycho eighteen-wheeler appeared and disappeared into thin air. Now, an ax murderer. Do you know what your problem is, Kyle Parks? You're as nutty as some of your old patients. Get a damn grip on yourself."

Kyle followed the driveway to the parking area behind the Inn. He turned off the car and nervously looked around. "Man, relax. Look at this beautiful place." He inhaled deeply, held his breath for a count of three, and then slowly exhaled. "You got this, Kyle." He muttered to himself as he opened the car door and hurried to the trunk. Kyle grabbed his luggage and bolted to the front of the Inn.

Kyle opened the oval beveled glass door and stared in awe at the beauty of the magnificent room. An elegant white coffered ceiling with three ornate Corinthian columns divided the large room in half. An exquisite crystal chandelier that sparkled like a cluster of diamonds hung in the center of the front section. An antique walnut claw foot table sat directly beneath the chandelier, placed on a purple and gold mosaic rug. A U-shaped arrangement of three purple couches in front of a white fireplace and an oval gold-framed mirror above it adorned the back wall below the balcony. The left wall of the room had a chest of ten drawers with a lamp, and the right wall had a large wooden counter where guests could check in.

Fresh-cut pine garland hung from the banister and fireplace, and the aroma filled the room. A tall Christmas tree with bright white lights and gold decorations stood by the spindle staircase.

"Gorgeous." Kyle smacked his gum as he stood at the door with his luggage at his side.

"Hello!" A lady shouted from another room. "I'll be right with you."

Kyle walked up to the counter and dropped his luggage on the floor. He turned and leaned against the thick walnut edge of the counter as he slowly surveyed the room. *I bet that whoever owns this place has a lot of money.* He thought as he smacked his gum loudly. *That damn chandelier is worth some megabucks. Kyle, ole boy, this might be your lucky ticket.*

"Can I help you?" A lady asked in a soft voice from behind the counter.

Kyle turned around and could not believe his eyes. The lady was breathtakingly beautiful. She had long, silky, dark brunette hair, and her espresso-colored eyes looked sweet, luminous, and mysterious.

"Can I help you? Or are you going to stare at me for the rest of the evening?" She giggled.

"I'm sorry, honey." Kyle foolishly grinned. "I wasn't expecting someone as beautiful as you. You're gorgeous. Such beauty in your eyes. I wasn't sure if you were a beautiful angel or a sexy devil, but now that I'm close, I can see heaven in your eyes."

"Oh, my!" She giggled. "That's pouring it on a little thick, but thank you."

"My name is Kyle Parks."

"I'm Cassandra Cooper, the owner of this Inn, but you can call me Cassie."

"Oh, a beautiful name for a beautiful lady." Kyle winked.

Cassie blushed and smiled shyly.

"Well, Cassie, honey." Kyle leaned across the counter towards her. "I need a room for tonight only."

"Well, Kyle." Cassie raised her left eyebrow and looked into Kyle's eyes. "You realize that it's the holiday season and only seventeen days until Christmas? Right?"

"Yes, sweetie, I realize that, but I ended up here by mistake." Kyle looked away from Cassie and started fidgeting with his watch. "Honey, I'm supposed to be in Atlanta, Georgia, right now. I can't explain how I ended up here, doll. I guess I took a wrong turn or something, but I can't go back out there. Sweetheart, the roads are dangerous, and my Corvette won't make it."

"Don't worry, I won't throw you back out on the streets," Cassie smiled and patted the top of Kyle's hand. "Also, you don't need to pour it on that thick, honey, because that doesn't work on me."

Kyle foolishly smiled, and his face turned red.

"Regardless of what kind of car you have, because of the snowstorm, all the roads will be completely impassable, and you won't be able to leave tomorrow either." Cassie opened the guest book. "The snowstorm is going to be a bad one, and the roads will be closed for at least a couple of weeks."

"Are you kidding me?" Kyle shrieked. "The ladies at the gas station, Jamie, Sesailee, and Brenda, didn't act like this storm was that big of a deal. Sesailee and Brenda told me I should be in Atlanta by tomorrow. In fact, Brenda was going to meet up with me at the Inn, and she was going to Atlanta, too." He nervously ran his fingers through his hair and smacked his gum. "Well, come to think of it, they told me about Strittmatter Country Inn, and obviously, there's no Country Inn by that name, so maybe they didn't know what they were talking about after all."

"Well, there's no other Country Inn around here, only this one. I don't know what gas station or who Brenda, Jamie, or Sesailee are that told you that, but I do know that you're not going anywhere until after Christmas." Cassie laughed. "The storm is going to last more than a day."

"Oh, my goodness," Kyle muttered, nervously tugging at his watch. "I can't believe this."

"Well, it could be worse," Cassie remarked with a smirk.

"I don't see how!" Kyle looked at Cassie and shook his head. "I can't even begin to explain what a terrible week I had, and I'm still experiencing. So, please tell me, how could this day get even more nightmarish?"

"Well, it's possible that I don't have any rooms available."

"What?" Kyle quickly interrupted. "What am I supposed to do now, doll?" He sternly looked at Cassie and smacked his gum.

"Well, that would certainly turn your day into a complete disaster, wouldn't it?" Cassie laughed. "You need to relax and quit pulling at that watch band before you break it." Then, she quickly pointed towards his mouth. "And please stop smacking that gum. You're driving me insane."

"Oh, that's a nervous habit." Kyle pulled the sleeve of his jacket over the watch.

Cassie handed him a tissue paper for his gum. "Yes, I can see and hear that."

Kyle spat out his gum and wrapped it in the tissue paper. "So, doll face, please tell me that you were joking and you have a room for me," He stuck the wad of tissue inside of his pocket.

"Well, this is my grand opening, and all my guests are by special invitation only." Cassie opened a drawer and searched through a stack of papers. "See." She handed Kyle an invitation. "Every guest received one just like that."

Kyle opened the card and raised his eyebrows as he read it. "You're letting your guest stay free?"

"Yes, it was supposed to be for four days, but they're stuck here through Christmas, just like you." Cassie grabbed the invitation out of Kyle's hand and threw it back inside the drawer. "I bought this place over a year ago and had it completely renovated. Just like I hand-picked each of my guests, I picked out every object in here."

"Well, you have exquisite taste." Kyle grinned. "That chandelier must have cost a pretty penny."

"Oh, I wanted only the best, and besides, money is no object."

"Well, Cassie, honey, you're my type of woman." Kyle winked. "I love a beautiful woman with good taste."

"You're doing it again." Cassie giggled.

"Doing what?" Kyle grinned. "Oh, I'm sorry. It's just my Southern charm. It just oozes out."

"Yeah, I guess." Cassie rolled her eyes. "I wanted this place to look magnificent and to provide my guests with an unforgettable experience. So, I poured a lot of my time and money into this place."

"I think you achieved your goal." Kyle looked around. "The Inn is spectacular, but it is not a moneymaker, considering the road ends directly in front of it and all the other businesses are in town."

"I don't know what you're talking about because the road continues up the mountain," Cassie snapped, looking annoyed as she stared into Kyle's eyes and waited for his reply. "For your information, this place is a money-maker because I'm booked solid through next year."

Kyle didn't want to upset Cassie further, so he remained quiet.

Cassie looked away from Kyle and flipped through the pages of her guest book. "Well, you're in luck," she grinned. "Maria didn't show up, so I have one room available."

"Oh, thank the stars!" Kyle heaved a sigh of relief.

"Well, I hope you don't mind, but it's on the third floor, and it's the room across from mine."

"No, not at all." Kyle grinned. "As long as it's not inside that little log cabin by the woods."

Cassie ignored his comment and jotted his name down in the book. "Grab your bags and follow me."

Kyle stopped and stared at the Christmas tree as they walked through the lobby towards the stairs. Cassie looked at his chiseled, tanned face as it glowed from the twinkling lights on the tree. His crystal blue eyes had a distant, faraway look as they filled up with tears.

"Are you okay?" Cassie asked.

Kyle ignored her and continued to stare at the tree.

"What's wrong?" Cassie gently placed her hand on top of his shoulder.

"This tree brings back a lot of fond memories," Kyle grinned. "This may sound a little strange to you, but the gas station had a tree that looked exactly like the one my Mom had every year. It brought back all the joyful and worry-free days of my youth. My Mom was so beautiful, young, and had such an enthusiasm for life, but she became very bitter when she got sick." Kyle quickly sat his suitcase down and wiped the tears from his eyes. "This tree is identical to the one I had with my ex-wife. That's the last time I can genuinely say I was happy."

"What happened with your marriage?"

"I guess I was the only one that was happy." A small, wistful smile appeared on Kyle's face as he looked at Cassie. "She left me for an old boyfriend that she dated over twenty years ago when she was in college."

"I'm sorry." Cassie's face turned red. "I hate a cheater!" She angrily remarked as she picked up Kyle's bag from off the floor and handed it to him.

"Well, I still love her, and I guess I always will." Kyle glanced back at the tree. "I hated what she did, and I wish that things would have worked out differently for us." Kyle smiled at Cassie. "But there's no getting past the broken trust."

"No, I agree. Once a cheater, always a cheater." Cassie grinned. "Well, Kyle, she will get what she deserves one day because what goes around comes around. Karma can be a real bitch."

"I think she did." Kyle chuckled.

"Let me show you to your room because I have to get up early in the morning." Cassie tucked her long hair that framed her tawny, flawless face behind her ears. "Tomorrow will be a busy day."

They walked up the stairs, and Cassie stopped on the second floor. Beautiful dark-varnished doors lined the white-painted walls down the purple-carpeted hallway. Small crystal chandeliers that hung from the ceiling produced a collection of rainbows that sparkled across the gold numbers above each doorway and illuminated each room.

"All my guest bedrooms are on this floor," Cassie whispered. "Please be quiet when you pass through here because a couple of guests are extremely bitchy."

Kyle grinned, and they continued up the stairs to the third floor, which looked identical to the second. They followed the hallway until it ended. Cassie inserted a key into the lock and twisted it. The door opened, and Kyle stepped inside.

A beautiful, deep cherry king poster bed filled most of the room. A lavender-down comforter with a fluffy purple blanket tossed across the bottom made the bed look cozy. Nightstands with matching brass lamps sat on each side of the bed.

"Gorgeous," Kyle blurted out as he tossed his bags on top of the bed.

An elegant white marble fireplace adorned the wall at the foot of the bed. A deep, purple Queen Anne chair with a small footstool sat in the front of it.

"I love this room." Kyle quickly stood in front of the fireplace as he continued to look around the room.

An enormous window occupied most of the wall on one side of the room, while a large mirror and dresser occupied the opposite wall.

"I'm glad that you like it because all of the rooms are the same." Cassie smiled. "My room is right across the hall, and there's a bathroom located at each end of the hallway."

"Okay."

"I'll see you in the morning." Cassie smiled as she handed him the key.

"Okay, you have a pleasant night." Kyle grinned. "Thank you, Cassie."

"You're welcome." Cassie walked out of the room and closed the door.

Kyle pushed his bags off the bed and flopped down on top of the comforter. He glanced around the room and noticed that there was no phone or television.

"Oh, goodness. This place is like stepping back in time." Kyle pulled his phone out of his pocket and looked for a signal. He held it up in the air and walked to the window. "I can't believe that the towers are still down. How am I supposed to entertain myself with no phone or internet service?" He glanced out of the window and noticed that the light was back on in the log cabin. "Why is that light on again?" He remained motionless as he stared intently and watched for the crazed ax killer to appear in the window. Suddenly, the light was off, and Kyle's heart pounded wildly. He waited in anticipation for someone to leave, but no one exited the cabin. "Does someone live there?" He stood quietly at the window for a few minutes. "Okay, Kyle, that's enough. Mind your own business." He hurried to the dresser, laid down the phone, and quickly looked in the mirror. "It could be worse," he mumbled, running his finger over his eyebrow, making sure every hair was in place. "Jennifer was a fool for letting you go." He went to the bed and flopped down, pulling the neatly folded purple blanket from the foot of the bed over him. Kyle squirmed around until he found a comfortable position.

"Well, at least I'm in a safe place and out of the snow." He closed his eyes and thought about the last time he saw Jennifer. She always behaved in a friendly, flirtatious way until she didn't get what she wanted. Kyle tried to recall the last time he saw Tim, Jennifer's husband. "He was nowhere around for the last two trips that I took up there. Come to think of it, Jennifer hasn't spoken about him for months. Maybe they broke up, and that's why she hasn't been quite the bitch towards me as usual." He smiled as he thought about how she begged him to stay, but it was too late for any of it. "Damn, I wished that things would have worked out differently," He mumbled and gripped the blanket tightly. He tossed and turned for a few minutes before finally drifting off to sleep.

An hour had passed, and Kyle was fast asleep. A loud thunderous engine roared outside, and a bright light flashed off and on repeatedly through the window of his room. It continued for several minutes, but Kyle remained in a deep sleep. Finally, the lights went out, and the engine's loud sound gradually diminished as it drove away.

~ 3 ~

MEET THE GUESTS

"Where are you going?" A lady shrieked.

"What?" Kyle groaned as he fumbled around for the edge of the blanket. "What's going on?" He squinted his eyes and glanced around the room as he slowly sat up.

"Hold up! Wait for me," the lady shouted from the hallway. "I forgot my bracelet in the bathroom!"

"Shh," Kyle loudly hissed. "Keep your voice down! People are trying to sleep," Kyle angrily shouted.

"I don't know what people you're talking about, man! Everybody is downstairs! It's breakfast time, dude," the lady shouted from the other side of the door. "You snooze! You lose!"

Kyle looked at his watch. "Eight o'clock! I can't believe that it's morning."

"Wait for me!" The lady shouted again. "Oh well, go ahead and stay in bed, dude! That's just more food for me!" She laughed as she galloped away from the door.

"Geez," he moaned as he slowly got out of bed and looked out of the window. "Oh, lordy, look at all of that snow. Cassie was right. My car would never make it out of here, so I guess I'm not leaving today. How depressing." He frowned as he looked towards the log cabin. "I can't believe my luck. Out of all the rooms in this place! I have to get the one that looks out at that damn cabin." He angrily pulled the lacey curtain halfway across the window and stopped when he noticed the large tire tracks embedded through the snow. He followed the tracks from the front of the Inn. They circled in front of his window and back towards the front. "That's strange. That must have been a large truck to get through all of that snow."

"Oh, well." He yanked the curtain closed. "I might as well make the best out of this crap," He grumbled as he walked to the side of the bed. "Where's my luggage?" He glanced around the room and noticed his bags stacked neatly by the door. "Who did that? Somebody must have been in my room." Kyle hurried to the door and swung it open. He looked down the hallway, but no one was there. "Surely, big mouth, who was screaming at the top of her lungs in the hallway, is responsible for this." He tossed his bags on top of the bed and pulled out a change of clothes. "I'm going to get to the bottom of this. No one is going to sneak into my room, especially with me in it."

Kyle quickly changed his clothes and headed downstairs. As he reached the bottom step, he stopped and searched the lobby for Cassie. An attractive blonde sat in front of the fireplace and immediately caught his attention. He watched as she dipped a chocolate bar into a jar of peanut butter while she dreamily gazed into the fire.

Kyle always had a weakness for blondes. He froze as she turned towards him and smiled.

"Oh, damn," Kyle shrieked. "She looks just like Jennifer."

"Excuse me!" Someone shouted from behind him. "Move it or lose it, buddy! I don't have all day to stand here while you gawk at Jill."

Kyle nervously laughed as he watched the blonde giggle and turned back towards the fireplace. He recognized the voice from the hallway earlier and angrily turned around. He chuckled and felt amused as he looked down at the short, chubby, dark brown-haired lady on the step behind him. "Oh, I'm sorry." Kyle grinned as he moved to the side and out of her way.

The short lady frowned and stuck her hands on her hips. "Mr. comb-over, do you see anything funny?"

"What did you say?" Kyle responded angrily.

"The question I asked was, Mr. comb-over, do you see anything funny?" She shouted.

"No, not really," Kyle smirked. "It's just that you're so short."

"I would rather be short than try to look like something I'm not! You know what I mean, man. Your shiny head blinded me all the way down the stairs," she glared into his eyes. "Now, move out of my way!"

"What's your damn problem?" Kyle clenched his jaw and bent down towards her face.

Loud laughter suddenly filled the room. Kyle watched as the short lady's face turned red with anger. She wildly waved her finger in front of his eyes. Her mouth moved continuously, but he never heard a word because of the boisterous laughter that came from the other room. Then, suddenly, she pushed him off the bottom step and hurried past him.

What is her damn problem? Kyle thought and became aggravated as he watched her waddle away from him. Finally, Kyle could not stand it any longer. The loud laughter abruptly stopped right as he shouted, "Have a nice day, stubby! You sawed-off piece of crap!" Kyle stopped abruptly when the pretty blonde turned towards him and gasped. He nervously smiled at her, but she shook her head in dismay and turned back towards the fireplace.

He blushed with embarrassment and walked away from the stairs. Kyle stopped and looked into the quiet room. About a dozen women sat in the dining room and stared at him as he smiled sheepishly in the doorway. *Maybe I should apologize because who knows how long I am stuck here with them,* he quickly thought.

"Ladies, I'm sorry that I acted that way. I am usually easygoing. I don't know what came over me," Kyle stuttered as he looked into their bewildered faces.

A young lady with red hair stood up and shouted, "Hey man, it's okay! She is stubby!"

Laughter filled the room once again. Kyle breathed a sigh of relief and hurriedly went to the front of the lobby.

"Can I help you?" A blonde-haired lady with enormous light blue eyes asked from behind the counter.

Kyle grinned and combed his thin hair with his fingers across his head. "You sure can, doll. My name is Kyle Parks, and I must have died and gone to heaven with all these beautiful angels around me." He leaned against the counter. "You must be the gorgeous angel in charge."

The lady giggled. "That's a pleasant thing to hear early in the morning." She smiled. "I hope the rest of my day goes just as well. My name is Cindy Blevins. You must be the man that Cassie told me about that arrived last night."

"Yes, doll." Kyle winked. "That's me."

"Well, of course, it's you," Cindy giggled. "It's only one other man here, and that's Richard Hagan. He's the maintenance worker."

"Are you kidding me?" Kyle chuckled. "Only two men with all these lovely ladies?"

"Honestly, there is only one." Cindy grinned and winked at Kyle. "Rick's married."

"Oh, what a shame," Kyle chuckled. "Are you married, doll?"

"No. Are you?"

"Oh, no, honey," Kyle smirked. "I'm as free as a bird."

"Oh, look who it is," the lady shrieked from behind him. "It's the big bald eagle stalking his next prey that just happens to be another blonde."

Kyle recognized the voice and angrily turned towards her. "Are you trying to get under my last damn nerve, or what's your problem? Oh, by the way, I have another question for you. Were you sneaking around in my room this morning?" He raised his eyebrows as he glared at the short brunette lady and waited for her to answer. "Well! Are you going to answer me?" Kyle felt terrible when she started to cry. "Look," Kyle patted her on the back as she wiped away the huge tears that rolled down her chubby cheeks. "I'm sorry that I was rude, but you were also rude." Kyle bent down and looked into her large brown eyes. "Let us start over. My name is Kyle Parks."

The lady looked at him and pouted. "My name is Irma Rios, and no, I wasn't sneaking around inside of your room!"

"Is there a reason you keep making smart remarks to me?"

"No, not really," Irma snapped.

"Why all the remarks then?"

Irma blushed. "Maybe I am being rude to you because I find you attractive, dude."

"Oh, really, honey," Kyle grinned. "I think that you're cute too." He bent down, stuck his face in front of hers, and winked. "Comb-over and all, huh, doll?" Kyle whispered in her ear.

Irma burst into laughter. "Yes, you bald eagle. Bird legs, comb-over, flat butt, and all."

Kyle was stunned at her remarks and promptly stood back up.

"Okay, Irma. Look at poor Kyle's face. Behave yourself," Cindy snickered. "Quit picking on the guest."

"I'll try." Irma grabbed a handful of mints from the bowl on top of the counter and walked off.

"That little faker! There isn't one tear in her eye. She's something else," Kyle remarked as he watched her enter the dining room.

"You said a mouthful," Cindy laughed. I think she enjoys making you feel uncomfortable. Pay her no attention, and she will eventually stop. Is there anything that I can help you with?"

Kyle smiled and turned towards Cindy. "Well, sunshine, I was looking for Cassie."

"It's no telling where she's at because she's been running around here like a chicken with her head cut off." Cindy laughed. "I planned on leaving tomorrow, but this storm messed that up."

"I know what you mean, sweetheart," Kyle sighed. "I needed to be some other place myself."

"I'm here to help Cassie, and she's still trying to do everything on her own."

"Oh, you don't work here?"

"God, no," Cindy chuckled. "That's my sister, and I love her, but we would end up killing each other."

"Oh, my," Kyle shrieked. "That sounds a little drastic."

"Not really," Cindy laughed. "You don't know Cassie."

"Well, beautiful," Kyle leaned across the counter. "My room is located on the third floor, directly across the hall from Cassie's. Somebody broke into my room while I was sleeping," he said quietly.

"Oh, no," Cindy gasped. "What makes you think that?"

"This morning, when I woke up, I found my suitcases stacked by the door. Last night, I pushed them off the bed onto the floor, so someone entered my room while I was asleep and placed my luggage by the door."

"I bet that it was Cynthia," Cindy chuckled. "She probably thought that the room was still unoccupied."

"Who is Cynthia?"

"She's the housekeeper. Oh, look! There she is," Cindy waved at a petite blonde woman across the lobby.

"Gezz," Kyle chuckled. "How many blonde women are staying here?"

"Over half the guests since you mentioned it," Cindy laughed.

"Lucky me," Kyle muttered.

"Can I help you?" Cynthia asked as she walked up to the counter.

"This is Kyle Parks." Cindy waved her right hand towards Kyle. "He is staying on the third floor, and he wants to know if you were the one who went inside his room?"

"Yes, I'm so sorry, but I thought the room was vacant," Cynthia apologized. "I left as soon as I saw you." She smiled. "I went inside your room to grab an extra blanket for another guest. I tripped over your luggage, and that's when I noticed you. I didn't want you to do the same, so I stacked them by the door. I would never have gone inside the room if I knew you were there."

"That's okay, sugar," Kyle grinned.

"If you need anything, just ask." Cynthia held her hand out in front of Kyle. "My name is Cynthia Morrow. Once again, I apologize."

"It's okay, honey. Don't worry about it." Kyle gently shook her hand. "I had a weird day yesterday and am still slightly on edge about it."

"I'm sorry to hear that," Cynthia smiled.

"It's going to get better." Kyle winked.

"I hope so," Cynthia grinned. "If you need anything, let me know."

"She seems nice," Kyle commented as Cynthia walked away.

"She is. Well, we solved that mystery." Cindy chuckled.

"Since we're talking about mysteries, who lives in that tiny log cabin next to the forest?" Kyle leaned against the counter.

"What cabin?"

"The one on that side," Kyle pointed in the direction of the cabin. "Why? Is there another cabin on the property?"

"No," Cindy quickly remarked. "Nobody lives there. Why would you ask something like that?"

"Well, doll," Kyle chuckled. "The lights were on at different times, and I was just curious."

"I don't know why the lights would have been on because it's an old workshop, and it's been sitting empty for over a year. Besides, you know what they say about curiosity and the cat," Cindy laughed as she shook her finger at Kyle. "Well, enough about that. Would you like to join me in the dining room?" Cindy walked from behind the counter and stood by Kyle.

"That sounds good," Kyle rubbed his stomach. "Honey, I'm hungrier than a tick on a teddy bear."

"You're so silly," Cindy giggled.

Cindy pointed towards each item as they strolled towards the dining room and told Kyle the history behind each piece. Kyle smiled and nodded his head, but his eyes never left the blonde in front of the fireplace.

They finally reached the couch, and Kyle smiled at the blonde lady while she struggled to remove a broken piece of chocolate from inside the jar of peanut butter. She looked up at Cindy and Kyle and smiled.

"Excuse me, but I'm sorry about what happened earlier," Kyle apologized.

"It's okay," The lady smiled and stuck the chocolate piece inside her mouth.

"That's Jennifer, my ex-wife's favorite too." Kyle smiled. "My name is Kyle Parks."

"I'm Jill Ecker."

"Please forgive me if I keep staring at you, but you remind me a lot of Jennifer. Your looks, actions, and voice are identical," Kyle chuckled. "I met her when I was visiting a friend in Maine."

"Oh," Jill laughed. "That's where I am from."

"Really?" Kyle's eyes widened.

"Yes, that's unbelievable," Jill smiled at the surprised look on Kyle's face.

"Well, Jill, since we're stuck here for a while, I'll make you a treat one night," Kyle grinned. "A peanut butter, hot chocolate smoothie. That's the drink that made Jennifer fall in love with me." Kyle winked.

"Okay, Kyle," Jill giggled. "The smoothie sounds delicious."

Cindy grabbed Kyle by the hand. "Let's go, Romeo! I thought you were starving like a tick on a teddy bear, and Jill doesn't look like a teddy bear." Cindy laughed.

Kyle blushed and foolishly giggled. "It was nice meeting you, Jill."

"You too," Jill smiled. "Enjoy your meal."

Suddenly, someone grabbed Cindy from behind.

"Hey, Cindy," The lady shouted as she walked around Kyle and looked at him up and down. "Dang!" She grinned and stood in front of the couch. "Is he your boyfriend?"

"Hey, girl. No, he's not my boyfriend. He's a guest," Cindy smiled. "I'm sorry about last night. They ought to be ashamed of themselves for how they acted."

"It's cool," She chuckled. "Irma, Loretta, and Jill came down and chilled for a couple of hours. We ended up having a blast."

"That's good." Cindy put her hand on Kyle's shoulder. "This is Kyle Parks. He arrived last night."

"Hello, Kyle, my name is Shannon Wright," she said as she sat down next to Jill. "Don't forget about tonight!"

"Oh, what's happening tonight?" Kyle asked.

"It's bingo night, but I want to sing some Christmas songs, too, if I can find a couple of people to participate."

Shannon chuckled. "Most of the guests went to bed at seven last night."

"Every night, we have something on the agenda. Last night was caroling. That is why everybody hid inside their rooms except Shannon and Callie," Cindy laughed.

"Don't worry about that," Kyle grinned. "I love to sing." Kyle cleared his throat as he took Shannon by the hand and began to sing. "*My heart melts when I look into those big eyes of blue. Beneath the moon and stars, I only love you.*" He stopped and winked. "What do you think, doll?"

"I'm speechless!" Shannon gazed in awe at Kyle. "Did you write that song?"

"Yes, I did. I wrote it for my ex-wife, Jennifer, for our fifth anniversary." Kyle looked at Jill and winked.

"That was beautiful," Jill quickly placed her peanut butter jar on her lap and clapped her hands. "Bravo!"

"Thank you, lovely ladies." Kyle bowed towards them.

"I think we might have a one-man show," Cindy giggled.

"My thoughts exactly," Shannon stated with a grin.

"I can't wait until tonight," Cindy grabbed Kyle by the arm. "Not only do we have one hot singer, but we also have hot chocolate. Lavivian makes the finest cookies and hot chocolate on the planet."

"What the hell?" Kyle muttered.

"What?" Cindy asked.

"Oh, nothing." Kyle nervously replied. "I'm not a big fan of hot chocolate."

"Oh, you will be," Cassie quickly remarked from behind Kyle, startling him.

"You scared me," Kyle patted his chest.

"You scared me," Cassie laughed. "I've been looking all over the place for you."

"He's been down here with me." Cindy patted Kyle on the back. "He met Irma."

"Oh, no," Cassie pouted. "She wasn't too rough on you, was she?"

"Well, it wasn't a pleasant experience," Kyle smirked.

"I'm sorry," Cassie grabbed Kyle's hand. "Did you have breakfast yet?"

"No," Kyle replied.

"Good, I'll go with you," Cassie smiled.

Cassie wrapped her arm around Kyle's left arm, and Cindy did the same with the right. Kyle could not help but smile as he strutted inside the dining room between two beautiful women clutched onto his arms.

Four oblong tables were evenly placed in the center of the rectangular dining room, each surrounded by six white padded chairs. A white tablecloth covered each table with a large artificial lavender rose bouquet in the middle of each one.

"Did Stubby finally leave you alone?" The red-haired lady with big blue-green eyes asked at the first table.

"Yes, honey, she did." Kyle grinned. "Thank my lucky stars."

"Irma does that to everybody that she likes. But honestly, I think she just likes to argue." She laughed. "My name is Candace Woodruff. My Mom, Cynthia, works here."

"Oh, I met her earlier." Kyle smiled. "She seems like a very nice lady."

She pointed across the table at a blonde-haired lady with green eyes. "This is my aunt, Patricia Noack."

"Well, beauty certainly runs in the family." Kyle smiled. "Thank you, Candace, for saving me earlier. I felt so embarrassed when everyone stopped laughing."

"Oh, they weren't laughing at you." Candace chuckled. "They were laughing at me."

"Candace was telling us a crazy story about the time that she visited New York." Patricia laughed. "You just shouted at Irma at the end of her story."

"Yes, no need to feel embarrassed about it." Candace smiled. "Everybody laughed at your comment because everyone in this room had a run-in with Irma."

"That's the truth," Cassie blurted out.

"Well, enjoy your breakfast, Kyle." Patricia smiled. "We will see you tonight at bingo."

"Yes, I'll see you lovely ladies tonight." Kyle winked.

They walked by the following table, and Kyle glared at Irma, but she never took her eyes off her plate. She sat alone at the end of the table with a massive plate of food in front of her.

They went to the last table and sat down. A lady with long blonde hair and light brown eyes looked up from her magazine.

"Good morning, Loretta." Cindy sat down and scooted her chair closer to the table.

"Good morning." Loretta smiled. "Well, we have a new guest."

"Hello, beautiful. My name is Kyle Parks." He reached across the table and held out his hand.

"My name is Loretta Cobb." She placed the magazine on the table in front of her and shook his hand.

Kyle noticed the dated cover, and it reminded him of when he was a teenager. "Where on earth did you ever find that old magazine?"

Loretta looked down with a puzzled look on her face. "It's not old. It just came out last week."

"Oh, I love it when they do a story about someone famous in the past. I had a poster of her hanging in my room until I moved out of my parent's house." Kyle laughed.

"You say some of the silliest things that I have ever heard." Cindy laughed.

He leaned forward across the table and tried to get a better look at the cover.

Loretta yanked the magazine off the table and placed it on her lap. "Once I have completed it, you may have it."

Loud laughter suddenly filled the dining room, and Kyle turned around. He watched as the noisy, giggling group of women sat down at the second table with Irma.

"Cassie, is this all of your guests?" Kyle asked.

"Yes, eighteen people are staying here. That includes five staff, me, and you." Cassie looked around the room. "I think you met most of them." She scowled at the women at the second table. "You will meet the rest tonight."

A lady placed a rolled-up cloth napkin with silverware in front of them and filled the coffee cups as she made her way around the table. She had her long chestnut-colored hair piled up on top of her head.

"Thank you, gorgeous." Kyle smiled. "What's for breakfast this morning?"

"Ham and cheese omelets, hash browns, and toast," she replied.

"Kyle, this is Cindy Etta Hagan, Rick's wife." Cindy poured some sweet cream into her coffee and sat the small silver pitcher in front of Kyle. "We call her Cindy Etta to avoid any confusion."

"Don't let her kid you," Cassie laughed. "The only one that gets confused is my sister."

"Hey," Cindy chuckled.

"Nice to meet you, Cindy Etta." As Kyle grinned, leaning toward Cindy, he patted her hand and whispered, "Someone was stuck on the letter C, and I can't blame them since they are so beautiful."

Cindy nudged Kyle's arm, blushing as she giggled.

"Cindy Etta and her mother-in-law, Lavivian, work in the kitchen. They prepare all the delicious food that you will enjoy during your visit with us. Cindy's husband, Rick, is the maintenance man." Cassie buttered a croissant and handed it to Kyle as she gave him a dirty look. "They owned an Inn on Virginia Beach, so they are knowledgeable about this business. They taught me everything. I couldn't have done it without them. I couldn't find a cook or someone to work maintenance in time for the grand opening, so they agreed to stay until I can find some people to replace them." Cassie smiled at Cindy Etta. "I know they are eager to get back to Indiana, so hopefully, I can find their replacement soon."

"We don't mind. I'm glad that you called me." Cindy Etta smiled, grabbed the empty silver pitcher from the table, and sat it on her tray. "I'll be back shortly with your breakfast." She smiled. "It was nice meeting you, Kyle."

"You too, honey," Kyle winked.

As they sat at the table, he looked around the room again. *How did I get this lucky?* He thought as he sipped on his coffee.

Loretta and Kyle laughed at Cassie and Cindy as they argued and picked on each other. They enjoyed their breakfast and the rest of the afternoon together. He felt drawn to Cassie, and he knew she felt the same about him. What Kyle first considered as bad luck now looked as though it might be the best thing that happened to him in a very long time.

$$\sim 4 \sim$$

BINGO NIGHT

Kyle was surprised at how quickly the day had passed and could not wait to spend the evening with Cassie and meet the rest of the guests. He hurriedly unpacked his bags and neatly placed his clothes inside the dresser.

He felt excited as he pulled his black Dolce & Gabbana hoodie over his head and admired himself in the mirror. "You sexy thing," Kyle smirked. He drenched himself with one of his expensive colognes and straightened his watch.

As Kyle combed his hair, he thought of all the beautiful women he had met earlier, but he could not get Jill and Cassie out of his mind. Jill looked identical to his ex-wife, Jennifer, when they first met years ago. Even though she betrayed him, he still deeply loved Jennifer.

Cassie was different from any woman that he had met before. She carried herself like a goddess, and a sense of mystery surrounded her. He loved how she spoke her mind, but he could tell that behind the sassy attitude. It was as if something from her past still haunted her.

Cassie changed the subject and avoided all the personal questions that he had asked earlier. In fact, she replied only to two questions: that she had been previously married and that she came from Ohio. *Her ex-husband must have really hurt her badly, just like Jennifer did me. Maybe that is why we have a strong connection. Plus, she's gorgeous.* He thought as he gazed at himself in the mirror.

"Now, don't be giving your heart away, stud," he winked at himself as he checked that every hair was perfectly in place. Then, he grabbed a handful of gumballs out of the side pocket of his suitcase. He suddenly remembered how much the gum and fidgeting with his watch irritated Cassie. "I guess I need to find a new habit." Kyle chuckled as he dropped them back into the suitcase. He removed his watch from his wrist and placed it on the dresser.

"Kyle!" Someone shouted from outside the door. "Are you ready to go downstairs?"

Kyle rushed and swung open the door. His big, bright smile quickly faded as he looked down at Irma. "Oh," he huffed. "It's you."

"Well, hell yes, it's me," Irma snarled. "What did you expect, your fairy godmother?"

"A damn troll would have been an improvement," Kyle mumbled as he stepped out of his room and closed the door.

"Well, I'm sorry, Mr. Dork Gabbana," Irma laughed as Kyle locked the door. "You're such a weirdo! Why do you have so many strange names printed on your hoodies?" she asked, heading down the hallway.

Kyle quickly caught up with her and grabbed her by the arm. "Are you kidding me?" he shrieked. "It's a famous name brand, and this hoodie cost me almost a thousand dollars."

"For that?" Irma laughed.

"Yes, for this," Kyle retorted.

Irma grabbed her shirt above her stomach and pulled it away from her body. "This shirt cost me nine dollars and ninety-nine cents. So, not only are you a dork, but you're stupid too," Irma laughed and hurried down the stairs.

Kyle chased after her as they argued the entire way.

"Okay! Okay!" Irma panted as she hung onto the handrail at the bottom of the staircase. "I give up. You win."

Kyle laughed and patted Irma on the back. "You better."

As Kyle looked across the lobby, his laughter suddenly stopped. Cassie and a man stood at the counter, huddled together. Kyle watched intently as Cassie gently rubbed her hand in a circular motion in the center of the tall, muscular build man's back. His short, groomed, salt-and-pepper hair and beard glistened against his tanned skin.

"What's wrong with you?" Irma shouted and looked across the lobby.

"Nothing," Kyle snapped.

"What are you staring at?" Irma shouted again. "Are you looking at Cassie?"

"Shut up," Kyle yelled.

Cassie quickly turned and looked at Kyle and Irma. "Kyle!" She shouted and waved. "Come here."

"Somebody is jealous! Somebody is jealous!" Irma chanted and skipped towards the dining room.

"Shut up, you fool," Kyle's face turned red as he glanced at Cassie, but her full attention was back on the other man. Kyle hurried towards them and cleared his throat as he approached, "I'm sorry about Irma."

"Oh, don't worry about that," Cassie turned around and smiled. "Kyle, this is Rick, Cindy Etta's husband."

"Oh," Kyle heaved a sigh of relief. "How are you doing?"

"Could be better." Rick smiled. "Well, Kyle, I heard a lot about you."

"All good, I hope." Kyle grinned.

"So far," Rick grabbed a book from off the counter. "Well, Cassie, I will talk to you later. Think about what I said."

"I will." Cassie looked worried as she watched Rick walk away.

"What's wrong?" Kyle asked.

"He wants to leave," Cassie grumbled.

"Why?"

"He wants to return to Indiana." Cassie shook her head. "I can't believe this crap."

"It will be okay." Kyle grinned. "I could replace Rick."

"I thought about this and told him he could leave as long as Cindy Etta stayed. He said that his wife and Mom, Lavivian, are leaving with him." Cassie angrily vented. "I offered Cindy Etta the job, not him or his mother. It's just like Cynthia. I offered her a job, and the next thing you know, she invited her sister and daughter to stay here." She chuckled. "Even my own sister showed up, and I haven't seen her in years."

"Why should that matter?" Kyle could tell Cassie wasn't telling him the whole story. He gently took her by the hand. "You needed the help, and thanks to Cynthia, Cindy, and Cindy Etta, you have extra guests to brag about their experiences at your Inn." Kyle patted her hand. "Take me, for instance. I wasn't planning on staying here, and I had never heard of Shivered, but now I have a nice place to visit again and tell my friends about."

Cassie looked at Kyle and grinned. "Not only are you handsome, but you're smart, too."

"I like to think so," Kyle winked. "If Rick wants to leave, let him. I can fill in for him. I'll even help out in the kitchen."

"What? Can you cook?" Cassie looked surprised.

"Can I," Kyle chuckled. "You will want to slap your mama after eating my gumbo."

"Well, I guess that problem is solved." Cassie laughed. "Besides, I don't know what I'm worried about because he can't leave because of the snow."

"That's true," Kyle agreed. "He is stuck here like the rest of us unless he drives that big old blue eighteen-wheeler."

Suddenly, someone pounded the piano keys, and a Christmas carol echoed throughout the room. Cassie's face tightened as she quickly covered her ears. Kyle chuckled at Cassie's reaction.

"They're just having fun." Kyle grinned.

"I know, but I'm not in the mood for that tonight." Cassie grabbed Kyle's hand, pulled him behind her, and hurried towards the piano. "Ladies! Ladies! It's bingo time!" She yelled as she waved her hands up in the air. "Let's go to the dining room so we can get started."

"Well, shucks," Shannon pouted, quickly banging on the piano keys. "We'll try this again after bingo, Callie."

"Sounds like a plan," Callie grinned.

"Maybe we can get Kyle to join us." Shannon smiled.

"I would love to," Kyle winked at Shannon and Callie as they walked away.

"Geez," Cassie rolled her eyes. "Come on, Kyle." Cassie grabbed Kyle's hand. "I'll introduce you to the rest of the guests."

They went into the dining room and stopped at the first table. A beautiful older lady with flaming red hair and green eyes caught Kyle's attention first.

"Ladies, this is our new guest, Kyle Parks." Cassie looked at the redhead and scowled. "He's stuck with us, so behave yourselves."

Kyle held out his hand in front of the redhead. "What's your name, doll?"

"My name is Pat Thompson." She reached up and shook his hand.

"You're stunning." Kyle grinned. "You look like a movie actress."

"Well, thank you, kind sir," Pat blushed.

"Oh, you got that right. Pat is quite the actress." The blonde lady laughed and slapped Pat on the back. "I'm Cathy Vedder, but you can call me Cat."

"Okay, Cat," Kyle noticed the woman next to Pat had a bright green plastic frog on the table in front of her. She had dirty blonde wavy hair, hazel eyes, a jade frog necklace, and an emerald frog pinned on her dark green sweater. "Sweetie, you must love frogs or green," he chuckled. "What's your name?"

"I'm LaDonna Koehne, and I love both. Green and frogs," she smiled and pointed at the plastic frog on the table. "This is Lucky."

Pat snatched Lucky off the table and stood up. "Let's see if Lucky works." She held the plastic frog in front of her. "Okay, Lucky, when I kiss you, you need to turn into a prince."

Everyone laughed out loud.

Pat kissed Lucky on the top of the head. "Well, girls, look," she pointed at Kyle. "Look who Lucky brought me. It's Kyle."

LaDonna laughed and grabbed the frog away from Pat. "He really does work." She sat the frog back in front of her on the table and patted his head. "He's for luck, not love."

Kyle laughed and looked at the brown-haired lady next to LaDonna. "What's your name, beautiful?"

"I'm Brenda Hutton," she smiled.

"You have the prettiest hazel eyes, honey." Kyle winked. "Do you like frogs too?"

"Nope, she's into fishes," LaDonna chuckled. "She loves to fish."

"Me too." Kyle leaned on the back of Cathy's chair. "Where are you ladies from?"

"We're all from Texas." Brenda pointed across the room. "Shannon is from Michigan. Jill is from Maine. Cindy and Cassie are from Ohio. Rick, Cindy Etta, and Lavivian are from Indiana. Everybody else is from Texas."

"Well, I'm from Texas, too," Kyle grinned.

"Brenda, what are you? An Atlas or just nosey?" LaDonna laughed.

"You ladies are funny," Kyle chuckled and looked around for an empty chair.

Cassie grabbed Kyle's arm and pulled him away from the table. "Let's go."

Kyle quickly looked back and shouted. "I'll talk to you, beautiful ladies, later!"

They all laughed at Kyle's silly expression as Cassie dragged him past Cynthia, Patricia, and Candace, who were seated at the following table.

"Come back, my prince," Pat shouted above the laughter.

"Oh, look, Loretta," Irma shouted from the third table. "It's Mister Doofus that spends too much money for someone else's name on his shirt."

Loretta, Shannon, Jill, and Cassie laughed as Kyle passed by and gave Irma a dirty look.

"You can sit up here between Cindy and me," Cassie pulled out her chair and waited for Kyle to sit down first. "Rick is going to be the bingo caller." Cassie sat down next to the large metal bingo cage.

"Hi, Kyle," Cindy placed a couple of bingo cards in front of him.

"Oh, just one card, honey." Kyle laughed and held up one of the cards. "I can only do one thing at a time."

"Are you sure?" Cindy grinned.

"Okay, Cindy," Cassie huffed and quickly grabbed the card away from Kyle and sat it in front of her. "Let's not turn this into something dirty."

"I wasn't," Cindy snapped.

"Yeah, right," Cassie rolled her eyes.

"No, I really wasn't," Cindy laughed as she patted Kyle's hand. "Cassie bought a lot of prizes for tonight's bingo game, so Kyle, you might want to play two cards."

"No, honey, one is fine." Kyle winked as he leaned towards Cindy and whispered. "For the record, doll, you can talk dirty to me any time."

Cindy blushed as she giggled.

Rick and his wife, Cindy Etta, walked up to the table. Rick stood behind the bingo cage, and Cindy Etta sat down next to him.

"Are you ready, Cassie?" Rick asked.

"Yes, I can't wait," Cassie sarcastically remarked, rolling her eyes.

Rick cleared his throat as he grabbed the microphone and pulled it towards him. "Okay, Ladies. Who's going to be the big winner tonight?"

"Me!" All the ladies shouted.

"Let the games begin," Rick turned the handle on the bingo cage, and everyone cheered. "B Thirteen!" As Rick continued to announce numbers, someone finally shouted.

"B-i-n-g-o!" Pat Thompson yelled. "I won! I can't believe I won the first game."

Cindy Etta went to the table and checked Pat's bingo card. "She's a winner," she shouted, handing her a large decorative basket filled with candies, fruits, and nuts.

"Okay, Ladies," Rick announced. "Are you ready for game two?"

"Yes!" All the ladies shouted.

The games continued for a couple of hours, and Kyle became noticeably quiet.

As Cindy leaned toward Kyle, she kept her eyes firmly fixed on her bingo cards. "I'm sorry that you haven't won a game yet, but I hope you're enjoying yourself." She waited for a reply, but he did not respond. Finally, she looked at him, and he was sound asleep. "Kyle, wake up," she laughed and nudged him on the side with her elbow.

"What?" Kyle opened his eyes and had a startled expression on his face.

"Those are my thoughts exactly," Cassie laughed. "I would rather be in bed sleeping than playing this crap."

The lights flickered, and a cold chill suddenly shot through Kyle. He nervously turned around and looked behind him.

"Are you okay?" Cindy asked. "What are you looking for?"

"What happened to the heat?" Kyle's voice quivered as he wrapped his arms in front of him.

"Nothing happened to the heat," Cassie replied quickly. "Why? Are you cold?"

"I'm freezing," Kyle looked at Cassie in disbelief. "Did you feel that blast of cold air?"

"No," Cassie remarked.

Rick glared at Kyle and gave him a dirty look.

"I can't believe that you're not cold," Kyle looked at Cindy. "Sunshine, is it chilly in here to you?"

"It feels perfect in here to me," Cindy remarked as she gently laid the back of her hand on Kyle's forehead. "You feel warm. Touch his face, Cassie."

"Shhh," Rick sternly looked at Cindy and Kyle as he covered the microphone. "Do you mind? Who cares if Kyle is cold or hot? We are trying to finish this game."

"I'm sorry," Cindy whispered in Rick's direction.

Cassie laid her hand on Kyle's cheek and leaned toward him. "Are you okay?" She whispered.

The lights flickered again, and the ladies started to panic.

"Please, everyone, remain calm," Rick waved his hand in the air and motioned for everyone to remain seated. "The storm is causing the lights to flicker, so it's nothing to get all worked up over."

Suddenly, the room went completely black.

"No," someone cried.

"Who was that?" Cassie shouted. "What's wrong?"

"It's me," Irma shouted. "I had one number left before I had a bingo."

"That's why the damn lights went out," Shannon shouted as the room erupted in laughter.

"I will try to find some candles, so please remain seated at your tables," Cassie shouted above the noise as she stood up. "I'll be right back. Cindy, keep an eye on Kyle." She held her hands in front of her and felt her way blindly through the room.

Cindy reached for Kyle's hand. "Are you okay?"

"Not really," Kyle's voice trembled. "I'm freezing."

"Yes, your hand is like ice," Cindy softly replied.

"What?" Kyle panicked and quickly rubbed both of his hands across his chest. "Cindy, that's not my hand!"

"No, it's mine," A voice roared in his ear. "I know what you did, and I'm going to make sure the same thing happens to you!"

"What do you mean that's not your hand, silly," Cindy chuckled as the hand slipped from her tight grasp.

"Charlie?" Kyle shouted. "Charlie, is that you?" He screamed as he stood up and looked around into the darkness.

"Kyle," Cindy quickly grabbed him by the arm. "What's wrong?"

Suddenly, the lights came back on, and all the ladies looked frightened as they stared at Kyle.

"I know that was Charlie," He muttered as his heart raced, frantically glancing around the room.

"Kyle," Cindy stood up. "Are you okay?"

"Where did he go?" Kyle looked nervously around the room.

"Who are you looking for?" Cindy asked.

"I'm looking for Charlie," Kyle snapped.

Cassie walked back into the room and noticed all the terrified faces on the ladies. "What's going on? Why does everyone appear as if they have just seen a ghost?" Cassie laughed. "It was just a blown fuse." She went back to the table and stood by Kyle. "Is anybody going to tell me what happened, and what the hell is everybody looking at?"

"I don't really know," Cindy looked at Kyle. "He started screaming something about Charlie. I grabbed his hand, and it felt like ice."

Cassie grabbed Kyle's hand. "What the hell is wrong with you people?" She tossed Kyle's hand away from her. "Kyle's hand feels warm to me, and please, will somebody say something."

"I think old Wimpy is scared of the dark," Irma shouted.

"He started freaking out," Pat imitated Kyle, and everybody laughed. "He acted just like that."

"Kyle, are you okay?" Cassie patted him on the back.

"Yes, I guess," Kyle's face turned red as he looked around the room. "I'm sorry about that, ladies."

"Who is Charlie?" Cindy asked.

"That was my old patient in Texas," Kyle replied.

"Patient? Are you a doctor? I can't believe that you're a doctor and you didn't tell me," Cassie excitedly chattered.

"No, I'm a home healthcare nurse, and Charlie was my patient," Kyle said, placing his hands over his face and shaking his head. "I don't know why I heard his voice."

"You're a nurse," Cassie chuckled. "The voice you heard must have been Rick's because it could not have been Charlie's since he lives in Texas. But, of course, this place is old. So, it may have been a ghost."

"Cassie! Don't tell him that," Cindy scolded. "He was scared."

"He was a little too scared if you ask me," Rick glared at Kyle intensely.

"He screamed like a girl," Irma laughed. "Old freaky deaky himself."

"That's not funny," Cindy grabbed Kyle's hand. "Oh! Your hand is warm now."

"I'm alright, Cindy," Kyle grinned. "Thank you for your concern, doll. I don't know what came over me." He looked at the ladies. "My apologies for my behavior."

"Okay, the show is over. Please return to your seats. Let's get the game started again," Rick grabbed the microphone. "We still have the grand prize to giveaway."

Everyone cheered as Rick cranked the handle on the bingo machine. Kyle held his head down, stared at his bingo card, and pretended to listen for the numbers, but he could not get that voice out of his head. Kyle knew that it was Charlie, but how could that be possible? Kyle thought about the last two years he spent with the Hanks and all of Charlie's threats. Kyle remembered one night in particular when Charlie grabbed him around his neck and threatened that if anything would ever happen to Deniese, he would track Kyle down and kill him.

"B-i-n-g-o!" Someone shouted and startled Kyle.

Cassie looked up. "Pat, you won again?" She laughed. "I think someone is cheating."

Everyone but Kyle gathered around Pat Thompson's table to see what was inside the large prize box.

"Oh my God," Pat shouted. "A fondue maker and a lava lamp."

"Who in the hell would get excited for that?" Kyle snickered as he watched Pat jump up and down. "Evidently, only that damn fool."

Cindy and Cassie returned to the table and sat down.

"Did you see the lava lamp, Kyle?" Cindy asked.

"Yeah, it was nice," Kyle looked away and rolled his eyes.

"It was nice, silly," Cindy laughed.

"Everyone, please take your seats," Cassie shouted. "It's time for hot chocolate and cookies."

"There she is," Irma squealed with excitement. "My favorite person and the best cook in the world, Lavivian." She pointed towards the kitchen door.

Kyle looked towards the door, and his jaw dropped. "Mama?" he stuttered.

A beautiful, petite, gray-haired lady walked into the room. She held a tray of cookies and hot chocolate in her hands. Except for Kyle, everyone in the room cheered. Her first stop was Cassie's table.

"Everything looks delicious," Cassie licked her lips. "This is my favorite time of day."

Lavivian sat the tray down on the table in front of Cassie. Her blue eyes twinkled as she smiled at Kyle.

"Lavivian, this is Kyle," Cindy patted Kyle on the arm and noticed the expression on his face. "What's wrong, Kyle?"

Kyle never replied.

"Have you seen another ghost again, or are you okay?" Cassie smirked.

"Mama?" Kyle's voice trembled.

"Mama," Cassie laughed heartily. "That's Rick's Mom, not yours."

"I'm Lavivian, honey, but you can call me Mama. I don't mind," she giggled and placed a cup of hot chocolate in front of him.

Kyle stared at the cup piled high with marshmallows, chocolate syrup, sprinkles, and a peppermint stick protruding from the top of the cup in disbelief.

"What's wrong, Kyle?" Cindy asked.

"My Mom made it the same way when I was a little boy," Kyle slowly pulled out the peppermint stick from the cup and looked up at Lavivian.

"Drink up, you stupid boy! We don't have all night!" Lavivian pushed the cup towards him.

"What did you say?" Kyle looked startled as he tossed the peppermint stick back into the cup and pushed it away from him.

"What's wrong?" Lavivian asked. "I can make you something else if you do not like hot chocolate."

"No, I don't want anything," Kyle looked at her. "Why did you call me a stupid boy and say we don't have all night?"

"What?" Lavivian became flustered and picked up the tray. "I don't know what you're talking about because I didn't say that."

"I heard you," Kyle snapped.

"No, I said to drink up, and I hope you like it," Lavivian looked confused.

"Mom," Rick abruptly interrupted as he walked up behind her. "Don't worry about him." He smiled at his Mom. "Go give the other guests their cocoa."

"Okay," she looked puzzled as she looked at Kyle and walked away.

Rick bent down over the table and looked sternly into Kyle's face. "Don't ever let me catch you talking to my Mom like that again. You understand."

"Yeah, man," Kyle nervously answered.

"Yeah, I thought you would," Rick stood up and followed his Mom.

"Why did you do that?" Cassie looked bewildered.

"Apparently, I misunderstood her," Kyle murmured nervously as Rick and Lavivian walked across the room.

"She told you exactly what she said, for you to drink up, and I hope you like it," Cassie pointed towards Lavivian. "Now, look at what you did. You got her all upset," she turned towards Kyle. "What got into you anyway? We had a nice, fun day, and you turn into something else tonight. You are seeing and hearing things that do not exist. What's wrong with you?"

"I am not feeling well," Kyle lowered his head. "I'll apologize to Lavivian in the morning. I think I will call it a night and go to my room."

"That's probably a good idea," Cassie scoffed.

"Yes, Kyle," Cindy softly smiled. "You look a little pale."

Kyle scooted his chair away from the table. "Okay, dolls, I will see you in the morning." He leaned over and hugged Cindy. "Thank you."

"Any time, Kyle," Cindy looked at him and smiled. "I hope you feel better in the morning."

"Me too," Kyle winked as he stood up. He turned towards Cassie and patted her on the back. "I'm sorry for ruining bingo night."

"Well, I hope you feel better." Cassie never looked at him. Instead, she took a big bite of her cookie and stirred her hot chocolate with the peppermint stick that protruded from the thick marshmallow topping.

Kyle hurried out of the dining room and headed towards his room. He went inside and flopped down on the chair in front of the fireplace. He just got comfortable when someone knocked on his door.

"Kyle!" A lady shouted.

Kyle did not answer.

"Kyle, it's me, Jill. Are you okay?"

Kyle remained quiet. After softly tapping on the door once more, she walked away.

"I can't believe that Jill came to my room, and I was too damn embarrassed to answer the door," he muttered as he got up and started a fire in the fireplace. He sat back down on the chair and propped his feet on top of the footstool. *What the hell is going on?* Kyle thought as he stared into the fire. *The Christmas tree at the store looked identical to the tree at my Mom's house. Then here, at the Inn, the tree looks the same as when I was married to Jennifer. Jill looks like Jennifer. Lavivian looks like my Mom. I know that was Charlie's voice. Why?* His thoughts were quickly interrupted by a loud beep.

"Is that my phone?" In a flash, Kyle jumped from the chair and grabbed his phone from the dresser. It showed one missed call. "Jennifer? How is that possible? How did that call come through without a signal?" Kyle tried to call back, but it was unsuccessful. Hurriedly, he moved around the room and searched for a signal.

"Maybe if I stand in front of the window." As he pulled back the lacey curtain, Kyle held his phone in the air and moved it in front of the glass. "Damn it," Kyle yelled. "Nothing!"

From outside, a bright light flashed in his eyes. He looked down angrily and froze in fear. In the snow, parked in front of his window, was the same blue eighteen-wheeler that terrorized him the day before. A tall, muscular man emerged from the truck wearing a red and black buffalo-patterned shirt. A short gray beard protruded from the brim of a black baseball cap that covered his face. The man stood in front of the bright headlights and looked up at Kyle. The lights glared against the back of the man's muscular body, making it impossible for Kyle to make out any details of his face. Kyle's heart wildly pounded as he stared at the tall figure. The man pulled an ax out from behind him and held it by his side. Kyle screamed and dropped his phone as he jumped backward away from the window. He quickly ran back to the chair in front of the fireplace and sat down. He brought his knees to his chest and wrapped his trembling arms around his legs as he stared into the bright light that radiated through the glass and filled the room.

"Why is this happening to me?" Kyle cried.

A few minutes later, as the truck drove away, the glow of the fireplace filled the room once again. Kyle stared at the window in fear and remained seated in the chair, unable to move.

~ 5 ~

DECEMBER 10

Knock-knock-knock!

"Huh, what?" Kyle quickly opened his eyes and glanced out the window. The gravel-gray sky was a welcome sight to his eyes. "Oh, thank goodness," he groaned in pain as he stretched his legs towards the floor. "I can't believe I slept in this uncomfortable chair all night."

Knock-knock-knock!

Kyle tried to stand, but he fell back into the chair. "Hold on," he grumbled. "I'm coming!" He held onto the arms of the chair and stood up slowly. He glanced around the room for his phone and noticed it on the floor by the lacey curtain. As Kyle slowly approached the window, he could hear the screeching winds of the dreadful storm outside. "What on earth?" Kyle muttered and hesitantly looked through the glass. He searched for the blue eighteen-wheeler, but the strong wind laden with blowing snow made it impossible to see anything.

Knock-knock-knock!

"I said hold on," Kyle angrily shouted as he picked up the phone off the floor and checked for a signal. "Crap! Please, somebody, anybody, please call me." He placed the phone next to his watch on the dresser and looked in the mirror. *Maybe that's Jill again.* He thought and quickly combed his hair. Then, he hurriedly sprayed on some cologne and rushed to the door.

"I'm sorry that it took me so long," Kyle's big smile quickly faded as he opened the door. "Oh, it's you," he rudely remarked.

"Didn't we have this same conversation yesterday?" Irma chuckled and waved her hands towards his face. "Poof! Your fairy godmother is here." She pushed Kyle aside and walked into his room. "So, what took you so long to answer the door?"

"Hey, who said that I wanted you in my room?" Kyle shouted.

Irma ignored him and stood in front of the fireplace.

"Well, I guess you just go wherever you want," Kyle grumbled. "It took me so long to open the door because I was busy, and if I knew it was you, I wouldn't have opened it. Besides, I thought you were someone else."

"Really? Who? Jill or Cassie?" She went to the door and poked her head out. "Oh, wait," she shouted as she looked down the hallway. "I do not see any of them." She chuckled as she returned inside and sat in the chair in front of the fireplace. "So, be happy that you got me, and besides, beggars can't be choosers."

"Why did you say Jill or Cassie?"

"Well, hell, I'm not blind," Irma laughed. "I've been watching you."

"Irma, I'm not in a good mood this morning, and you're making it worse," Kyle leaned against the opened door and motioned for Irma to get out.

"You're always in a bad mood, so what's new," Irma laughed. "Well, I noticed that you haven't slept in your bed and have the same clothes on as you did yesterday. Why is that?"

Kyle shut the door and sat down on the edge of the bed. "Since it doesn't look like you're leaving any time soon," he smirked, "I have a question for you."

"What?"

"Did you ever see a blue eighteen-wheeler?"

"All the time," Irma laughed.

"Really," Kyle looked shocked. "I can't believe it."

"I dated a man that drove a blue eighteen-wheeler about five years ago," Irma boasted.

"No," Kyle angrily shouted. "Did you ever see one here? At the Inn?"

"No," Irma snapped. "Why?"

"A truck tried to run me off the road on the way here, and the same truck was parked outside of my window last night."

"For real?" Irma gasped. "What happened?"

"He flashed his lights until I came to the window. Then he climbed out and stood in front of the truck with an ax."

"What?" Irma shrieked.

"Yes, doll. He just stood there and stared at me. I was so scared that I thought I would have a heart attack. I couldn't get a good look at him, but his beard and muscular build reminded me of Rick. He wore a black baseball cap, and the large brim hid his face." Kyle clenched his fist against the bed. "I wished I could have gotten a better look, but the lights from the truck were too bright." Kyle tapped his chest with his hand. "I know in my heart that it was Rick."

"No, it couldn't be Rick, but it does remind me of John. He acted like a nut and always wore a black cap," Irma laughed.

"Who is John?"

"That's the guy I dated that drove a blue eighteen-wheeler."

"That's impossible," Kyle chuckled. "Why would he show up here?"

"Oh, hell," Irma shrieked. "Do you think that he might be stalking me?"

"Stalking you?" Kyle burst into laughter. "Are you serious? Now that's funny."

"What is so damn funny about that?" Irma snapped. "John was mad when I broke up with him."

"Why did you break up with him?"

"I found out that John was married, and he also had a bunch of girlfriends." Irma's eyes sparkled as she looked at her silver bracelet. "He gave me this, and it meant the world to me at the time." She tugged at her bracelet, and a slight smile appeared on her face as she read the words engraved across the top of the silver bar. "My Honeybee." She looked teary-eyed at Kyle. "We had some good times. I miss him."

"I know what you mean," Kyle grinned. "It is sometimes difficult to let someone go, regardless of how bad the circumstances were."

"It sure is," Irma smiled. "I wear this bracelet every day to remind myself of the pain that he caused me and never to let someone take advantage of me again."

"Well, they say that every experience in life serves a purpose." Kyle watched as Irma rubbed her finger softly across the silver bar on the bracelet. "Irma, doll, I'm sorry that I laughed at you."

"That's okay, Kyle." Irma smiled. "Well, change your clothes, and let's go downstairs for breakfast."

"That sounds good." Kyle grabbed some clothes from the dresser. "I'll be right back."

Ten minutes later, Kyle returned to his room and saw Irma staring out the window.

"Oh no! Is he out there again? What does he want from me?" Kyle babbled as he stood motionless at the door.

"What? Calm down, man," Irma chuckled and pointed, pressing her finger against the glass. "I can barely make it out, but is that a house?"

"Yes, it's a little cabin. Why?" Kyle rushed to the window and stood next to Irma. "What's going on?"

"Nothing, dude," Irma laughed. "I could barely see it through all the snow that's falling. I didn't know Cassie had another house on this property." She looked at Kyle as he nervously combed his fingers through his hair. "You need to calm down, man."

"I know that I need to calm down, but to tell you the truth, Irma, I'm scared."

"There's nothing to be scared of," Irma softly stated, patting Kyle on the back. "I'm sure it's just someone picking on you because I haven't seen or heard anything, and believe me, I would be able to detect any strange energies."

Kyle immediately tried to think of all the people he crossed over the years, and it was too many to count. "You might be right about that one." He nervously smiled at her.

"Well, let's go downstairs." Irma grinned as she rubbed her belly. "I'm starving."

"Okay, doll."

Kyle closed and locked the door behind him as they exited the room. When they reached the bottom of the stairs, they knew something must have happened. Cassie and Cathy were in front of the fireplace, and Cathy seemed upset.

"I wonder what's wrong?" Irma tugged at Kyle's hoodie as she rushed past him.

"It's no telling in this place," Kyle muttered to himself and hurried to catch up with Irma.

"I'm sure that Pat is fine." Cassie smiled and hugged Cathy as Irma and Kyle joined them.

"What happened?" Kyle asked.

"Cat said that she went to Pat's room, and Pat wasn't there," Cassie replied.

"Where could she be?" Cathy asked.

"I'm sure she's around here somewhere," Cassie said, looking into Cathy's eyes.

"I hope so," Cathy replied bleakly.

"Well, she can't go too far in all this snow." Irma patted Cathy on her back. "Don't worry. She'll show up."

"Well, I have a few things to take care of before everyone gets up and moving. Kyle, will you keep Cat company for a while?" Cassie asked.

"Yes, Cat, go sit down in front of the fireplace, and I'll be there in a second." Kyle smiled.

"I'll keep an eye out for Pat," Cassie quickly remarked as Cathy walked away.

"Do you think that she will be okay?" Kyle watched Cathy as she sat down on one of the purple sofas. "She seems to be extremely upset."

"She'll be fine. She's a nervous type of person anyway. If anybody can cheer her up, it's you. Thank you, Kyle," Cassie said with a smile. "This shouldn't take too long. I'll be right back."

Cassie hurried off, and Kyle joined Cathy on the couch. Irma sat on the large white brick hearth of the fireplace and stared nervously at the Christmas tree.

"Don't worry, Cat," Kyle reassured her. "As Irma said, Pat couldn't have gone far. She will show up."

"I doubt it," Cathy bleakly replied.

"Why would you say something like that?" Kyle asked.

"Pat is a creature of habit. She is up at six every morning, showering and getting ready for the day. By seven o'clock, she's either reading the newspaper or writing yesterday's events in her diary. Pat is the only true friend that I have left since my husband Frosty died." Cathy lowered her head. "Frosty and I had a few problems about a year ago because I had an affair. Pat and I were dating the same man, and that is how I met Pat. She helped me get my marriage back together. A few months later, Frosty died from a heart attack."

"Oh, my goodness, girl," Kyle wiped the tears from his eyes with his sleeve and grasped Cathy's hand. "I can't believe he died. Isn't that sad, Irma?" He waited for Irma to respond. "What do you think, Irma?" He quickly turned and looked at her, but she looked deep in thought as she stared at the Christmas tree. "Irma," he shouted.

Irma jumped. "What?"

"Did you hear a single word that Cat said?" Kyle turned and looked at the Christmas tree. "What are you looking at?"

"Nothing," Irma snapped back. "Yes, I heard her."

Kyle rolled his eyes and looked back at Cathy. "I'm sorry about your husband."

A soft smile appeared on Cathy's face. "I'm just glad that we were able to put our differences behind us, and we were happy before he died."

"Yes," Kyle said, gripping Cathy's hand even more tightly. "Don't worry about Pat. Maybe she decided to take a walk and change up her morning routine." He smiled. "She's around here somewhere."

"I hope that you're right," Cathy replied in a soft voice.

Something flashed from outside through the window. Kyle quickly looked towards the oval glass door across the lobby.

"What's wrong?" Cathy asked.

"I'll be right back." Kyle hurried to the door and looked out of the window. In front of the Inn, he saw a person in a red jacket by one of the tall cedar trees. "Cat! Come look," he shouted.

Cathy ran to the door and looked out of the window. "What?"

"That must be Pat over there," Kyle shouted excitedly and pointed.

"Where?" Cathy held her face closer to the window as she tried to look outside. "I can't see anything." She turned towards Kyle and looked sternly into his eyes. "It is extremely windy and snowing heavily, which makes seeing anything impossible. What kind of sick joke are you trying to play on me?"

"What?" Kyle shrieked. "You can't see that person with a red cap and jacket walking by the cedar tree?"

"What's going on?" Cassie asked as she approached Cathy and Kyle.

Kyle pointed out the window and looked at Cassie. "Do you see anybody by the tree?"

Cassie looked out and chuckled. "I can't see anything."

Kyle quickly looked again, and the person was gone.

"I don't think that was funny, Kyle," Cathy scowled at him. "I'm going to my room. But, Cassie, if Pat shows up, please let me know?"

"Of course I will." Cassie grinned and watched Cathy as she stormed off towards the stairs. "Well, you just made a new friend," she laughed.

"I swear I saw someone," Kyle muttered as he looked out the window again.

"I don't think that anybody in their right mind would even try to go out there. Besides, you can't see five feet in front of you. There's no way that you saw anyone by the tree because you can't even see the tree," Cassie pulled Kyle away from the window. "Well, I guess you're stuck with me the rest of the day, Mr. Popular." Cassie wrapped her arm around his. "We have buttermilk waffles this morning, so let's go eat."

"Okay." Kyle glanced towards the fireplace for Irma, but she wasn't there. "I wonder where Irma went?"

"I'm sure she is working on someone's nerve wherever she is," Cassie muttered.

Cassie kept Kyle busy the rest of the morning and afternoon around the Inn. They talked about their childhoods and realized they had a lot in common. Kyle spoke about Jennifer, but Cassie kept her past relationship private and changed the subject every time Kyle asked.

"Well, the day went by quickly. Don't you think so, Kyle?" Cassie grabbed her key from out of her pocket as they exited the top of the stairs.

"Very much so," Kyle replied, patting Cassie on the back. "I really enjoyed it."

"I'll see you in a little bit." Cassie smiled as they stood at Kyle's door. "Thank you for helping me with everything today. I enjoyed your company." She went to her room across the hallway and opened the door. "I'm starting to like you a lot," she giggled.

Kyle blushed, saying, "I like you too."

"Stay away from the window. I don't want you to see the lady in red again." Cassie laughed as she shut the door.

"She's never going to let me live that one down," he muttered, feeling a little sheepish as he quickly went inside his room. He rushed to the mirror and smiled at himself. "She likes me," he cheered as he looked down at his phone. "Oh no," he shouted. "A missed call from Catrina McSpadden." He tried to call her back, but again, there was no signal. Frantically, he rushed to the window and waved the phone up in the air. "Please! Please," he pleaded. Kyle tried for a few minutes and finally gave up.

He started to walk away when he noticed a large black bag directly below his window in the snow. "What is that?" Kyle tried to examine the bag when it suddenly disappeared in front of his eyes. "What the hell is going on around here?"

"Kyle, are you ready?" Cassie shouted from the hallway outside of the door.

Kyle placed his phone back on top of the dresser and opened the door. "I'll be ready in a second."

Cassie stood by the door and watched Kyle briskly comb his hair.

"Cassie, what's the story behind that old log cabin?" He reached for his watch, but it was gone.

"What?" Cassie asked as she went to the window and looked out. "Why would you ask about that old place?"

"Well, I noticed a light on in the cabin a couple of times."

Cassie turned towards him but did not respond.

"Do you see the big black bag?" He grunted as he kneeled in front of the dresser and looked underneath.

"What bag?" She watched as Kyle frantically dug through the dresser drawers. "What are you looking for?"

"My watch is missing." He rushed to the window, but everything was cloudy and blurry due to the heavy snowfall.

"The weather is getting worse," Cassie remarked as she raised her eyebrows and watched his strange behavior.

"Oh, my goodness," Kyle shrieked. "You can't see anything."

Cassie looked at him and laughed. "That's what I told you earlier." Cassie walked towards the door. "What bag?"

What the hell is happening? One minute, I can see clearly outside, and it's not snowing, and the next minute, it's snowing so hard that I can't see anything. I can't tell her about the weather or the bag because she already thinks I'm nuts. Kyle thought as he turned towards her with a big silly grin on his face. "Oh, I thought I brought a black bag with me, but I must have left it behind."

"Geez," Cassie laughed. "Come on, and let's go downstairs. You can look for your watch later."

My watch was on my dresser this morning when Irma was here. He thought as he followed Cassie to the door.

"Are you going to be okay this evening?" Cassie asked as she closed the door. "I hope we don't have any more episodes like last night."

"No, I'm okay, doll."

"I hope so," Cassie quickly remarked.

They went downstairs and into the dining room. Kyle smiled at all the ladies as he walked by. Finally, they sat down at the last table with Loretta and Cindy.

"Good evening, beautiful ladies." Kyle smiled as he gently pushed Cassie's chair closer to the table for her and sat down.

Cindy and Loretta giggled.

Kyle noticed Cathy and Pat were absent as he glanced around the room. "Where's Cat?" he asked. "Did anyone talk to her? What happened to Pat?"

"Cat is up in her room," Cindy replied. "I think that Pat is with her."

"Oh, that's good," Kyle breathed a sigh of relief. "I was worried about her. She was pretty angry with me today."

"Yes, we all heard about the woman in red," Loretta laughed as she watched Kyle blush with embarrassment.

Cindy Etta walked up to the table. She sat a pitcher of iced tea and a basket of yeast rolls in front of Cassie. Her green eyes glowed as she glared at Kyle and gave him a dirty look. "I'll be back in a second with your steak and baked potatoes, ladies." She rolled her eyes and walked away.

"What's wrong with her?" Kyle whispered to Cassie.

"I can't believe you have to ask me that," Cassie muttered, looking into Kyle's eyes. "She didn't like how you spoke to Lavivian last night."

"I'll apologize to Lavivian when I see her." Kyle looked up and nervously grinned when he saw Rick, instead of Cindy Etta, holding the food tray. "Good evening, Rick," he stuttered.

"Here's your food, ladies." Rick gently sat the plates in front of Cassie, Cindy, and Loretta. "Enjoy." He held Kyle's plate ten inches above the table in front of Kyle and dropped it. Everything fell off the potato, and the plate was a mess. "Oops," he smirked, sticking the tray under his arm and walking away.

"He loves you," Loretta chuckled.

"I can see that," Kyle huffed as he placed the topping back on top of the baked potato.

They finished dinner, and everyone gathered for hot chocolate and cookies in front of the fireplace. Kyle sat on the couch next to Cassie. He smiled when he saw Jill and patted the sofa excitedly for her to sit next to him. *How sweet is it going to be to sit in the middle of Cassie and Jill,* he thought as he grinned foolishly at Jill. Suddenly, pain shot up his arm as someone pounced on top of his hand.

"Ouch," he yelled and turned his head away from Jill. "Irma!" He yanked his hand out from underneath her. "I should have known it was you."

"Sorry, Jill, but I'm sitting here," Irma snapped, laughing as she watched Jill walk away.

"You're a real jerk," Kyle lashed out. "You know that I wanted her to sit by me."

"Too bad," Irma sighed, wrinkling up her face and wiping both eyes with her fists. "You little cry baby."

"Okay, will you two stop your stupid arguing," Cassie scolded. "I swear."

"Well, let's play a game," Shannon shouted.

"Let's play truth or dare," Irma quickly replied.

"Oh, damn," Kyle chuckled. "What is this? Grade school. I haven't played that since I was twelve years old."

"I want to go first," Irma shouted and turned towards Kyle. "Truth or dare?"

"Are you kidding me?" Kyle shook his head in disbelief.

"Truth or dare?" Irma raised her voice and looked at Kyle sternly.

"Okay, truth," Kyle grumbled.

"Who do you like more? Jill or Cassie?" Irma giggled.

"I like both the same," Kyle replied with a smug look on his face. "Okay, LaDonna. Truth or Dare?"

"Dare," LaDonna chuckled.

"Make a funny face and keep making it for two minutes while the game continues."

"That's easy," LaDonna crossed her eyes, and everyone laughed. "Brenda, truth or dare?"

"Dare," Brenda giggled as she looked at LaDonna's crossed eyes.

"Drag your butt on the floor like a dog from one end of the room to the other."

Brenda scooted across the floor, and everyone laughed. Everybody kept the game silly and fun. Lavivian came out with the hot chocolate, and Kyle asked for a cup of coffee instead. He apologized to Lavivian, Cindy Etta, and Rick for how he acted last night. Lavivian and Cindy Etta accepted Kyle's apology, but Rick did not. After a couple of hours, the game became more serious and personal.

"Cynthia, what is the one secret you haven't told many people?" Patricia asked.

"I'm scared of the dark," Cynthia sighed. "Shannon, truth or dare?"

The lights started to flicker.

"Oh, no," Shannon grumbled. "Not this again. Truth."

"If you had to walk through a pitch-black forest, who would you want to take with you? Kyle or Rick?"

"I would take Rick because he doesn't get scared as easily as Kyle," Shannon laughed.

The lights suddenly went out. The warm glow of the fire filled the room and illuminated everyone's face.

"Now, that looks scary," Irma remarked, looking at Kyle and giggling.

"Everyone, continue the game, and I'll go check the electrical box." Cassandra stood up. "Rick, will you come with me? I might need your help."

Rick followed Cassie out of the room.

"Irma, truth or dare?" Shannon asked.

"Dare and make it a good one," Irma responded with a chuckle.

"Okay," an evil smile spread across Shannon's face as she rubbed her hands together. "Try to scare someone without them knowing it's you before the next two players finish their turns."

"I love it!" Irma sprung up with excitement. "Give Loretta the next one for me!" Shouting, she bolted out of the room.

"Okay, Loretta, truth or dare?" Shannon asked.

"Truth."

"Have you ever murdered or thought about murdering someone?" Shannon asked.

Suddenly, the fire in the fireplace went out, and the room went completely dark. Kyle frantically searched for someone to hold on to, but he was alone on the couch.

"Yes, you did, boy," a woman's voice cackled from behind the couch. "You are a cold-hearted, self-centered piece of shit!"

Kyle quickly turned around. He began to choke over the odor of stale cigarette smoke as it filled the air. He could feel the woman's warm breath against his face as she leaned over the back of the couch.

"What's the matter, boy?" The woman's voice rattled. "Did old Walter the cat get your tongue?"

"Mama?" Kyle stuttered.

"What are you staring at, boy?" She shouted. "We don't have all damn night!"

Kyle turned around and screamed in terror. The lights came back on, and everybody stared at Kyle as he sat and trembled with fear.

"Oh, my God!" Irma jumped out from the back of the couch.

Kyle turned quickly around and angrily shouted. "It was you! Why would you sneak up behind me in the damn dark and say those things?"

"I don't know what you heard, but I didn't get a chance to do anything. You started screaming as soon as I got behind the couch. You freak," Irma yelled as she rubbed her neck. "Why did you do that to me?"

"What? I didn't do anything to you," Kyle snapped.

"What's going on now?" Cassie shouted and rushed up to Kyle.

"Irma scared Kyle while the lights were out. I'm sure that Irma didn't mean to frighten him that badly. It was part of the game." Cindy pointed at Shannon. "Ask her. That was Irma's dare."

"Yes, that was her dare, but I didn't mean for her to scare him to death," Shannon remarked.

"I'm going to my room," Kyle hissed as he patted Cassie on the shoulders. "I have a headache and had enough of this stupid game anyway."

"Are you sure that you are all right?" Cassie tried to grab Kyle's hand, but he quickly pulled away.

Kyle turned and faced the group of ladies. "I did have fun tonight." He glared at Irma and gave her a dirty look. "Until someone scared the crap out of me."

Irma stuck her tongue out at Kyle.

"Well, goodnight, lovely ladies." Kyle nervously smiled. "Irma!" He stuck his tongue out at her and made a face as he turned back towards the stairs. "You too, Rick," he shouted as he walked away.

Everyone laughed. Kyle went to his room and checked his phone, but there were no new missed calls. The wind whistled through a gap in the window as he looked out. "At least the snow finally stopped, or did it? Around this place, who knows," he groaned as he yanked the curtain across. Kyle changed his clothes and got ready for bed when he noticed a light flashing outside. "Oh, no! I hope it's not that truck again!" Slowly, he approached the window and peered out. Kyle observed a man wearing the same red and black buffalo plaid shirt as last night, walking towards the log cabin with a flashlight. The man went to the side of the place and disappeared for a few seconds. When he returned to the front, he flashed his flashlight towards the Inn before entering the cabin. Kyle watched as the light came on inside the cabin and stared intently at the cabin's window until the light finally went out. He waited a few minutes for the man to leave, but no one exited the cabin. He glanced towards the front of the

Inn for the blue eighteen-wheeler, but it was nowhere in sight.

"Oh, well, that's just great. The psycho with the ax must live there, and that's why Cassie doesn't want anyone to know," Kyle grumbled, walking away from the window. "I'm tired of worrying about all of this. I wish this damn storm would end so I could go back home," he bitched, as he flopped down on the bed and stuck his hands up under his head.

I had a good day except for stupid Irma's little prank. I wonder how she knew what my Mom, rest her evil soul, used to say to me. Suddenly, he remembered the incident that had happened the previous night with Lavivian. *Ole Nosey must have overheard me, but I wonder how she knew about Walter and my Mom's smoking habit. Tomorrow, I will have a little chat with Ms. Prankster. I want to know how she found out the details about my Mom and why she took my watch. I hope that she didn't ruin my chance to get with Cassie. She probably thinks that I'm a real nut case. I'll have to pour the ole Southern charm on her tomorrow, hopefully changing her mind.*

He tossed and turned until he finally found a comfortable position in the center of the bed and drifted off to sleep.

~ 6 ~

DECEMBER 11

"Hey man, are you up?" Irma shouted from the hall-way as she pounded on the door.

"What?" Kyle sat up in the middle of the bed and slowly looked around the room.

"I know you're in there," Irma said, jiggling the door-knob.

"Hold on, Irma," Kyle grumbled as he briskly got out of bed and opened the door. "I'm glad you're here because I want to talk to you."

"I want to talk to you too," Irma grinned as she looked at him up and down. "Step aside, you half-naked man." She pushed Kyle out of her way and walked inside. "At least you got your pajama bottoms on this morning and not the same clothes as the day before?" She laughed as she sat down in the purple Queen Anne chair.

Kyle ignored her comment and sat down on the foot-stool in front of her. "When you were here yesterday, did you happen to see my watch?"

"No, I didn't," Irma quickly replied. "Why?"

"I left it on the dresser, and now it's gone." Kyle lowered his head into his hands. "It's an expensive watch and has a lot of sentimental value to me."

"Oh, no," Irma gasped, glancing around the room. "I'm sure that you will find it. It has to be in here somewhere."

"I hope so," Kyle sighed. "What did you want to talk to me about?"

"I wanted to talk to you about what happened last night." Irma had a worried expression on her face. "When I snuck up on you and hid behind the couch, you turned around and said something. What did you say?"

"Well, hell," Kyle chuckled and looked at her stupidly. "You should know because you had your damn face right up to mine."

"No, I didn't," Irma quickly remarked.

"Yes, you did," Kyle retorted. "I would like to know how you found all those details out about my Mom. For example, how did you know that my Mom smoked, and about the cat, Walter, that I had when I was a boy?"

"What are you talking about?"

"About my cat, Walter, damn it," Kyle shouted. "How did you know about all the mean names that my Mom called me and that she smoked like a damn chimney?"

"Kyle, I swear to you, that wasn't me. Please, believe me," Irma pleaded.

"What do you mean?" Kyle angrily raised his voice. "You admitted in front of the whole room that you scared me because it was your dare."

"I never said that. Cindy did," Irma cried out as tears filled her eyes.

"Why are you crying?" Kyle snapped.

"I'm scared," Irma cried. "That's why I'm crying."

"Scared! I'm the one that should be scared," Kyle chuckled. "Tell me, Irma, why would you scaring me make you afraid?"

"I always had the ability to see and communicate with the dead, and I think that you have an evil spirit around you," Irma spoke softly as she gazed at Kyle. "Ever since you arrived, I've been watching you. I think whatever you saw or heard the other night during bingo is after you."

"My dead Mom?" Kyle burst into laughter. "That's who I thought it was."

"I knew you would think I'm crazy," Irma shouted above Kyle's loud chortling.

"I sure do," Kyle replied with a smirk. "My Mom looked identical to Lavivian, which caught me off guard. That's all there is to it. So, there's no evil ghost chasing after me. Besides, she's been dead for twenty years. Don't you think that she would have caught me by now?"

"Kyle, last night, I could barely see your big dumb head before I squatted down behind the couch," Irma's voice began to tremble. "As I sat behind you, I imagined how funny it would be when I jumped up and scared you. Suddenly, something pushed me to the floor and held me down by my neck." She pulled the collar on her sweater down and exposed the markings on her neck. "I heard you say something, and then you screamed. When I stood up, you started accusing me."

Kyle closely examined Irma's neck. "Something definitely had a tight grip on you." *Or she might have done it to herself,* he thought. "In any case, Irma, I do not believe in evil spirits, and I am tired of trying to figure out what's going on here. So next time you see the ghost, just ask them what they want. Last night, I saw the guy who drives the blue eighteen-wheeler, and it's apparent that he lives in the log cabin by the woods. I don't know why Cassie doesn't want anyone to know, but I guess she has her reasons."

"Oh gosh," Irma shrieked. "He lives there?"

"Kyle?" Cassie shouted as she tapped on the door.

Kyle's jaw dropped as he leaned closer to Irma, whispering, "Do you think she heard us?" His eyes darted towards the door.

Irma shook her head and shrugged her shoulders. "No, I don't think so," she whispered back.

"Come on in, Cassie," Kyle shouted.

Cassie opened the door and looked shocked when she saw Irma inside the room.

Irma nervously grinned as she stuttered, "G-g-good morning, Cassie."

"What are you doing in here?" Cassie asked. "I didn't know that you and Kyle were best buddies."

"She likes harassing me," Kyle laughed.

"Yes, I do," Irma replied as she stood up. "Well, Kyle, I'll talk to you later." She quickly headed out of the door, stopped in the hallway, and looked back into Kyle's room. "Later, Gator!"

Cassie pushed the door shut before Kyle could reply. "Yes, later, much later," Cassie muttered.

"That was a little rude. Don't you think?" Kyle chuckled.

"Yuck! What a way to start the day," Cassie muttered, sticking out her tongue and looking disgusted.

"She's not that bad."

"Maybe not to you." Cassie went to the window and looked out. "It's snowing heavily again." She pointed towards the cabin. "You still can't see anything." She turned and walked away from the window. "Oh, well!" She opened the door. "I'll be downstairs in my office. Come and get me after you change your clothes or put some clothes on, and we'll have breakfast," she said, giggling.

"That sounds good." Kyle patted his bare chest and smiled as he watched Cassie close the door behind her. He rushed to the window and looked out. "Oh, no! It will be a little snowstorm, but it won't last long," he said jeeringly. "Well, thank you, Jamie, Sesailee, and Brenda. A little snowstorm, my ass! Now, I'm stuck in this place." He checked his phone, but there were no messages or missed calls. "Come on, someone, please call me." After plugging his phone into the charger, he placed it back on the dresser. He then changed his clothes and went downstairs.

When Kyle reached the lobby, he saw Jill sitting on the couch. *She is so beautiful.* He thought as he gazed lovingly at her while she sipped on her cup of coffee.

"Kyle!" Irma grabbed him from behind.

Kyle jumped and turned towards her. "Do you enjoy scaring me?"

"What did Cassie say?" Irma whispered. "Did she hear what we were talking about?"

"No, I don't think so because she didn't say anything," Kyle muttered.

"Oh, good," Irma breathed a sigh of relief. "Let's go have some breakfast."

"I would love to, doll, but Cassie wanted me to go with her." Kyle smiled and gently patted her shoulder. "Maybe we can have lunch together?"

"No, that's okay," Irma snapped. "I don't need a charity lunch!" She stuck her tongue out at him and angrily stomped away. "You can go back to stalking Jill!"

"She's something else," Jill chuckled and sipped her coffee.

"She sure is," Kyle laughed as he walked up to her. "Jill, honey, I meant to apologize to you about the other night. I didn't answer the door because I was too embarrassed about what happened earlier that evening."

"What are you talking about, Kyle?" Jill looked confused as she looked into his eyes.

"A couple of nights ago, when you came to my room and knocked on the door," Kyle replied.

"Kyle, that's sweet of you to apologize to me, but I never came to your room."

"Sure, you did," Kyle chuckled. "You knocked on the door, said it was you, and asked if I'm okay."

"That wasn't me," Jill smiled. "Maybe that was Irma pretending to be me. You know how she likes to joke around with everybody."

Kyle glared towards the dining room. "Yes, Irma would certainly do that." He looked at Jill and grinned. "Well, hon, it probably was Irma, or wishful thinking."

Jill giggled and sipped her coffee.

"Let me make good on my promise," Kyle smiled. "I'll be right back. Don't go anywhere!"

"Okay, I'll wait right here," Jill grinned as she watched Kyle run towards the kitchen.

Kyle was back a few minutes later and had something behind his back. "I got a surprise for you," He said with a big silly grin on his face. "I promised you that I would make you one." He beamed with pride as he held a tall cup piled with whipped cream in front of him.

"Oh, what's that?" Jill reached for the cup.

"It's my famous peanut butter and hot chocolate smoothie," Kyle winked as he handed it to her. "Be careful, now. That's the drink that made my ex-wife fall in love with me."

Jill giggled as she took a sip. "Oh, that's delicious." Jill took another sip. "That's the best smoothie I have ever had."

"Well, there you are," Cassie shouted across the lobby. "Let's go eat. I'm starving."

"Doll, I'm glad you like it," Kyle winked. "I'll talk to you later."

"Okay, Kyle," Jill smiled as she held up her cup. "Thank you."

Kyle walked briskly away and caught up with Cassie. They entered the dining room and sat down in their usual spot with Cindy and Loretta. Kyle kept watch for Cathy and Pat during breakfast, but they never showed. After breakfast, he helped Cassie again with chores around the Inn for the rest of the day.

"Thank you for helping me, Kyle. The last two days have been so much easier with your help." Cassie smiled as she unlocked the door to her room.

"My pleasure, doll," Kyle winked. "It makes my day go by faster. What's tonight? Hide and seek? Pin the tail on the donkey?" He laughed.

"It's card night tonight, and Lavivian is making her delicious lasagna. So, don't be lollygagging like you did this morning. Besides, hide and seek is tomorrow night," Cassie laughed as she went inside and closed the door.

"Oh, damn, I hope she's joking," Kyle muttered as he went inside of his room.

He was on his way to the dresser when he tripped and almost fell. He looked down, and one of his large travel bags sat in the middle of the floor.

"What the hell?" Kyle picked up the heavy bag and placed it on the bed. He unzipped the top and found all of his clothes crammed inside. Kyle found his watch in the side pocket and became furious when he discovered that somebody had busted the band into pieces and shattered the watch's face. Kyle looked at the top of the dresser for his phone, but it was gone. He frantically searched the bag and found the phone hidden at the bottom, underneath his clothes. "Oh, thank goodness, at least my phone is in one piece. Who would do something like this?" he raged. "This is the last straw!" He threw his clothes back into the drawers and placed his phone on the dresser. In a hurry, he changed his sweater, stuffed the broken watch into his pocket, and made his way downstairs.

When he reached the bottom of the stairs, he saw Irma staring at the Christmas tree. He glanced at the tree and grabbed Irma by the arm. "Why are you staring at the tree? That's the second time that I caught you doing that." He looked down at Irma's face. "What do you keep looking at?"

"Cassie has appalling decorating skills," Irma wrinkled her nose in disgust.

"What?" Kyle shrieked. "Cassie has impeccable taste. Why on earth would you say something like that?" Before Irma could reply, Kyle jerked her by the arm and pulled her closer to him. "Never mind! I forgot who I am talking to because you don't even know your name brands," he chuckled. "I need to talk to you."

"What now?" Irma rolled her eyes.

"Someone destroyed my watch." He pulled the broken watch out of his pocket and showed Irma.

"Where did you find it?" Irma gasped.

"While I was helping Cassie today, someone packed my bag and put the busted watch inside the side pocket." He drew his lips in tightly. "I'm so damn mad. This watch meant a lot to me. Who would do something like that?"

"I don't know, but you need to tell Cassie."

At that moment, he spotted Cassie across the lobby by the check-in counter.

"Irma, I'll talk to you later. I see her," Kyle rushed across the lobby and grabbed Cassie by the arm.

"Geez, I know I told you no lollygagging, but you were moving so fast I thought you would run me over," Cassie laughed.

"I need to show you this," Kyle reached inside his pocket and placed the broken watch on top of the counter.

"What happened?" Cassie asked while she examined the pieces.

"Someone packed all my clothes away in one of my bags while I was helping you today. Then, they did this to my watch and stuck it in one of the side pockets," Kyle angrily vented. "Who would do something like that? This watch was expensive and had a lot of sentimental value to me."

"I'm sorry," Cassie put her arm around Kyle's waist. "I don't know but one person who would do something so mean and heartless. I think it was Irma."

"Irma?" Kyle looked shocked. "I don't think she would do anything like that, especially to me."

"Then you don't know Irma too well," Cassie replied bluntly. "I think we need to confront everyone and get to the bottom of this."

"It's too late now, and I don't want to go around and blame people," Kyle sighed.

"If you like, I'll buy you a new one," Cassie smiled.

"Oh, no! I don't want you to do that. Besides, I have money to replace the watch if I want, but it's the memories behind the watch that I can't replace," Kyle smiled.

"I'm sorry," Cassie smiled and hugged Kyle. She picked up the watch and noticed something engraved on the back. "C.H., congratulations on 40 years of service. Who's C.H.?" Cassie asked as she handed Kyle the watch.

"Huh?" Kyle looked at the back of the watch. "Oh, that's my uncle." *That damn Charlie stuck his name on everything.* He thought as he quickly put it away in his pocket.

"Oh, that's why you are so upset," Cassie replied with a pouty expression on her face.

"Yes, good old Uncle Charlie," Kyle muttered under his breath.

"What did you say?" Cassie quickly asked.

"Nothing," Kyle snapped.

"Well, as you said, it's nothing that we can do about it now," Cassie patted Kyle on the back.

"No, I guess it's not that big of a deal." Kyle looked into Cassie's eyes. "Thank you for listening."

"You're welcome," Cassie grinned. "Let's go check out the dining room. Cindy says it looks just like a Las Vegas Casino."

They stopped at the doorway of the dining room. Gold, shiny curtains covered the white walls around the entire room. Two vintage slot machines lined the left side of the room, and roulette, blackjack, and a craps table lined the right. A large stage filled the back wall.

"Oh, I can't believe it," Cassie gasped, looking around the room in astonishment.

"Oh gosh," Kyle chuckled. "I might actually enjoy myself tonight."

"I hope so," Cindy giggled as she entered the room. "Tonight, Kyle, no hot chocolate. We're having drinks, real drinks. Vodka, whiskey, anything that you want."

"Oh, now I know that I'll have a good time," Kyle laughed.

"Cindy, this looks great," Cassie hugged her.

"We had costumes to wear, but it's too cold." Cindy pointed towards the back wall. "Lavivian prepared lasagna and a bunch of different types of finger food for tonight's dinner, and we're setting up a buffet table by the stage."

"You thought of everything," Cassie smiled. "Well, let's get this party started."

The room filled up quickly. Shannon was the DJ for the event. Rick, Cindy Etta, and Cynthia worked at each of the tables. Cindy was the bartender, and Lavivian kept the buffet full. Kyle, Cassie, and Callie played at Cindy Etta's blackjack table most of the night. Kyle kept watch and looked around the room periodically for Cathy and Pat.

"Okay, it's karaoke time," Shannon announced. "Who's first?"

"Me," Callie shouted and ran onto the stage.

"I must have a buzz because the karaoke isn't bothering me?" Cassie laughed as she sipped on her daiquiri.

Kyle laughed as he looked around the room again. Patricia, Candace, and Irma stood at Cynthia's craps table, while Jill, Loretta, and Brenda sat at Rick's roulette table. He looked at the slot machines for Cathy and Pat, but only LaDonna was there.

"Who are you looking for?" Cassie asked.

"Cat and Pat, they're not here," Kyle looked worried. "Don't you find that strange?"

"Not really," Cassie sneered and raised her left eyebrow. "I hope that you're not going to have another episode and make a spectacle out of yourself."

Kyle ignored her comment and motioned for Cindy Etta to give him another card.

Callie came back to the table and sat down next to Kyle.

"You must love to sing?" Kyle grinned.

"I love it," Callie smiled. "Reading and singing are two of my favorite activities."

"Well, Callie, would you like to join me on stage?" Kyle asked.

"Yes," Callie shouted. "I would love to."

Kyle and Callie sang a duet, and everyone cheered. Shannon and Callie sang most of the night and kept the entertainment going. Kyle sang the song that he wrote Jennifer, and all the ladies went wild. LaDonna had her plastic frog, Lucky, on top of her slot machine and won big. Everybody had fun, and the most significant part of the night to Kyle was that it was completely uneventful. Kyle helped Cassie, Cynthia, and Cindy get the dining room back in order for the next day.

A couple of hours later, they completed their work for the night, and Cynthia and Cindy retired to their rooms. As Cassie and Kyle walked toward the stairs, Kyle stopped in front of the Christmas tree. He had a smile on his face as he gazed at the lights.

"What's wrong, Kyle?" Cassie asked. "You're not thinking about your ex-wife again, are you?"

"No," Kyle grinned. "For the first time in a very long time, I am happy and will spend Christmas with friends."

"Aww, that's sweet," Cassie hugged him.

"Cassie," Kyle grabbed her hand and looked into her eyes. "I just met you a few days ago, and I know that this may sound rushed, but I feel very drawn to you. I can't explain it, but it just feels right to me. I really like you and hope I'm not scaring you."

"Not at all," Cassie grinned. "I feel the same way about you."

"You do?"

Cassie wrapped her arm around Kyle's waist, and they headed upstairs.

"I had a good time tonight, Cassie," Kyle smiled. "I think that was the most fun that I had in a while."

"Me too," Cassie grinned and unlocked the door to her room. "I wish that every day could be like this."

"Yes, me too."

"Well, good night, Kyle," she smiled as she opened the door. "Thank you for helping with everything. It means a lot to me."

"You're welcome, doll." Kyle winked. "Have sweet dreams."

Cassie giggled as she entered her room and closed the door behind her.

Kyle went inside his room and checked his phone. There were no missed calls or messages. He was about to go to the window and look outside, but he changed his mind.

"I'm not going to ruin a good evening by looking at that damn log cabin or for that devilish eighteen-wheeler," Kyle laughed as he changed into his pajamas. "It's best to let sleeping dogs lie."

Kyle lit the fireplace and stood in front of it. "What a wonderful day I had." The flames danced and flickered as he watched and thought about his day. Then, he fluffed up the pillows and climbed into bed. *I hope the rest of my stay is just as good.* Kyle thought as he found a comfortable position and drifted off to sleep.

Knock-knock-knock!

Kyle never moved. He was sound asleep.

Bam-Bam-Bam!

"What the hell?" Kyle sprung out of bed. "Who is it?" He angrily yelled.

"It's me, Lavivian," she replied softly.

"Lavivian?" Kyle hurried to the door and swung it open. "Lavivian, what on earth are you doing here?" He turned and glanced at the clock by the bed. "It's one o'clock in the morning."

"I heard a noise, and I want you to check it out for me," Lavivian smiled meekly.

"What's wrong with Rick? Why didn't you get him to check it out?"

"I don't want him. I want you."

"Well, I guess. Give me a minute so I can get a shirt on."

He was about to close the door, and Lavivian quickly stuck her hand up and stopped the door from closing.

"Kyle, just come to my room when you get a shirt on." Lavivian pointed down the hallway. "It's the last door next to the stairs."

"Okay," Kyle closed the door. "What on earth? Why didn't she get Rick or Cassie?"

Kyle picked up the sweater that he had worn earlier off the floor and quickly slipped it over his head. He stepped into his slippers on the way to the door.

"Who in the hell hears a noise at one o'clock in the morning?" Kyle grumbled as he angrily swung open the door.

Immediately, a strong, foul, musty odor made Kyle wrinkle up his nose. "Ewwww, what's that smell," he gagged as he stepped out of his room into the pitch-black hallway. "What happened to the lights?"

He quickly returned to his room for his cell phone, turned on the flashlight, and returned to the hallway. The walls were no longer white but dirty and stained, with large holes. As he lowered the light to the floor, the once deep purple shag carpet now appeared worn and matted.

"What the hell?" Kyle sprinted to his room in a panic and plowed into the closed door. His heart raced with fear as he tried to open the locked door. "Please open! Please open," he pleaded. Then, suddenly, he felt someone grab his shoulder. He turned quickly around and pointed the light down the hallway, but no one was there.

"Get a grip, man." Kyle closed his eyes tightly as he muttered, "This can't be real. Breath Kyle. One, two, three." He opened his eyes and noticed the broken, dirty chandeliers.

Kyle quickly pounded on Cassie's door. "Cassie! Cassie! Help me, please," Kyle desperately shouted, but Cassie never answered. He frantically twisted on the doorknob, but it wouldn't turn. "Cassie! Please! Help Me," He cried. "Oh, damn! Where is she?"

Kyle apprehensively turned away from the door and pointed his flashlight down the long, creepy, dark hallway to the opposite end. He watched in terror as Lavivian's door slowly opened, and a warm glow poured out of the room. Kyle waited anxiously for Lavivian or a familiar face to appear, but no one exited the room. He nervously tried to open his door again, but it wouldn't budge. His hand uncontrollably shook as he pointed the light back down the hallway. *I guess that I have no choice but to go down there.* He thought as he gripped his phone tightly and slowly crept towards Lavivian's room.

"Lavivian?" Kyle whimpered as he got closer to the door.

He cowardly stepped inside and glanced around the room. The bare walls were gray, and a dark blue comforter covered the full-size bed. A black recliner with a football blanket tossed across its back was in front of the fireplace. *This room looks familiar,* he thought. He fearfully walked to the dresser, and his stomach clenched when a large brass coin tray caught his eye. His eyes widened with fear as he read the initials D.M. engraved on the side. *That's impossible. He's dead.* Kyle thought as he quickly turned to leave.

"Well, it's about time that you showed up," the blonde-haired man grumbled from the recliner. "I thought that you might have gotten your little panties in a twist and quit."

Kyle's jaw dropped open, and he trembled with fear.

"What's wrong with you?" The blonde-haired man shouted. "Just don't stand there. Toss another log on the damn fire. It's freezing in here."

Kyle grabbed his chest and felt like he was going to pass out.

"Well?" The man shouted.

"D-Dondi? Dondi Morrow?" Kyle stuttered.

"K-Kyle, Kyle Parks?" Dondi imitated Kyle's voice as he grabbed his chest and rolled his eyes. He pulled the blanket from behind him and reclined back in the chair. "Well, I'm not Santa Claus, but you must think I am the way that you drained my bank account," he grumbled as he tossed the blanket across his legs.

"How can this be?" Kyle muttered.

"Quit playing games, damn it," Dondi shouted. "Throw another log on the fire and get me my damn nightly cocoa before I get up and light a fire under your ass!"

Kyle ran out as fast as he could down the hallway towards his room.

"Run faster, you little assmonkey!" Dondi's loud voice echoed. "We don't have all damn night!"

"Please be unlocked," Kyle murmured as he twisted the doorknob and rushed inside. He quickly locked the door and pushed the purple Queen Anne chair in front of it. Then, he flew into bed and hid under the covers.

"Why is this happening to me?" He remained motionless, too scared to move, as a tear ran down his cheek.

~ 7 ~

DECEMBER 12

Knock-knock-knock!

Kyle sprung up from the bed and looked at the door. The purple Queen Anne chair was back in front of the fireplace.

Knock-knock-knock!

"Give me a second," Kyle shouted as he swung his legs to the side of the bed and rubbed his head. "Dondi, I haven't thought about you in years." He mumbled as he sat on the edge of the bed and glared at the purple chair. "That was one hell of a dream." He looked on the floor by the dresser, and the sweater that he wore the night before was still there. "It was so vivid, and the odor in the hallway was horrendous."

Knock-knock-knock!

He angrily stood up and went to the door. He reached for the doorknob and suddenly stopped. *What if I'm still dreaming and Lavivian is outside my door again? Or worse yet, Dondi!* He thought as his heart raced.

"Who is it?" Kyle asked in a shrilled voice.

"It's the big bad wolf, you idiot," Irma shouted. "Don't make me huff and puff and blow your door down."

Kyle opened the door, slowly poked his head out, and peered down the hallway as Irma pushed her way inside.

"What the hell is wrong with you this morning?" Irma laughed. "Since when did you start asking who it is and sounding like a girl?"

"Irma, don't start with me this morning," Kyle snapped, slamming the door shut. "I had a rough night," he grumbled as he ran his fingers through his hair and sat on the foot of the bed.

"Really? What happened?" Irma sat down in the chair.

"Just a bad dream," Kyle's voice quivered. "It's not worth repeating."

"Well, dude, it's clear to see that it rattled you," Irma replied, glancing down at her bracelet. "I had a lot of nightmares, too, after I broke up with John. The one that I'll never forget is when he tied me up to a tree and left me in the middle of nowhere. He told me it was for my own good because his wife found out about all his mistresses, and she's crazy. Then, finally, after a couple of days, an old man and lady found me."

"What?" Kyle shrieked. "What kind of maniac did you go out with to dream something like that?"

"Dude, he was crazy, but I think his wife was crazier," Irma nervously tucked her bracelet under the sleeve of her sweater and looked at Kyle. "The strangest thing that happened after the nightmare, John disappeared."

"What?" Kyle shrieked.

"Yes, I couldn't believe it. The police came to my house. It was right after Christmas last year, and they questioned me. I explained to them that I hadn't seen John in four years because I found out that he had a list of girlfriends and was also married, so I broke up with him."

"Whatever happened to him?"

"I don't know," Irma sighed. "That man haunted my dreams for four long years, but after that nightmare of being tied to the tree, that was the last time I dreamt of him. It was like John was trying to warn me about something."

"Yes, doll, it sounds that way to me."

"John's friend and co-worker at the trucking company reported him missing, not his wife," Irma scowled. "The police told me that they were having problems locating her. I asked him where he lived a couple of times, but he told me he lived in his big blue truck," she chuckled. "I would not pass out my address if I was married and cheating on my spouse."

"That's the truth," Kyle grinned.

"Damn cheater," Irma smirked. "I'm glad that's all behind me."

"I bet," Kyle replied as he opened a drawer in the dresser and pulled out a hoodie and a pair of jeans. "Well, honey, let me change my clothes, and we'll go downstairs for breakfast."

"Cool, I'm starving," Irma quickly groaned as she rubbed her stomach.

"Me too," Kyle said as he grabbed his toiletry bag from the top of the nightstand. "All that running in my nightmare last night made me work up an appetite." He laughed. "I'll be right back."

Kyle took a deep breath as he slowly opened the door. He looked down the hallway before he stepped out of the room. He looked back at Irma and foolishly grinned as he closed the door behind him.

A few minutes later, he returned to his room and saw Irma at the window.

"Oh no," Kyle shrieked. "Don't tell me! The psycho is back at the log cabin." He ran to the window and stood by Irma.

"Man," Irma laughed. "That dream really freaked you out." She pointed outside. "It's not snowing as hard, and this is the first time that I can clearly see the cabin."

"Oh, geez," Kyle shook his head. "Look at all of that snow on the ground. I'll never get out of here."

"Don't be silly," Irma chuckled. "You'll be out of here one day, but not any day soon." She looked back towards the cabin. "That is a creepy-looking place. Is that a pond between the cabin and the woods?"

"Yes, it is," Kyle looked shocked. "I can't believe that I never noticed that before."

"There is obviously something extremely distressing about that place," Irma's voice cracked as she turned towards Kyle.

"My thoughts exactly," Kyle looked at Irma. "The first night that I arrived, I saw a man swinging an ax in the window, like he was butchering something."

"Really?" Irma shrieked.

"I think the man driving the blue eighteen-wheeler lives there, but I don't know why it's such a big secret." Kyle walked away from the window.

"I don't know why someone would want to live there," Irma muttered as she stared out the window.

"Me neither," Kyle agreed as he stood in front of the mirror and combed his hair.

"Let's go downstairs," Irma quickly trotted to the door. "That cabin is creeping me out."

"Me too," Kyle opened the door and motioned for Irma to go first. "After you, honey."

Irma walked out and waited for Kyle as he locked the door. When they reached the bottom of the stairs, Irma stopped in front of the Christmas tree.

"Why are you stopping?" Kyle asked.

"Look!" Irma pointed towards the top of the tree.

Kyle looked up when a sudden argument between Cassie and Shannon in the dining room caught his attention.

"I wonder what's happening? Let's go see!" Irma grabbed Kyle's hand and quickly pulled him behind her.

When they entered the room, they saw Rick with an angry look on his face as he stood between Shannon and Cassie.

"Calm down," Rick shouted. "Arguing isn't going to help the situation."

"What's going on?" Kyle asked.

"Callie is missing," Cassie snapped.

Cynthia entered the dining room and quickly walked up to them. "What's going on? Is everybody okay?"

"I told Cassie that she needs to do something instead of walking around with her damn head in the sand," Shannon shouted. "Pat, Cathy, and now Callie. How many more people need to disappear before she decides to do something?"

"What do you want me to do?" Cassie yelled.

"Call the sheriff," Shannon demanded.

"I can't! I told you that the phone line is down."

"That's another thing," Shannon raised her eyebrow and gently shoved Rick out of her way. "Where exactly is this phone? I would think each room would have a phone for the guest."

"The phone is in my office," Cassie glared into Shannon's eyes. "Why your room does not have a telephone is none of your business. Besides, you're staying for free anyway."

"Cassie is right," Kyle quickly interrupted.

"What," Shannon scowled and turned towards Kyle.

"I mean about the phone line being out," Kyle nervously stuttered and watched in disbelief as Rick shrugged his shoulders and had a cocky grin on his face. *He's really enjoying this,* he thought.

"How would you know anything about the damn phone lines when we don't have a phone?" Shannon remarked.

"I stopped at a gas station the day that I arrived, and the phone line was down. So, with all of the bad weather and snow, there's no way that it's repaired yet," Kyle patted Cassie on the back. "Would you like for me to check their rooms?"

"Yes," Cassie grabbed Cynthia's arm. "Go with him."

Kyle and Cynthia quickly went to Callie's room on the second floor.

"Callie?" Cynthia tapped on the door and waited for a few seconds. Finally, she unlocked the door, and they went inside the room.

"Did you make the bed this morning?" Kyle asked as he looked around the room.

"No," Cynthia timidly replied. "I don't start cleaning the rooms until after breakfast."

"Look, Cynthia," Kyle's voice nervously cracked. "Those are the clothes that Callie wore last night."

"Oh, it sure is," Cynthia looked at Kyle worriedly. "This doesn't look good."

"I agree, honey," Kyle bent down and pulled out the boots that Callie wore yesterday from under the bed. "She wore the same boots every day since I met her."

"That's her favorite pair," Cynthia anxiously looked around the room for any other signs. Then, finally, she noticed that Callie's rings and necklace were on top of the dresser. "Kyle, how could she just disappear?"

"I don't know," Kyle nervously combed through his hair with his fingers. "Let's go check Cathy's room."

They walked down the hallway to the last door and stopped. Once again, Cynthia tapped lightly on the door and waited a few seconds before she unlocked it.

"Geez," Kyle blurted out as he walked inside. "All the rooms are really identical."

"Yes, they are. Knowing Cassie, she got it for a bargain price, and that's why they're all the same," Cynthia remarked.

"What are you talking about?" Kyle chuckled. "Cassie has plenty of money."

"Is that what she told you?" Cynthia chuckled. "She did before she stuck every dime into this place."

Kyle ignored her and walked to the side of the bed. "Did you make this bed?"

"No," Cynthia stood at the door and looked around the room. "I haven't been in here since Pat's disappearance. I knew Cathy was too distraught, and I didn't want to disturb her." She walked to the purple Queen Anne chair and picked up Cathy's white cashmere sweater. "Now, I wished that I would have."

"Where would she go without her sweater?" Kyle glanced around the room and noticed Cathy's shoes by the bed. "There's something strange going on around here."

"Definitely," Cynthia tossed the sweater on the back of the chair and dashed to the door. "Come on, Kyle. Let's go to Pat's room."

Kyle rushed out of the room and followed Cynthia back down the hallway. They stopped at the last door, and Cynthia quickly unlocked it.

"Oh, no," Cynthia shrieked. "Look, Kyle."

The fondue maker and the lava lamp Pat won on bingo night were still inside the bag on top of the bed. The large fruit basket was sitting on top of the dresser. By the door, a half-eaten apple was on the floor.

"What the hell is going on?" Kyle looked around the room.

"We need to tell Cassie," Cynthia shouted as she walked back out of the room into the hallway. "Something bad happened to them."

"Wait, Cynthia," Kyle darted towards her. "Let me tell Cassie in private. We need to keep this quiet."

"What," Cynthia cried out. "Are you kidding me? Why?"

"I don't want to upset everyone. Besides, we don't really know what happened to them," Kyle turned around and closed the door.

Cynthia hesitated a moment and looked at Kyle. "I guess you're right."

When they reached the bottom of the stairs, Kyle and Cynthia could hear the loud commotion that was taking place in the other room. Irma frantically waved her arms up in the air and ran up to them.

"Kyle," Irma shouted above the noise.

"What's going on?" Kyle looked at Cynthia.

"Come on," Irma quickly grabbed Kyle's hand and pulled him behind her as she ran towards the dining room. "Everyone is panicking over Pat, Cathy, and Callie missing."

"Here comes the answer man," Shannon shouted as they entered the room. "What did you find? Did you find Callie?"

Kyle approached the group of women with apprehension as he looked into their worried faces.

"Well?" Shannon's eyes turned ice blue, and she threw her hands up in front of her.

"No, there's no sign of them anywhere," Kyle's nervous voice cracked as he stared at Shannon's stern face.

"Oh, my God," Loretta gasped. "What happened to them?"

"That's the million-dollar question," LaDonna glared at Cassie. "We are all trapped here because of the weather so they couldn't have gone far."

"Exactly," Cassie agreed.

"Well, if that's the case, where are they?" Patricia muttered to Candace.

"I wished that I knew," Candace wrapped her arms around Patricia's and her Mom's waists. "We should have gone on that cruise instead of this place."

"Kyle, did you find anything inside of their rooms?" Cindy asked. "Anything odd or out of place?"

"It looked like Callie and Cathy changed their clothes but never made it to bed. Pat's room had her bingo prizes on top of her bed and a half-eaten apple on the floor,"

Cynthia softly stated, glaring at Kyle. "He wanted to keep it a secret."

Kyle quickly lowered his head and looked down at the floor.

"Why would you want to keep something like that a secret?" Cindy Etta angrily shouted.

"Maybe he's behind the disappearances," Rick abruptly remarked.

"What?" Kyle quickly raised his head. "No," he gruffly replied.

"This is why Cynthia should have kept the rooms a secret," Cassie angrily looked at Cynthia. "We don't know what happened to them, and we are not going to start accusing people." She glanced at Rick as she gently pulled Cindy towards her. "We are going to divide up into teams and search every inch of this place. Patricia, Candace, Cynthia, and Cindy will search the basement. Lavivian, Cindy Etta, Loretta, and Rick, the first floor. Brenda and Irma, you're going to the third floor with Kyle." Cassie handed Kyle a ring of keys to unlock the rooms. "LaDonna, Jill, and Shannon, you will go to the second floor with me."

They all divided into their groups and left the dining room.

"What do you think happened, Kyle?" Brenda asked as they reached the top of the stairs.

"Well, I know for a fact that Kyle is not involved," Irma smugly stated.

"I don't know what happened, but I know that I didn't have anything to do with it. I don't know why Rick would say something like that." Kyle pointed towards the end of the hallway and said, "I guess we can start in my room."

Kyle nervously stood in front of Lavivian's room and waited for Brenda and Irma to go in front of him. He started to follow them when he heard a noise inside the room. He stood in silence and pressed his ear to the door.

"So, what idiot put my little assmonkey is in charge?" Dondi laughed.

Kyle frantically ran towards Brenda and Irma.

"What's wrong with you?" Brenda chuckled.

"You didn't hear that?" Kyle gasped as he quickly unlocked the door.

"I didn't hear anything," Brenda remarked as she entered Kyle's room. "Did you, Irma?"

"Nope," Irma chuckled as she walked past Kyle.

Brenda walked around the room and stopped at the window. "What exactly are we looking for?"

"Anything that belonged to them," Kyle stated, standing by the door.

"Or their bodies," Irma cackled like a witch and rubbed her hands together.

"Stop it, Irma," Kyle shouted when he saw the fearful expression on Brenda's face.

"The whole searching thing is pointless," Brenda muttered as she went and stood by Kyle.

"I'm sorry if I upset you, Brenda, but I think all this is just a big waste of time too," Irma flopped down on the Queen Anne chair and looked at Kyle. "Honestly, if someone is behind Pat, Cathy, and Callie missing, do you think they would be stupid enough to leave evidence inside their room?"

"No, not really," Kyle replied, motioning for Irma to get up. "Cassie is counting on us to search the rooms, so we better do it."

"What are you? Cassie's puppet," Irma grumbled as she stood and walked out.

After searching Cassie's room, they went next door. Kyle was surprised when he realized the room belonged to Rick and Cindy Etta. Despite rigorously searching the room, Kyle found nothing.

"It's unbelievable that there's nothing here," Kyle muttered as he looked under the bed.

"It's unbelievable that you don't know who stays on the same floor as you," Irma laughed.

"No, I really don't," Kyle chuckled. "I presumed it was all staff, but I thought Cindy would have the room next to Cassie."

"Cindy is in the room next to you. So, you, Cindy, Cynthia, and Lavivian are on that side. Cassie, Rick and Cindy Etta, Loretta, and Jill on this side." Irma chattered as she opened the door.

"Jill?" Kyle squealed with excitement.

"Yes, Jill," Irma rolled her eyes and looked at Brenda. "Kyle has the hots for Jill and Cassie."

Brenda looked at Kyle and giggled.

"Don't pay any attention to Miss Know-it-all," Kyle muttered, walking to the door. "Let's go check the rest of the rooms."

Brenda and Kyle discussed fishing and the various fish that they caught as they searched the rooms. Brenda also spoke about her love of cooking and baking.

"You know, honey," Kyle grinned. "Cassie needs a cook because Rick and his family are eager to go back home to Indiana. So, if you're interested, why don't you talk to Cassie about the job."

"Really?" Brenda smiled. "I'll talk to Lavivian this evening about it. I'm helping her prepare tonight's dinner."

"Why would anyone want to stay and work here," Irma gawked at Kyle. "Finally, the last room."

Kyle's eyes widened with fear as they approached Lavivian's room. Standing in front of the door, he nervously fumbled through the keys and appeared uneasy.

"What's wrong?" Irma asked.

"Nothing," Kyle replied, slowly opening the door and peering inside. He felt relieved when he saw that the room was the same as his.

"This is stupid! What possibly can Lavivian be hiding? She's like a mother to all of us," Irma grumbled as she stood in the hallway.

Kyle quickly closed the door and locked it. "You're right, Irma. I don't think we have to go in there." He looked at Brenda. "Do you?"

"No," Brenda grinned. "Let's go."

They went downstairs and sat in front of the fireplace.

"Everyone must still be searching for them," Brenda commented as she looked around. "What's taking them so long?"

Kyle quickly stood and looked towards the dining room. "Dolls, I'll be right back." He briskly walked to Cassie's office and went inside. He glanced around the room but couldn't find the phone Cassie had mentioned earlier. So, he looked for a phone jack but couldn't find any. "Why would she lie about a phone?" he murmured as he walked out of the office.

"Why were you in there?" Cassie asked as she met him outside the office door.

"Oh, I was looking for you," Kyle nervously replied and foolishly grinned. "Did you find anything?"

"Nothing," Cassie grumbled. "I knew it would be a big waste of time, but I had to do something to quiet everyone down, at least for now."

They sat down in front of the fireplace and waited for everyone to join them. Lavivian, Cindy Etta, and Brenda went to the kitchen to prepare dinner. Cindy, Cynthia, Patricia, and Candace joined them about an hour later.

"What took you so long?" Cassie asked. "It was just one room."

"One big room," Cindy chuckled. "It was dark in a lot of the areas, and we wanted to be thorough." Cindy pointed at Candace. "Thank God that she found a couple of flashlights."

"That basement is dark, musty, and nasty," Patricia commented in a disgusted tone and crinkled up her nose.

"Well, I am glad that everyone is concerned about the condition of the basement and preparing dinner. Hell with Callie, Pat, and Cathy, right?" Shannon angrily shouted. "I'm going to my room." She stood and walked towards the stairs.

"Shannon, don't be angry. Come back and sit down," Loretta pleaded. "Nobody can do anything. We all are scared and worried about the situation, but we are trapped here. We can't leave or get help, so what do you want us to do?"

Shannon stopped and turned back towards the group. "I don't know, but I can't sit here and act as though nothing happened," she said, glaringly at Cassie. "If I'm not down in the morning, you'll know it was my turn to disappear!" She turned and went up the stairs.

Suddenly, the front door flew open, and a strong blast of cold air filled the lobby. Kyle jumped up and rushed towards it. He grabbed the doorknob and leaned against the door to close it, but it wouldn't budge. Then, Kyle noticed that someone had on an old, familiar pair of work boots in the doorway. He looked up, and the man was Charlie.

"I'm coming for you," Charlie bellowed.

Cassie pushed Kyle out of the way and slammed the door shut. "What's wrong with you?" Cassie shouted. "The lobby is freezing now! Why were you standing there like a statue?"

"You didn't see him?" Kyle stuttered.

"Oh, no," Cassie moaned. "Don't start that crap again."

"It's dinner time," Brenda announced as she stood in front of the dining room door. "I made chicken and dumplings, and Lavivian baked a delicious peach cobbler for dessert."

The ladies stared at Kyle and slowly made their way into the dining room as he awkwardly smiled. Cassie stood beside him and waited until everyone was out of the room.

"Kyle, please stop," Cassie pleaded. "I don't know what you think that you're seeing or hearing, and maybe you really are, but please stop. Everyone is suspicious of you and thinks you're behind the disappearances."

"What," Kyle shrieked. "Why me?"

"Because they had all been here for a week before you arrived, and nothing had happened," Cassie explained. "Suddenly, you appeared, and people began to disappear."

"That's ridiculous," Kyle huffed. "I can't believe that they would think that."

"Well, they do, and I don't want you to keep adding to their ludicrous accusations by your peculiar behavior."

Kyle stared in silence towards the dining room for a moment. "I guess I can understand why they believe that, and thanks for telling me," Kyle hugged Cassie.

"Kyle, I like you, and I believe you," Cassie looked into his eyes. "You're a good, honest man." Cassie smiled. "Let's go and enjoy our dinner."

"Okay," Kyle smiled meekly. *That's the first time in my entire life that someone called me good and honest.* He thought as they walked towards the dining room. He looked at Cassie and grinned. *Maybe I can be good and honest with Cassie by my side.*

The mood was quiet and dismal as everyone ate their meal. After dinner, Kyle went straight to his room. He checked his phone, but there were no missed calls or signal. He changed his clothes and sat on top of the bed.

"I can't believe all the ladies think I'm behind Pat, Cathy, and Callie's disappearance. I bet Rick started the rumor, and that's why he made that remark earlier." He fluffed two of the pillows and stacked them on top of each other. Then he pulled the blanket on top of himself as he rested his head on the pillows. "Maybe I should leave. I may be able to walk to the gas station if I wear enough layers of clothing, and I know that Jamie and Sesailee will help me get off this godforsaken mountain."

Finally, after tossing and turning for a while, he fell to sleep.

A loud noise in the hallway jolted Kyle awake, and he abruptly sat up on the edge of the bed.

Whack! Whack! Whack!

He could hear a man and woman arguing in the distance. Kyle's eyes widened, and his heart pounded. *What is that?* He thought as he tried to remain calm. Suddenly, something fell against his door, and he heard a woman scream.

"I told you to shut up and stay in the room," A man's voice roared from the hallway.

Kyle crept to the door and pressed his ear against it. He waited for a few minutes until the hallway was completely quiet. Kyle slightly opened the door and peeked out when suddenly, the man with the red and black buffalo plaid shirt appeared. Kyle's body stiffened, and his chest pounded as he peered through the tiny opening into the dark hallway. Kyle watched as the man bent down and pulled the drawstring closed on the large black bag in front of his door. He tried to see the man's face, but the large brim on the black baseball cap kept his face covered.

The man suddenly stood up and moved the large black bag away from the door. Kyle slowly opened the door a little wider and poked his head out. The man whistled an eerie tune as he walked down the hallway and dragged the bag behind him. He watched as the man disappeared into the darkness and heard the sound of his whistle becoming fainter and fainter.

"I know that is Rick," Kyle grabbed the cell phone for light and quickly stepped out of the room to follow him. The hallway was dark and musty, just as it was last night when Lavivian came to his room. *I hope that Dondi isn't waiting for me.* He thought as he hesitated momentarily, then bolted past Lavivian's room and down the stairs.

He heard the whistling intensify as he ascended the staircase and entered the lobby. He followed the eerie sound echoing through the dining room into the kitchen.

Kyle abruptly stopped outside the kitchen door when the whistling suddenly ended. He turned off the flashlight and stood in silence for a few seconds. *Maybe Rick went outside,* he thought and turned the flashlight back on.

Kyle opened the door and stopped in his tracks. The light glowed against the man stooped over the bag in the middle of thc kitchen. As the man stood and released the drawstring, an arm with a silver bar bracelet flopped out of the bag.

"Irma," Kyle shouted.

The man kicked the arm towards the bag and rushed towards him. Kyle screamed as he turned around and bolted through the dining room and up the stairs to his room. He slammed and locked the door. His heart hammered in his chest as he leaned against the door. Suddenly, the doorknob jiggled as the man tried to open the door. Kyle ran to the purple Queen Anne chair, placed it in front of the door, and backed slowly away. The man pounded so loudly that he thought the door would break.

Finally, the man stopped hammering and started to whistle. As Kyle turned frantically towards the bed, he tripped over a pair of slippers, hit his head on the corner of the dresser, and fell to the floor.

~ 8 ~

DECEMBER 13

Knock-knock-knock!

"Kyle, are you okay," Irma shouted. "Are you in there?"

Knock-knock-knock!

"Oh, no! Not Kyle. Please let him be in there," Irma whimpered. "I'm going to get Cassie."

"Wait," Kyle cried out as he opened his eyes.

"Kyle," Irma joyfully shouted. "Thank God! Open the door!"

"Give me a minute," Kyle looking up from the floor. His head pounded as he slowly sat up. The room appeared blurry. He gently touched the bump on his forehead and noticed the chair in front of the door. "Oh, crap, last night really happened," he moaned as he stood up and held on to the dresser, closing his eyes and lowering his head, trying to snap out of it.

"Kyle," Irma shouted. "What's wrong?"

As Kyle staggered to the door, he grabbed the chair's top back rail for dear life while pushing the chair slightly to the side. He nervously tugged at his shirt before opening the door.

"What happened to you?" Irma quickly grabbed Kyle and helped him to the foot of the bed. "Sit down," she held on to his arms as he sat down. "Where did you get that big ole goose egg from?" She gently touched his forehead.

"Ouch," Kyle shouted and pulled his head backward. "Damn, Irma, that hurts, but I'm so happy to see you that I don't care."

"I'm sorry," Irma grinned.

"Sure, you are," Kyle grumbled.

"What happened?"

"I fell and hit my head on the corner of the dresser," Kyle moaned.

"What?" Irma tried to touch his head again, but he jerked her hand away.

"Doll, you're not going to believe this, but I know who the person is behind the disappearances."

"Who?" Irma shrieked.

"It's Rick," Kyle kept a watchful eye on the door as he told Irma the story about what happened last night. After he finished, he looked at Irma's tear-filled eyes and her terrified face. "Honey, are you okay?"

"He had someone chopped up inside the bag, and you thought it was me," Irma sobbed. "We all are going to die."

"I know that I am because he saw me and chased me back to my room."

"What are we going to do?"

"I don't know," Kyle sighed. "Cassie lied to Shannon about having a phone in her office. In fact, there's no phone or phone jack. Not that it matters because the lines are down, but why would she lie about something like that?"

"Beats me, man," Irma got up and went to the window. "Even Mother Nature is against us. Look, Kyle. The snow is falling heavily again."

"Are you kidding me?" Kyle slowly stood and looked outside. "Last night, I thought about walking to the gas station. It's about a mile and a half away. I know that I can get some help for all of us there. What do you think?"

"I think that it's worth a try," Irma glared out the window towards the front of the Inn. "If we stay here, we're going to die. I would rather die in the snow than get chopped up. The wind is way too strong to leave today, and you need at least a day to recover from that bump on your head."

"You're right," Kyle looked at Irma. "So, will you go with me?"

"Right on, man," Irma grinned. "I wouldn't let you go by yourself. I think that I should stay with you at night, too."

"I would love that, honey," Kyle smiled. "To tell you the truth, I'm scared to be alone, especially after the last couple of nights."

"Me too," Irma sat down on the bed. "Do you think that you really saw Rick or that you were sleepwalking?"

"It's no way that I was sleepwalking," Kyle blustered. "Why would you say that?"

"Well, the night before, you had that horrible nightmare, and last night you saw Rick. I know without a doubt that Rick doesn't care for you, and if he ever had a chance to scare you, he would," Irma chuckled. "I can even picture him chasing after you, but I don't think that he's a murderer."

"Whatever," Kyle scowled. "Think what you want, but I know what I saw."

"Well, tonight, we'll find out if you're sleepwalking or if something is happening," Irma stood up. "Are you feeling better?"

"Yes, a little bit," Kyle grinned. "I could really use a cup of coffee. How about you?"

"Yes. I hope Lavivian made her delicious honey-glazed biscuits," Irma licked her lips as she rubbed her belly.

"Nothing spoils your appetite," Kyle chuckled and opened the door.

"Are you going to change your clothes?" Irma laughed.

Kyle looked down at his pajamas and blushed. "Give me a minute." He grabbed a change of clothes from the dresser and walked out. A few minutes later, Kyle was back. "Okay, honey, let's go." He tossed his pajamas on top of the chair and held the door open for Irma.

"Beauty and brains first, drab and dorky last," Irma shouted as she laughed and rushed past Kyle.

When Kyle and Irma reached the bottom of the stairs, they saw Cynthia in tears in front of the fireplace and rushed to her side.

"What's wrong, Cynthia?" Kyle hugged her. "Did something happen to Candace?"

"No, my sister Patricia is missing," Cynthia wailed.

"Oh, no," Irma shouted.

"I'm sorry, honey," Kyle hugged Cynthia tightly.

"Don't tell me that bullshit about she's around here somewhere like Cassie just did," Candace angrily shouted from behind Kyle. "That makes four people that just suddenly wandered off, according to her." She pulled her Mom away from Kyle and wrapped her arms around her. "I told you, Mom, we should have left when Pat and Cathy disappeared."

"That's not what I was going to say, Candace, because I don't believe they just wandered off like that," Kyle turned and glanced around the room for Cassie. "I think that something bad happened to them."

"What?" Cynthia cried. "Why would you say something like that?" She grabbed Kyle by the collar of his shirt. "That's my sister!"

"Great job, moron," Rick grumbled as he approached the group. "Why would you say something like that? Unless you're behind it!"

"He's not behind anything," Irma shouted. "I'm tired of everybody blaming Kyle!"

"Then what happened to his head?" Rick pointed at Kyle. "By the size of that knot above his eye, he must have been in one hell of a brawl."

"He fell and hit his head on the corner of the dresser," Irma stepped in front of Kyle.

"Yeah, right," Rick laughed.

"He did," Irma angrily shouted. "I know because I found him on the floor."

"Who's missing today?" Shannon asked as she exited the stairs.

"My sister," Cynthia cried out.

"Okay, ladies and gentlemen," Cassie shouted as she walked towards the group. "Let's try to get to the bottom of this and stop accusing people!"

"Oh, what's your plan?" Candace sarcastically remarked. "Oh, wait! I know! Let's divide into groups and search this place," she rolled her eyes and hugged her Mom. "We searched this damn place so many times that I know the location of every spider web. So, obviously, that doesn't work. Something happened to them. They are not hiding or taking a damn stroll through the deep-ass snow."

Jill, Loretta, LaDonna, Brenda, and Cindy came downstairs and sat nervously on the sofa in front of the fireplace.

"She would never leave without saying something to me," Cynthia wept.

"Oh, my God," Cindy's voice squeaked. "Patricia's missing?"

"Yes, and Cassie wants us all to go on another useless hunt," Candace snapped angrily.

"I think that we should," Loretta quickly interrupted.

"Why?" Candace raised her voice and turned towards her. "It's pointless!"

"At least we're trying to find them," Loretta remarked. "Honestly, I think it's pointless too, but what else can we do?"

"Loretta and Cassie are right," Jill said, standing by Candace. "I'm sorry about your aunt, but we have to keep searching for them. Unfortunately, we don't know what to do and don't have many options but to search."

"Candace, honey, they're just trying to help," Cynthia sniffled.

"Okay, Mom," Candace hugged Cynthia. "I'll go along with this nonsense for you."

"Divide into the same groups and search the same floor as yesterday," Cassie grabbed Cynthia by the hand. "If you don't feel up to it, you can stay with Rick."

"No, I want to go," Cynthia wiped her eyes.

"Okay, everybody, meet back here," Cassie shouted.

Lavivian and Cindy Etta entered the room and watched as everybody divided into groups.

"What's going on, son?" Lavivian asked as everyone hurriedly left the room.

"Patricia's missing," Rick grabbed his Mom and Cindy Etta by the hand. "I knew we should have left when we had a chance."

"What are we going to do?" Cindy Etta looked into Rick's eyes worriedly.

"We're going to stay together at all times. As soon as we get a chance to leave, we're gone," Rick looked at Lavivian. "Mom, I want you to pack up your things and move into our room."

"I think that's a good plan," Lavivian agreed.

"We'll pack up your things after dinner," Rick nervously glanced around the room. "I guess we should help with the search. Remember, stick together!"

An hour later, the groups slowly gathered in front of the fireplace.

"Well, ladies, did you find anything?
Kyle asked.

"Not a thing," LaDonna muttered and looked at Cindy.

"Nothing," Cindy replied and looked at Kyle.

"Where are they?" Kyle sighed and noticed the frightened expression on Irma's face as she stared at the Christmas tree. "Irma, what are you looking at?"

"Look!" Irma pointed at the top of the tree. "What is that?"

Cassie quickly went to the tree and pulled one of the four objects off the pointy pine branch.

"What is it?" Brenda asked.

"A homemade doll," Cassie's eyes widened as she flipped it around.

Everyone rushed towards her. She held the white burlap doll up in the air with the name Patricia embroidered in gray across the chest.

"It looks like a voodoo doll," Shannon shrieked.

Cassie quickly pulled the yellow doll down from the tree with Cathy written across the chest. "What is this? Is this supposed to be someone's idea of a sick joke!"

Rick watched Kyle's eyes widen with fear and nervously ran his fingers through his hair.

Cassie angrily yanked the purple doll with Callie and the red doll with Pat's name embroidered on it from the tree. "Irma," Cassie shouted. "When did you first notice these voodoo dolls on the tree?"

"A couple of days ago," Irma snapped. "Why?"

"Before you start jumping down Irma's throat, I think you need to question your buddy, Kyle," Rick sneered. "Look at his face."

Cassie quickly turned towards Kyle and held the four dolls up in front of him. "Do you know where they came from?"

"Before I arrived, I found them in the trunk of my car." Kyle nervously stuttered as he glanced around at all of the ladies' bewildered faces.

"I told you, Cassie," Rick shouted. "I knew he was behind all of this!"

"No! Wait," Kyle cried out. "Let me explain."

"Okay, explain!" Cassie demanded.

"The day that I arrived, I stopped at a gas station. When I opened the trunk to get my jacket, I found a box with the same dolls wrapped in black tissue paper inside. The people that I worked for, Charlie's wife, Deniese, collected these dolls. Charlie told me that the dolls were evil. I panicked and threw the box of dolls away in the trash can by the gas pumps, and then I left," Kyle nervously glanced back around at the ladies' faces.

"Bullcrap! If you left the dolls at the gas station, how did they end up here?" Rick went up to Kyle and glared into his eyes. "I'll tell you how. You've been acting freaky since day one. You're taking these women at night and doing God knows what to them," Rick said, snatching one of the dolls from Cassie's hand and holding it in front of Kyle's face. "Then you're hanging one of these things on the tree like it's a joke," he tossed the doll in Kyle's face. "You're sick!"

Kyle looked at Cassie. "Believe me! I have nothing to do with any of this! I promise you! Someone must have been watching me at the gas station. When I threw the box away, they got it and decided to follow me."

"So, you're telling me that somebody followed you here?" Cassie asked.

"Yes," Kyle replied.

"Oh, man, come on," Rick blurted out as he shook his head.

"It makes sense," Cassie agreed as she picked the doll up from the floor and placed all four of them on top of the mantel.

"What?" Rick shouted in disbelief.

"Think about it," Cassie grabbed Rick by the arm. "Nothing happened until Kyle arrived. He claims that he doesn't have anything to do with the missing woman, and I believe him."

"Well, I don't," Rick quickly remarked.

"I believe him, too," Cindy swiftly moved by Kyle's side. "I don't think that there's an evil bone in his body."

"He's too much of a scaredy-cat to be a murderer," Irma chortled.

"You got that right," Shannon agreed.

"Ladies. I hate to interrupt, but dinner is almost ready," Cindy Etta announced.

"How can anybody think about food in a time like this?" Cynthia cried.

"Mom's right!" Candace became angry as she glanced around the room at the nonchalant look on the ladies' faces. "What's wrong with everyone? Don't you realize that if we stay here, sooner or later, we're all going to die! We can't sit around and act as though nothing happened."

"What do you expect us to do?" Brenda asked.

Candace raced to the front door and gripped the doorknob tightly. "I'm leaving," she shouted, looking back at the ladies. "I'm going to get us some help."

"Candace! Wait," Cynthia cried. "Don't go! I can't lose you too."

"I have to try, Mom," Candace grabbed a black coat that hung on the coat rack by the door and ran out.

"Wait," Cynthia screamed and glanced at Rick and Kyle. "Why are you just standing there? One of you, go after her!"

Rick and Kyle ran to the door and swung it open, but Candace was gone.

"She'll be back," Rick said as he shut the door. "That thin black coat won't keep her warm."

"No," Cynthia wailed as she rushed towards them.

Cassie hurried and grabbed Cynthia. "Calm down," Cassie hugged her. "Rick is right. She'll be back. It's too cold to stay out there too long." Cassie gently led Cynthia back in front of the fireplace. "Do you want to stay down here or go back to your room?"

"I'll stay here and wait for Candace," Cynthia whimpered.

Everyone gathered back in front of the fireplace. The room stayed quiet except for an occasional whisper between the ladies.

Cassie noticed Lavivian standing by Cindy Etta in front of the dining room door. "Ladies, Lavivian and Cindy Etta made us a lovely dinner in the midst of all this craziness. I know that no one has much of an appetite, but we need to keep up our strength," Cassie stood and reached out her hand towards Cynthia.

"I can't," Cynthia cried.

"It's okay, Cassie," Lavivian smiled. "I'll make some broth and bring it out here for her."

All the ladies slowly made their way to the dining room. Kyle entered last and sat next to Cassie. The sound of the silverware as it scraped against the plates echoed through the quiet room.

"Mmm, yummy," Irma broke the silence as she squealed with excitement when Lavivian entered the room with the dessert. "Fudge cake!"

"Do you think that Candace came back?" Kyle whispered to Cassie.

"I don't know," Cassie snapped. "Why are you whispering?"

"Because everyone is scared," Cindy grumbled. "Look around, Cassie. Look at their faces."

Cassie turned and glanced around the room. "I don't know what they expect me to do?" She muttered.

"I don't think there's anything that you can do, honey," Kyle gently patted Cassie's hand and softly smiled. "We're all trapped here."

"That's the truth," Cassie agreed as she smiled at Lavivian. "Thank you for the delicious meal."

"You're welcome," Lavivian grinned as she sat the dessert plate in front of Cassie.

"Kyle, I hope you enjoy it," Lavivian pushed a plate with an extra-large slice of cake in front of him. "It's an old family recipe."

"It looks scrumptious," Kyle smiled.

They finished dessert and returned to the lobby to check on Cynthia, but she was gone.

"Candace must have returned," Cindy smiled and grabbed the dolls off the top of the mantel. "Cassie, I'm putting these inside your office."

"Are you ready, roomie?" Irma slapped Kyle on the butt.

Kyle jumped and nervously chuckled as he looked at Cassie.

"What?" Cassie looked horrified.

"We decided it would be better if we stayed together," Kyle stuttered, pulling at his sweater's sleeve. "I've been having a hard time sleeping, and last night, I fell and hit my head."

"Hmm," Cassie raised an eyebrow and gave Irma a dirty look. "I'm speechless. I didn't realize that the two of you became so close, but I guess it's all starting to make sense now."

"What?" Kyle blurted out. "It's not what you're thinking. We are only friends."

"For now, Kyle, we are friends, but I might get lucky after tonight," Irma laughed and headed up the stairs.

Cassie rolled her eyes and quickly walked away. She turned back towards Kyle before she entered the office and slammed the door. He shook his head and went upstairs.

"Oh, great job, Irma," Kyle grumbled and went upstairs. As he unlocked the door to his room, Irma rushed towards him with her arms filled with clothes.

"Move it or lose it," Irma shouted as she hurried past him and dropped her clothes on the floor by the dresser. "I'm excited about having a roommate, aren't you, Kyle?" She flopped down on the Queen Anne chair and propped up her feet on top of the footstool.

"Yes, until you told Cassie," Kyle looked at his phone on top of the dresser for any missed calls. Then, he quickly hid it under the clothes inside of the top drawer.

"What are you hiding?" Irma chuckled.

"Nothing," Kyle snapped and sat down on the foot of the bed. "Why did you say that to Cassie? Now, you ruined any little chance that I had with her."

"What," Irma laughed. "Cassie doesn't want you."

"Not now," Kyle flopped back on top of the bed. He looked at Irma and grinned. "She was jealous."

"Yes, she was," Irma giggled.

"Are you going to be okay sleeping in the chair?" Kyle asked.

"Yes. I'll be fine," Irma said, standing and turning off the lights. "I feel better having you in the room with me." She grabbed the blanket from the foot of the bed and sat back down.

"Me too, honey," Kyle mumbled. "Me too."

A few hours later, a loud thump against the door woke Kyle. He quickly sat up and looked at Irma. She had her head covered with the blanket.

"Irma," Kyle whispered. "Irma, wake up."

Irma pulled the blanket off her head and had a confused look on her face. "What?" She shouted and glanced around the room.

"Shhh!" Kyle hissed as he raised his index finger in front of his lips.

An eerie, whistling sound from the hallway echoed through the room as Irma's eyes widened with fear. She tucked her feet up in the chair and pulled the blanket back over her head.

"Irma," Kyle whispered as he stood at the foot of the bed. "You hear that noise?"

"Yes, I'm not deaf," she whispered from under the blanket.

Kyle crept to the chair and pulled the blanket off her. He pinched her on top of the arm as hard as he could.

"Ouch," Irma shouted. "What the hell is wrong with you?"

Kyle quickly covered her mouth with his hand. A beam of light glowed through the window and filled the room.

"Oh, no," Kyle muttered. "Not the eighteen-wheeler."

"Where's the light coming from?" Irma stood and grabbed Kyle's arm as she peered out of the window.

"You can see the light?" Kyle looked relieved.

"Yes, and if you pinch me again, you're going to see your lights get knocked out," Irma scoffed.

The light flashed through the room and suddenly went out.

"Do you think that they're still out there?" Irma whimpered.

Kyle shrugged his shoulders as they slowly headed to the window.

"Oh, my God," Irma pointed. "Look, Kyle."

They watched as a person wearing a long dark coat and carrying a flashlight made their way through the deep snow towards the cabin.

"Is that Candace?" Irma shrieked.

"I don't think so," Kyle muttered. "That person is a lot bigger."

The person walked to the side of the cabin and disappeared.

"Where did he go?" Irma shouted.

In an instant, the man emerged from behind the log cabin with a large, black bag behind him and proceeded to drag it through the doorway.

"That's the black bag that I told you about this morning," Kyle excitedly pointed out the window.

"The one with body parts," Irma shrieked.

"Yes," Kyle grabbed Irma by the arm and glared towards the cabin.

Irma clutched Kyle tight. "I'm scared," she said.

"Me too."

They stayed at the window for hours until the light inside the cabin finally went out.

"Okay, Irma. Whoever that was should be leaving any second," Kyle nervously rattled.

"Oh, my gosh," Irma gripped Kyle tighter.

They waited in suspense for someone to leave, but no one ever left.

"What happened?" Irma released Kyle's arm and backed away from the window. "Why didn't the person leave?"

"I think that person lives there." A feeling of nausea swept through Kyle as he rubbed his stomach and sat on the foot of the bed. "My stomach is in knots."

"Mine too," Irma grabbed the blanket from the chair and sat beside him. "Can I stay next to you tonight?"

"Sure, honey." The two of them climbed into the bed, and Kyle wrapped his arm around her as she curled up beside him.

"I don't want to die," Irma's voice nervously cracked.

"Me neither, honey," Kyle muttered. "Me neither."

~ 9 ~

DECEMBER 14

As Kyle awoke from a deep sleep, he felt an intense pain in his chest. He took a deep breath and immediately opened his eyes.

"Irma," Kyle's voice mumbled against Irma's chest. Finally, he pushed her off of him and quickly rolled out of her way.

"Why did you do that?" Irma moaned as she opened her eyes. "I was comfortable."

"Yes, I guess you were," Kyle sat up and rubbed his chest. "You piled up on me as if I were a pillow for your personal pleasure."

"Don't get all turned on," Irma chuckled. "Nothing happened." Irma stood by the bed and dropped the blanket.

"Oh, Irma, you're naked," Kyle shrieked and covered his eyes.

"I'm not naked. I have my bra and panties on," Irma angrily grabbed her shirt off the floor and slipped it over her head. "I bet you wouldn't be covering your eyes if I looked like Cassie or Jill."

"Doll, I didn't mean it that way. It just surprised me, that's all." Kyle grinned. "The last time I saw a woman lying half-naked was ten years ago."

"Well, as I said, don't get all turned on. I sleep in my bra and panties every night," Irma griped as she pulled her stretchy pants over her chubby hips. "Maybe tonight I will sleep naked, so you'll know the difference."

"Don't threaten me with a good time," Kyle smirked and got out of bed.

"Crazy," Irma laughed and went to the window. "I can't believe that someone lives there."

"I can't believe that someone besides me actually witnessed it." Kyle stood at the window next to Irma. "Everyone else was not aware of anything I saw or heard."

"That's not true. Remember the night we played truth or dare? Someone grabbed me by my neck."

"I had initially thought you made it up, but now I believe you." Kyle patted Irma on the back.

"I hope Candace was able to locate help for us or at least found a safe place to stay the night." Irma looked at Kyle. "Do you think that she made it?"

"No, honey, I don't think that she did," Kyle muttered as he lowered his head.

"There's something in my gut that says no as well," Irma sighed and looked at Kyle. "Are you serious about leaving?"

"Yes, doll." Kyle looked surprised. "I hope that you're still going with me."

"Definitely."

"Let's go after dinner tonight." Kyle pointed outside towards the front of the Inn. "We'll leave through the kitchen and head up the driveway towards the road. As long as we layer our clothing enough, we should be fine."

"I think so, too." Irma smiled and walked to the dresser.

"I don't think that we should tell anyone about our plan."

"Me neither. I promise that I won't tell." Irma grabbed a brass tray off of the top of the dresser and held it up in the air. "What's this?"

"What?" Kyle turned around and looked at Irma. His face turned pale, and his jaw dropped.

"What's wrong with you?" Irma chuckled. "You look as if you have just seen a ghost."

"Where did you find that?" Kyle rushed up to Irma and grabbed it out of her hand.

"It was right here on top of the dresser," Irma placed her hand over the spot where it had been. "Why? What's the big deal?"

"Since we've been honest with each other," Kyle looked into Irma's eyes. "This brass coin tray belonged to a patient of mine who died."

"Oh," Irma looked startled. "So, you keep it with you for a memoir."

"No, honey," Kyle groaned. "That man hated me."

"So why do you keep the tray?" Irma chuckled.

"Remember when I told you that I had a bad dream?"

"Yes."

"Well, the man that owns the tray was part of that nightmare," Kyle looked down at the coin tray. "His name was Dondi Morrow. He broke his legs in an accident, and he hired me to take care of him for six months. We were around the same age and had a lot of things in common. I thought it would be a dream job, but he hated me."

"Why?"

"I don't know," Kyle placed the tray back on top of the dresser. "He called me names until the day that he mysteriously died." He looked at Irma. "That means if you can see the tray, it wasn't a bad dream the other night. It really happened, but how can that be?"

"There are a lot of things around here that do not make any sense," Irma muttered.

"You're not lying about that one, doll," Kyle stated. "That's why we need to leave as soon as possible."

"Exactly."

"Well, let's go downstairs and see what's happening," Kyle quickly pulled a hoodie out of the dresser drawer and slipped it over his head.

When they reached the bottom of the stairs, Kyle looked up at the Christmas tree for any dolls. Irma peeped around Kyle's back and saw Cassie staring at them. She quickly stuck her hand in Kyle's back pocket as she blew a kiss in Cassie's direction.

"Well, look who decided to join us," Cassie smirked. "The honeymooners."

"That's not nice, Cassie," Cindy huffed. "I would stay in your room if you would let me."

"Yeah, Cassie," Irma smirked. "Don't be jealous."

"Where's Cynthia?" Kyle asked and tried to change the subject.

"She's in her room," Cindy said, her face becoming worried as she looked at the Christmas tree. "Candace never came back, so hopefully, she made it. There wasn't a doll with her name on it this morning, so that's a good sign."

"Kyle, can I talk to you?" Cassie extended her hand toward Kyle and looked at Irma. "Without your sidekick."

"Yes, honey," Kyle smiled and grabbed Cassie's hand.

Cassie and Kyle walked off, and Cassie looked back at Irma. Irma stuck out her tongue at her, and she did the same thing back at Irma. They went inside the office, and Cassie closed the door.

The office was small and cozy. Bookshelves packed with statues and plastic flowers lined the wall, but no books or pictures, which Kyle thought was odd. A large oak desk with a black office chair and two purple padded chairs in front of the desk filled the room.

"What do you want to talk to me about?" Kyle asked as he pushed one of the purple chairs closer to the desk and sat down.

"I want to talk to you about Irma," Cassie said as she sat down behind her desk.

"Irma?" Kyle chuckled. "What about Irma?"

"I don't think that she's the right person for you," Cassie replied as she crossed her arms across her chest. "She is devious and manipulative."

"Irma?" Kyle laughed. "I don't think so."

"Trust me," Cassie angrily remarked. "She is. Irma will tell you and agree with anything to get what she wants."

"Why do you think that?" Kyle immediately thought about last night and how frightened Irma was. "What would she possibly want from me?"

"Money, sex, who knows?" Cassie shrugged her shoulders. "Maybe she's just pretending to be your friend to get information out of you."

"Well, I don't believe it."

"Are you having sex with her?" Cassie glared into his eyes.

"Lord, no," Kyle shrieked. "She's not my type."

"So, you're really just friends?"

"Yes."

"Oh, thank goodness," Cassie smiled and relaxed her shoulders.

Kyle watched as Cassie's demeanor quickly changed. *She's jealous,* he thought.

"I thought it might have been something more by the way Irma acted when she came downstairs this morning."

"No, honey," Kyle grinned. "It's only one person that I'm interested in, and that's you."

Cassie blushed and softly giggled as she opened one of the drawers and pulled out a stack of papers. Kyle leaned back in his chair and noticed a small trash can underneath the desk next to her. The dolls that Cindy brought to the office were inside. *Why would she throw them away?* He thought as he tried to examine the dolls without Cassie noticing him. A burlap doll was laid on top, with Candace's name embroidered in hot pink. *Oh, no! Candace is missing. Cindy said that there wasn't a doll on the tree.*

"Hello," Cassie yelled and scared Kyle. "What are you looking at?"

"Nothing," Kyle nervously replied. "I was thinking about what you said about Irma."

"Oh, don't worry about that," Cassie chuckled. "We're done with that." She held up a piece of paper. "I found this in Cathy's room." She handed it to Kyle. "Cathy started writing a letter but never finished it. I think the person she was writing to, Dorothy, is Pat's daughter."

"Dorothy, I know who is responsible," Kyle read with a puzzled look on his face. "That's it?"

"I think she was interrupted because the ink line from the last word goes across the paper."

"Yes, I think so too," Kyle looked back down at the paper. "That would explain the half-eaten apple on the floor. Do you think she was able to figure out who was behind all of this?"

"Who knows," Cassie rolled her eyes. "Pat was a little on the bizarre side." She chuckled. "Don't you remember bingo night?"

"Oh, yes," Kyle laughed. "She kissed Lucky the frog. I thought that she was funny."

"Funny?" Cassie grumbled. "Weird is more like it."

Kyle glanced around the room. "Cassie, where's the phone that you said was in here?"

"Oh, I put it away since it's not working." Cassie reached over the desk and grabbed the paper away from Kyle. "Why?"

"I wanted to check and see if the lines are still down," Kyle grinned.

"The repair will not take place until after the storm. It's nothing new to me. I've been through this before." Cassie shoved the paper into the stack and put it back into the drawer.

"The weather is bad," Kyle remarked. "Do you think Candace is okay?"

"I'm sure she is," Cassie muttered as she stood and went to the door. "Wherever she is."

Why is she lying about the doll? Kyle walked toward Cassie as he thought. *But, then again, she might not want to cause Cynthia any more pain.* Cassie smiled at him as he walked by and grabbed his arm.

"I know that you saw the dolls in the trash can," Cassie whispered in his ear. "Keep it to yourself because I don't need another lynching led by Shannon again."

"Don't worry," Kyle sighed with relief. "I knew that you had a reason for doing that."

"See," Cassie pointed across the lobby. "They're all standing in front of the Christmas tree waiting to see who's next."

"You did the right thing by throwing it away," Kyle grabbed Cassie's hand, and they joined the group of women.

"Well, I guess the killer took last night off," Shannon sarcastically remarked as she stared at the top of the Christmas tree.

"Yeah, but how long will that last," LaDonna muttered.

"That's the truth," Loretta agreed.

"Look, ladies," Cassie walked through the center and broke up the group. "Candace did not return, so she had to arrive safely. Right?"

"That's true," Jill smiled and looked at Brenda.

"Thanks to Candace, we should have somebody arrive here at any moment to help us." Cassie smiled. "If they're not here today, they'll surely be here tomorrow."

"What do you think, Kyle?" Brenda asked.

Kyle glanced around at the women's concerned faces and thought, *you need to be worried, fools. Cassie just fed you a plate of false hope.*

"Well?" Shannon demanded and placed her hands on her hips.

Kyle looked nervously at Shannon. *She looks as though she's ready to choke somebody herself.* "Yes, we'll be fine," He smiled. "Candace is probably with the sheriff now."

"I hope so," Cindy Etta joined the group of ladies. "Lavivian wants everybody in the dining room. She made buttermilk waffles."

"Oh, yes," Irma squealed with delight as she scurried to the dining room.

"It would be nice if that one disappeared for good," Cassie mumbled and turned toward the women. "It's just a matter of time before our help arrives, so enjoy your breakfast, ladies."

The mood lightened as everyone grew hopeful that help would soon arrive in each hour that passed. Everyone spent the day in the lobby and kept a close eye on the front door. Finally, Cynthia came downstairs and joined them that afternoon. Everyone boasted about Candace and knew that she would succeed. Darkness fell as evening approached, but everyone's hopes remained high as they gathered back in front of the fireplace after dinner.

"Well, ladies, let's give Lavivian and Cindy Etta a big round of applause for the wonderful dinner," Cassie loudly announced. "Also, Brenda, for the scrumptious dessert."

Everyone cheered.

"It doesn't look as though anyone is going to rescue us tonight, but I'm sure they will be here as soon as possible," Cassie said with a smile. "I am going to call it a night, and I suggest you ladies do the same."

"I think so, too," Loretta grinned as she patted Cassie on the back. "I will finally get a good night's sleep since everything has been happening for a long time."

"Yes, me too," Irma cheered.

Cassie glared at Irma and rolled her eyes as she headed upstairs. Everyone followed and went straight to their rooms. Cassie hurried and entered her room before Kyle and Irma could catch up with her.

"What's wrong with your woman?" Irma laughed as she entered Kyle's room.

"She doesn't like you staying here with me," Kyle replied, glancing at Cassie's room before closing the door.

"Oh, my God, is that a news flash?" Irma chuckled as she flopped down on top of the bed.

"What are you doing?" Kyle shrieked. "We need to leave."

"Leave. Why?" Irma sat up and stared at Kyle with a bewildered expression on her face. "Why should we go? Candace is probably on her way back here with the sheriff."

Kyle sat down beside Irma and placed his hand on her knee.

"What is it?" Irma asked.

"I promised that I wouldn't say anything," Kyle lowered his eyelids and looked at the floor. "Candace didn't make it. Cassie found a doll on the tree this morning and took it down before anyone could see it."

"What the hell," Irma cried. "So, the whole day was nothing but bullshit."

"Cassie had to hide the doll, Irma, because everybody, especially Cynthia, would have been devastated."

Irma stayed silent, and after a while, she shook her head and agreed.

"I didn't understand why she hid the doll at first, but I understood as the day progressed, and I watched everyone in better spirits." Kyle looked at Irma. "Everyone would have argued, fought, and accused each other, resulting in utter chaos."

"Yes, they would have." Irma wiped the tears from her eyes. "Poor Candace. I feel so bad for Cynthia." Irma stood and grabbed Kyle's hand. "We need to get out of here and get them the help they were waiting for."

Kyle smiled and stood by Irma. "Let's do this."

As they layered their clothes, Kyle turned away from Irma and opened the dresser drawer. He quickly checked the phone for any missed calls and stuck it inside of his jacket. Next, he pulled out two flashlights from another drawer and handed one to Irma.

"Where did you get that?" Irma asked.

"During the search in Rick's room yesterday, I stumbled upon them." Kyle wore two knitted hats and a pair of thick wool gloves to cover his head and hands.

"I'm ready," Irma whispered as she tied the strings from her cap that covered her ears under her chin.

"Ok, be super quiet," Kyle spoke softly as he placed his finger in front of his mouth. "Shh!"

Irma and Kyle crept down the hallway and stairs to the kitchen. Kyle watched as Irma grabbed a cupcake from off the counter and shoved it inside of her mouth. He opened the kitchen door quietly, and they hurried outside.

"Damn, Irma," Kyle shook his head as Irma licked the icing from her lips. "Are you always hungry?"

"As a matter of fact, I am," Irma hurriedly pulled out her gloves from her jacket and slipped her hands inside. "When I'm nervous, I eat." She looked frightened at Kyle. "I'm scared," she shouted above the loud roar of the strong wind.

Irma held Kyle's hand, and he pulled her behind him as he made his way to the front of the Inn.

"Don't walk so fast," Irma huffed. "The snow is deep, and I have short legs!" She jerked his hand for him to stop. "Look! The snow is up to my knees!"

Kyle stopped and turned toward Irma. "If we move too slow, we'll freeze to death," he shouted and released her hand. "Come on!" Kyle made it to the front of the Inn and watched as she struggled to keep up with him. "Maybe this isn't a good idea, Irma. I don't think that you'll be able to make it."

"I'm fine," Irma gasped and tried to catch her breath. "Just move a little slower."

"Okay," Kyle shouted as he pointed to the tree-lined driveway. "That way leads to the road. Don't turn on your flashlight until we get to the driveway. The Christmas lights will light the way until then."

The icy wind pierced their faces and felt like a thousand needles pricking their flesh. Irma clutched tightly onto Kyle's hand as they trudged slowly through the deep snow towards the driveway.

"We made it, Irma," Kyle gasped. "Hopefully, the rest of the way won't be as bad. The trees should block most of the wind."

"The rest of the way?" Irma panted. "We're only at the front of the Inn." She pointed back to where they began. "Unless I turn into the abominable snowman, I seriously doubt if I'm able to make it all the way to the gas station."

Kyle pointed his flashlight down the dark, tree-lined driveway. "Irma, at least go to the road." Kyle yanked Irma's hand exasperatedly. "If we can make it to the mailbox, you can go back to the Inn, and I'll walk to the gas station alone."

"I don't know," Irma shrugged her shoulders as she glared up the long driveway. "I thought that I could make it, but that looks scary up ahead, and I'm tired."

"Irma," Kyle pleaded. "If we don't get help, we'll die."

Irma hesitated for a few seconds before she nodded her head to continue. The wind howled through the trees as they continued up the driveway. Then, suddenly, someone appeared in the distance by a big, crooked tree, and Kyle stopped.

"Did you see that?" Kyle shrieked.

"See what?" Irma glanced ahead.

"Up there," Kyle moved the beam of light slowly across the driveway, and the bright glow flickered through the trees into the darkness. "It looked like a person."

"It probably was a bear," Irma chuckled.

"There are no bears in December."

"Oh, that's right," Irma rolled her eyes. "They're in hibernation like we should be."

"Look," Kyle shouted and pointed into the light. "There it is."

In the distance stood a lady with red hair and wearing a long pink robe.

"Is that Pat?" Irma quickly hid behind Kyle.

"It looks like her, but how can that be?" Kyle grabbed Irma's hand.

The lady stood motionless as her long robe waved rapidly in the wind. Irma and Kyle trudged slowly through the snow toward her.

"Pat," Kyle shouted. "Is that you?"

Irma gripped Kyle's arm tightly as the lady slowly turned towards them. Her flaming red hair framed her face, which was pale as the moon, with deep shadows under her protruding cheekbones. Her eyes were black as coal. She lifted her thin arm in the air and pointed in the road's direction.

"Run, fools, run for your life," Her voice bellowed over the howl of the wind.

Kyle and Irma screamed with terror. As Kyle turned, he ran into Irma and fell backward into the snow. He watched as the lady crept closer to him and was too scared to move. Kyle tightly gripped the flashlight like it was a weapon when suddenly, Irma grabbed his arm and jerked him back up from the ground. They quickly high-stepped their way through the snow and across the driveway into the tree line's thick underbrush. Kyle pulled Irma down next to him and hid behind a snow-covered bush.

"Oh, damn," Kyle gasped for air.

"Was that Pat?" Irma wheezed.

"Yes, I think so," Kyle muttered as he peered over the snow mound in the direction of the woman. "I don't see her." He stood and helped Irma up. "It's not safe to stay here."

"I'm not going back alone, Kyle," Irma's voice trembled. "I'm going with you."

Kyle grinned and hugged her. "I wouldn't let you go back there, Irma." He pointed at a path between the trees. "I think that we should stay off the driveway and take this path."

Irma nodded her head and agreed.

The path covered with underbrush and deep snow made the walk more difficult, but Kyle and Irma felt safer than walking in the open. Then, after a while, Kyle suddenly stopped, and Irma glanced around.

"Why?" Irma shouted.

Kyle turned quickly around and covered Irma's mouth with his hand. "Shh!" He frowned and motioned with his eyes in the direction he wanted Irma to look.

Irma put her hand on Kyle's waist as she leaned slightly past his chest and peered out from behind him. She gripped his waist tightly, and her jaw dropped. Kyle hurried and placed his hand back over her mouth.

"Don't scream," he whispered.

"Is that Patricia and Candace?" Irma stuttered softly.

"Yes, I think so," Kyle muttered. "But, I don't plan on finding out. Let's go this way."

Kyle held Irma's hand and pulled her behind him as they briskly walked away from the two ghostly figures. They walked for hours when, finally, they came to a clearing.

"Where are we?" Irma huffed and folded her arms across her chest. "I'm freezing, Kyle."

"I know, honey, me too," Kyle held the flashlight in front of him and moved the light slowly around the area. "How can this be?"

"What?" Irma turned her flashlight in the direction of Kyle's. "Is that the log cabin?"

"Yes," Kyle looked confused. "How is that possible? We were going in the opposite direction."

"I don't know, Kyle, but I'm scared," Irma tugged on Kyle's jacket. "I think that we should go back to the Inn."

"Look, Irma," Kyle pointed towards the log house. "The light is on."

Irma watched as Kyle walked towards the cabin. "No, Kyle," Irma shouted. "Don't go over there."

Kyle ignored her, so she hurried through the deep snow after him. When they were almost to the front of the cabin, the light went out, and the front door flew open. They stopped in horror as a tall, dark image stood at the door. Kyle flashed his light towards it and caught a glimpse of the man's face. The man suddenly raised a bloody ax above his head.

"Run, Irma," Kyle screamed at the top of his lungs.

Suddenly, as Irma turned, she lost her balance and fell face down on the frozen pond.

"Irma," Kyle screamed as he flashed the light behind him. "Where arc you?"

Irma held the flashlight tightly as she placed her fist on top of the ice to help her get up when she saw something underneath her. She turned the light towards the pond and screamed with terror.

"Irma," Kyle grabbed her and pulled her off the ice. "Get up! He's coming!"

The bloody ax suddenly fell next to Irma in the snow. Kyle jerked Irma off the ground and pulled her behind him as they ran towards the Inn.

When they reached the Inn, Kyle swung open the kitchen door and yanked Irma inside. He slammed the door and locked it.

Irma leaned against the counter and grabbed her chest. "I can't breathe," She huffed.

"Come on, Irma," Kyle grasped her hand once again and pulled her behind him up the stairs and into his room.

"Are you okay, doll?" Kyle asked as he locked the door.

Irma remained silent as she flopped down in the chair in front of the fireplace. Kyle tossed a couple of logs onto the grate and started the fire. He added a few more logs and looked at the blank expression on Irma's face.

"What's wrong, doll?" Kyle asked as he sat on the footstool in front of her.

"I'm going to die," Irma started to cry.

"No, you're not," Kyle placed his hands on her knees. "Why would you say something like that?"

"When I fell on top of the pond, I saw something under the thick layer of ice," Irma whimpered.

"What did you see?" Kyle asked.

"Me," Irma bawled.

"You saw yourself under the ice?"

"Yes," Irma dried her face with the sleeve of her jacket.

"Maybe it was just your reflection on the ice." Kyle worriedly grinned. "It was dark, and we were scared."

"No," Irma quickly interrupted. "I know what I saw."

Kyle placed pillows and a purple cover from the bed on the floor in front of the fireplace. He took Irma by the hand, and they sat down on the blanket. He wrapped his arm around her and cradled her against his chest as they leaned back against the pillows. They remained quiet as they gazed into the flickering flames of the fire.

~ 10 ~

DECEMBER 15

Kyle awoke to find Irma still cradled in his arms.

"Hey, doll," Kyle gently squeezed her. "Are you okay?"

Irma opened her eyes slowly, then suddenly jerked and sat up as she glanced around the room.

"Calm down, honey," Kyle gently rubbed her back. "You're okay. It's morning, and we're safe inside my room."

Irma jumped up and ran to the window. Her face looked worried as she gazed outside.

"What's wrong, Irma?" Kyle swiftly went and stood next to her.

"No wonder I feel sick to my stomach every time I look at that place," Irma glared at the log cabin. "I'm going to die, Kyle. That image in the ice was a warning, like a premonition, that I'm going to die there."

"Don't be silly, doll," Kyle chuckled. "It was dark, and we were scared. What person wouldn't be scared? That freak with the plaided shirt was chasing us. I honestly think that you saw your reflection on the ice. Don't you think that makes more sense?"

"Sense?" Irma glared at Kyle. "Name one thing about last night that makes sense. We saw Pat, Patricia, and Candace. Besides, if it was just a reflection, why were my eyes solid white?"

Kyle stared silently out of the window at the cabin.

"This place is evil," Irma boldly remarked.

"I think so, too," Kyle had a worried expression on his face as he turned toward Irma. "It all started that day when I drove through Chattanooga. I was on seventy-five one minute, and the next, I'm here. I don't believe in ghosts, spirits, and all of that, but I'm a believer after last night."

"My belief in ghosts has always been strong, but I have never actually seen one until now." Irma patted Kyle on the back. "I know that you don't believe me, but that was me in the pond trapped under the ice, just like that was Pat, dead with the black, evil eyes."

"Irma, right now, I don't know what I believe anymore." Kyle continued to stare at the cabin. "What do you think is his part in all of this? I think he's taking the women and murdering them."

"Who's part?"

"Rick," Kyle marveled at Irma's foolishness. "The man who opened the door in the cabin with the red and black plaid shirt. You couldn't tell that it was Rick?"

"No, when the door flew open, all I saw was a dark figure with an ax."

"Well, believe me, I did," Kyle replied in a raspy tone. "I can't believe that you didn't see his face."

"Should we tell the others?"

Kyle thought about it for a while and shook his head. "No, Irma. I don't think that they would believe us. Everybody likes Rick, and you don't even believe that he could be a murderer. Furthermore, Cassie will get mad at us for not discussing it with her first."

Irma remained quiet and finally agreed.

"I believe that we should try again to leave."

"I don't know," Irma replied as she stared out of the window. "The snow is so deep, and the wind cuts right through me."

"We don't have a choice, doll." Kyle patted her on the back. "Either we stay here and die or take our chances out there."

"I guess you're right," An expression of solemnity filled Irma's face. "My life is worth taking a chance, and I'm not giving that damn ax murderer an easy kill."

"Me neither. Well, let's get ready and go downstairs." Kyle went to the dresser and took his phone out of his pocket. He had a missed call from Jennifer's husband, Tim. Kyle tried to call back, but there was no service. Kyle looked back at Irma. She was busy changing her clothes, so he quickly shoved the phone back inside the drawer. *It figures that Tim would manage to get through. I really need to talk to him.*

Kyle and Irma arrived downstairs to find all the guests gathered around the Christmas tree. Kyle knew from the look on Cassie's face that something terrible had happened.

"What's going on?" Kyle asked.

"Why don't you ask her?" Shannon pointed at Cassie.

"I know that you took the doll off the tree and hid it," LaDonna shouted in Cassie's face.

"Did you take Candace's doll off the tree, too?" Cynthia angrily yelled.

"Enough," Cindy shouted and stood in front of Cassie. "I'm tired of everybody jumping my sister! If she said there was no doll, there wasn't one. End of story."

"Then where is Brenda?" LaDonna shouted. "Six people are missing, and I presumed that they are dead."

Irma and Kyle glanced nervously at each other.

"Will you please do something," LaDonna said, pushing Cindy out of her way. "That's all we are asking you to do. You own this place, and it's your responsibility that we are safe. At this rate, we will all be dead by Christmas."

"What do you want me to do? I am stuck here just like you," Cassie angrily replied as she leaned closer to LaDonna's face. They glared into each other's eyes when Rick walked into the room.

"That's enough!" Rick quickly made his way into the center of the group. "Enough! What do you want Cassie to do? We can't leave. We have no way of communicating with anybody. So, if you think that you can leave, then leave!" He looked at Kyle. "What's wrong with you?"

Kyle's face looked pale, and his body trembled with fear. No words came out of his mouth when he tried to answer.

"Whatever, man," Rick snarled as he walked away.

So, what are we going to do?" Shannon sarcastically remarked. "Oh, I know! We're going to search this place!" She threw her hands up in the air. "Well, go ahead and count me out. Hopefully, Candace will show up today and rescue us." She grabbed Loretta by the hand and headed to the dining room. "We might as well stay nourished and wait our turn. Maybe we can whip their ass," she snickered and looked at Cassie as they exited the room.

"What's wrong with you?" Irma whispered to Kyle.

"Did you notice Rick's shirt?" Kyle whispered back.

"Yes, why?"

"That's the same red and black plaided shirt that the killer wears. I told you that it's Rick."

"What are you two whispering about?" Jill asked.

"Nothing," Irma snapped.

Kyle nervously smiled. "Jill, we're going to the dining room. Would you like to join us?"

Cassie quickly grabbed Kyle's arm. "Before you go, I want to talk to you."

"Irma and Jill, go ahead. I'll be there in a minute," Kyle grinned as he watched them walk away, then turned towards Cassie. "What do you want to talk about?"

Cassie glanced nervously around to make sure that they were alone. Then, she pulled a white burlap doll from the pocket of her sweater and held it in front of her. "Look, it's Brenda's doll."

Kyle's eyes widened as he read Brenda's name written in blue across the chest. "Oh, no," Kyle shrieked. "What the hell is happening?"

"I don't know!" Cassie quickly crammed the doll back inside of her pocket. "Somebody has to be hanging these damn things on the tree, but who?"

"Why are you hiding them?" Kyle lowered his voice when he saw Cindy looking at them from the other room.

"Why would you ask me something like that?" Cassie looked surprised. "You have just witnessed their behavior."

"Because you can't hide it," Kyle raised his voice and threw his hands up in the air. "There are only twelve people left, Cassie. So, sooner or later, the truth will come out. When it does, all hell will break loose, especially if you keep hiding the damn dolls."

Cassie lowered her head and thought about it for a few seconds. "You're right."

"They are going to think that you're behind the disappearances and turn against you." Kyle gently pushed the hair away from Cassie's face and tucked it behind her ears.

"Kyle, I don't know what to do," Cassie softly replied, looking tenderly into his eyes. "I need you. I could use your advice, but you're always around Irma. She's not the only one who is scared. I'm scared, too."

"I know, but Irma's not as bad as you think." Kyle smiled. "In fact, she has been a good friend to me, and I probably should tell you something."

"What?"

Kyle hesitated a few seconds and looked into Cassie's eyes. "While we should have discussed it with you first, we attempted to leave last night after dinner."

"Who?" Cassie frowned. "You and your little side-kick?"

"Yes, but we didn't get very far," Kyle glanced around the room for anyone before he continued. "Somehow, we got turned around and ended up at the log cabin. Rick came out of the door swinging an ax and chased us back to the Inn."

"Rick," Cassie shrieked, looking bewildered. "Are you sure it was him?"

"Yes, doll, I stared straight at him." Kyle grabbed Cassie's hand. "Are you mad?"

"No, not at all," Cassie gently squeezed his hand and released it. "I'm so glad that you're okay and that you tried to help us, but I hope next time you will trust me enough to tell me in advance."

"I'm so relieved," Kyle sighed. "So, what do you think we should do about Rick?"

"I am not sure at the moment," Cassie looked worriedly through the dining room doorway. "Give me some time for all this to sink in, and I'll let you know. So, you honestly think that he's behind all of this?"

"Yes," Kyle watched as Rick came out of the dining room and headed up the stairs. "I saw him. He's a murderer."

"Murderer?" Cassie looked alarmed.

"Yes, we saw Pat's ghost."

"What?" Cassie stopped talking when she saw Cindy approaching.

"Well, everyone has calmed down except for LaDonna." Cindy hugged Cassie. "Are you alright?"

"Yes," Cassie smiled.

"I'm glad." Cindy turned to Kyle. "Believe it or not, Irma calmed everyone down. She reminded everyone that Candace should be back at any time to save us."

"Well, I'd be damned," Kyle muttered.

"Oh, that's a surprise," Cassie remarked, patting Kyle on the back. "Maybe it's a good thing that she is hanging out with you."

"I think so," Cindy agreed. "I need your help with something, Cassie."

"Oh, okay," Kyle grinned. "You two go take care of whatever it is, and I'm going to join Irma and Jill in the dining room."

Kyle watched Cindy and Cassie briskly go up the stairs as he moved towards the dining room.

"Hurry up, man," Irma shouted when Kyle entered the room.

Kyle rushed to the table and sat down.

"What took you so long?" Irma asked as she pushed a cup of coffee across the table in front of him.

"Cassie wanted to discuss a few things with me." Kyle looked at Jill and grinned.

"Well, it must have been a long list of things because it took you forever," Irma rolled her eyes when she noticed the sheepish look on Kyle's face as he stared at Jill. "Would you like for me to leave?" She asked sternly.

"What are you talking about?" Kyle chuckled.

"Mister googly eyes," Irma said, looking at Jill and making goo-goo eyes. "I'm in love."

"Irma," Jill laughed. "Behave, silly."

Cindy Etta placed a plate of pancakes and bacon in front of Kyle. "If you need anything else, let me know."

"This looks delicious, honey," Kyle grinned. "Thank you." He watched Cindy Etta as she walked away and noticed Rick by the dining door. Kyle's heart pounded as Rick passed their table and opened the door for Cindy Etta. He smirked and stared back at Kyle as he stood by the kitchen door.

"What's wrong with you?" Irma chuckled.

"Your face is as white as a ghost," Jill grabbed Kyle's arm.

Rick lifted his hand to his stern face, pointed towards his left eye, and quickly pointed at Kyle.

"What's wrong, Kyle?" Jill stood and moved closer to Kyle. "You're shaking like a leaf."

Irma turned in the direction Kyle was looking and asked, "What do you see? It's nothing there."

"I'm okay," Kyle motioned for Jill to sit back down as he leaned closer to Irma. "Rick knows that I know it's him," he whispered.

"Can I have everyone's attention," LaDonna shouted as she stood up. "The guest list is dwindling, and we better figure out something to do before it's too late."

Cynthia's voice was nervous as she shouted, "Candace should be back here at any time!"

"Cynthia, I hope so, but we better decide what we're going to do just in case she doesn't." LaDonna worriedly looked at her. "I don't want to end up like poor Brenda, Callie, and the rest of them."

"Don't worry," Shannon shouted. "I'll think of something." She went over to LaDonna and Cynthia's table, and all three walked out of the room together.

"Do you mind if I join y'all?" Loretta asked.

"Have a seat, Loretta." Jill grabbed the chair next to her and gently pushed it away from the table. "I've been waiting for you."

Loretta sat down and looked at Kyle's pale face. "What happened?"

"Oh, he's okay," Irma mumbled as she shoveled a large piece of pancake into her mouth.

"Kyle, do you think that someone is coming for us?" Loretta asked.

Kyle looked into Loretta's face and saw the fear in her eyes. "I'm not going to lie to you. No, honey, I don't think anyone is coming."

"So, you don't think that Candace made it?" Loretta's eyes widened.

"No, honey, I don't," Kyle sighed.

Loretta looked quickly at Jill and tilted her head towards Kyle. "Ask him!"

"Ask me what, honey?"

"We want to leave," Jill said softly. "Will you come with us?"

"Of course," Kyle looked at Irma. "What do you think?"

"The more, the merrier," Irma mumbled.

"Every day, someone disappears, and we are all trapped. If we stay, we're just waiting for our turn to die." Jill looked at Loretta. "We decided that if we are going to die, we would rather die trying to escape than sitting here doing nothing."

"Definitely," Loretta agreed.

"Let me be honest with you, dolls. We tried to leave last night but did not make it very far." Kyle sipped his coffee as he stared worriedly at the kitchen door.

"What's going on between you and Rick?" Loretta asked. "There is so much tension between you two that you could cut it with a knife."

"Rick's the killer," Irma blurted out as she stuffed the last of the pancakes into her mouth.

"What," Jill shrieked. "How do you know that?"

"Geez," Irma moaned. "He saw him."

"Irma," Kyle angrily raised his voice. "Thanks a lot. Now, he will surely come after me."

"Rick knows that you saw him?" Loretta's eyes widened as she glanced towards the kitchen.

"I didn't want to say anything until I knew for sure." Kyle angrily glared at Irma. "A man chased us with an ax last night by the log cabin. Rick is wearing the same shirt today as the man wore last night. I caught a quick glimpse of his face, and he looked like Rick."

"Judging by the way he's acting today, I think you're right," Loretta said softly.

"That explains the tension between the two of you." Jill grabbed Kyle's arm. "You better be careful."

"Oh, don't worry about me, doll," Kyle grinned at Irma. "The two of us are always together and never alone."

"I moved Loretta into my room because I'm scared to be alone too." Jill worriedly grinned. "So, what time do you want to leave tomorrow?"

"Let's plan on six in the morning." Kyle looked at Loretta and Jill. "Is that a good time for you?"

"That's perfect." Jill stood up. "Loretta, let's go back to our room. I don't feel much like socializing today." She smiled at Kyle. "You are the only one that I trust."

"Me too," Loretta smiled.

"Thanks, ladies," Kyle foolishly grinned. "We will see you in the morning."

Kyle watched as Jill and Loretta walked out of the dining room.

"Do you ever stop," Irma laughed as she made googly eyes. "I bet if Jill ever held an ax up to your throat, you would be trying to catch a kiss instead of running for your life."

"You're probably right," Kyle chuckled. "Well, let's go back to the room before Rick comes out of the kitchen."

"Okay." Irma gathered all the banana nut muffins from her table, piled them up on her plate, and walked around the room, grabbing them from each table. She was at the last table, and she noticed the disgusted look on Kyle's face. "You'll thank me later when you're hungry."

"Twenty muffins, Irma? Really?" Kyle shook his head as Irma scurried towards the stairs.

"Kyle," A woman's voice cried out.

Kyle quickly turned and glanced around the room. "Irma, wait," he shouted. "Did you hear that?"

"Kyle," she cried louder.

"Who is that?" Irma suddenly stopped halfway up the stairs.

"It sounded like Deniese," Kyle muttered as he nervously looked toward the dining room.

"There, you dork," Irma shouted as she pointed to the top of the stairs and pressed the plate of muffins against her chest. "She's up there!"

Kyle quickly looked up the stairs, but no one was there. "Where did she go?"

"How should I know? What do I look like, the tour guide of Cassandra's Country Inn?" Irma's heart sank as she lowered the plate of flattened muffins away from her chest. "Damn, I ruined the muffins."

"Is that all you are concerned about?" Kyle sneered. As he raced past her, he grabbed her arm and pulled her up the stairs behind him.

"Would you slow down," Irma grumbled. "You're making me leave a trail of crumbs, and we're definitely not Hansel and Gretel."

"Well, thank goodness for that!" Kyle suddenly stopped halfway down the hallway. "Look, Irma, did you leave the door open?"

Irma looked at the door and frantically scurried closer to Kyle. "No, I'm sure that I locked it."

They heard laughter inside the room as they crept closer to the door.

Irma's eyes widened as she pressed the plate against her chest and grabbed Kyle by the shirt, pulling him towards her. "Do you hear that?" She whispered. "I'm not going in there."

"Come on," Kyle muttered as his strong fingers pried her hand off his shirt.

They stood in the hallway by the door, and Kyle peered inside.

"Do you see anyone?" Irma softly asked.

"No, doll."

As Kyle and Irma slowly entered the room, he noticed that his cell phone was on top of the dresser.

"Look, Kyle," Irma shouted, pointing at a box in front of the fireplace.

Kyle turned around, and the color quickly drained from his face. His hands trembled as he crept towards it.

"What is it?" Irma asked.

Kyle picked the box up and placed it on top of the chair. "It looks like the box that I threw away at the gas station." He anxiously opened it and looked inside. He closed his eyes and stood motionless for a couple of seconds. He could hear his heart as it throbbed in his ears, as a feeling of dread crept up from the pit of his stomach. Then, he slowly reached inside the box lined in black tissue paper and pulled out a black burlap doll with matching feathers around a small clay face.

"Those are the same dolls that are on the tree," Irma shrieked. "Why are they here?"

"I don't know," Kyle's voice quavered. "This is the same box that I found in my car's trunk the day I arrived and threw it away at the gas station."

"So, that's the box that you were talking about the other day. If you threw it away, how did it get here?" Irma went to the chair and looked inside. "Look at all of the dolls."

Suddenly, pain shot up Kyle's arm, and he dropped the doll.

"What happened?" Irma looked down at the doll and then at Kyle. "Who's Charlie?"

"I don't know," Kyle snapped and snatched the doll from off the floor.

"Hold on just a second," Irma raised her eyebrow and looked at Kyle. "Charlie, didn't you shout that name during bingo?"

"Yes, I shouted that name, but it doesn't mean any-thing." Kyle quickly shoved the doll back inside of the box. "Besides, there's more than one Charlie on this earth."

Irma picked up the box and placed it on the bed.

"What are you doing?" Kyle angrily asked.

"I'm going to search for an Irma doll." She pulled the doll out of the box and placed it on the bed. "Okay, Char-lie." She pulled a green one out and looked suspiciously at Kyle. "Deniese." She picked up five more and laid them in a straight line on the bed. "Dondi, Annie, Lucky, Frank, and Emily." She did not see her name as she looked through the remaining five dolls. "I'm glad that my name isn't on one." She picked up the one with Dondi written across the chest and looked at Kyle. "This is the man that you told me about." She pointed at the green doll on the bed.

"Look, Irma," Kyle replied, quickly tossing the dolls back inside of the box. "I don't know the meaning behind these dolls. The only thing I know is that I had nothing to do with the missing women from this Inn."

"I know that." Irma placed the doll with Dondi's name back inside the box and closed it. "I told you before, and I still believe that someone is after you."

Kyle's phone buzzed and vibrated on top of the dresser.

"What's that?" Irma shrieked.

"It's my cell phone," Kyle rushed to the dresser and looked at his phone. He had one new message.

"A cell phone!" Irma laughed. "Whatever, man!"

Kyle darted to the window and opened up the messages. *A message from Charlie? How is that possible?* He thought.

"If you had a phone this whole time, why didn't you call for help?" Irma smirked.

How can it be Charlie? The message stated, "It's me." *What the hell?* As he watched for a signal, he raised his phone around his head.

"Stop it, man!" Irma laughed. "That's not even a real phone! You're going to make me pee in my pants!"

"What the hell are you laughing at?" Kyle went back to the dresser and opened the drawer.

"I never saw a phone like that before." Irma chuckled as she wiped the tears from her eyes. "That's some funny stuff." She imitated Kyle as she waved her hand around like a robot in the air and made an angry face.

"Of course, you haven't," Kyle scoffed, placing the phone in the drawer. "You aren't familiar with designer clothes either."

"Okay, you got me on that one," Irma giggled. "Kyle, you crack me up. I needed that laugh. You made me forget about dying for a second." She grinned. "Look, I know that you're not behind the disappearances, but you better hide that box to be safe because if Rick finds it, he will convince everyone it's you."

"You're right, doll." Kyle took the box and shoved it under the bed.

Irma sat in front of the fireplace with the plate and tried to salvage the rest of the muffins. Kyle stood silently at the window, deep in thought. *How can that be? All those dolls were my victims. Charlie and Deniese didn't know about any of them, and how did I get a text from Charlie?*

"Hey, Kyle," Irma shouted. "Let's play spades and take our minds off all of this for a couple of hours. I managed to save seven muffins."

Kyle sat down on the floor in front of Irma, and they played cards the rest of the day.

"I'm starving," Irma moaned as she rubbed her stomach.

"Me too, doll," Kyle smiled. "Thank you, Irma."

"For what?"

"For being a friend and keeping my mind occupied on other things. I don't think that I would have been able to make it without you."

"I feel the same way about you." Irma grinned. "Okay, enough with this mushy stuff. Let's go downstairs."

They went downstairs, but no one was there. So, Kyle and Irma looked in the dining room and saw Lavivian at one of the tables.

"Hey, honey," Lavivian shouted as she stood up. "Where's everyone?"

"I guess that nobody is hungry." Kyle smiled.

"Oh, that's silly," Lavivian chuckled. "You have to eat." She patted Kyle and Irma on the back. "I'll make the two of you a couple of cheeseburger platters, and you can take them to your room if you like."

"That's perfect," Kyle grinned. "Thank you."

The lobby remained deserted as they headed back upstairs with their meal.

"Where's everybody?" Irma asked.

"I guess everyone decided to stay in their room." Kyle had a worried expression as he glanced at the Christmas tree.

"Don't worry," Irma chuckled. "That was the first thing that I looked at."

As they exited the stairs and headed to Kyle's room, Jill swung open her door.

"I knew it was you," Jill smiled. "We'll see you in the morning."

"We'll be ready, doll," Kyle winked.

Jill giggled and closed the door.

"I can't wait," Irma remarked as she rolled her eyes.

Kyle and Irma sat on the blanket in front of the fireplace and ate their meal. They spent the rest of the evening in front of the fire and made plans to leave the Inn the next morning.

~ 11 ~

DECEMBER 16

Knock-knock-knock!

Kyle rushed and opened the door.

"Good morning, Kyle," Jill said with a smile. "I'm sorry. I'm a little early, but I was too excited to sleep."

"That's okay," Kyle replied. "I've been up since four o'clock arguing with Irma." He pointed at the large lump in the center of the bed, covered with blankets. "She decided that she wasn't going with us after we sat on the floor most of the night and had it all planned because it's too cold for her to go out."

"Loretta backed out too," Jill giggled.

"Oh, so it's just you and me." Kyle appeared flustered as he turned and looked at Irma.

"I'm not going to waste my energy pulling the cover off my head," Irma shouted from underneath the cover. "This is like your dream come true, so go for it, googly eyes."

"I'll lock the door," Kyle nervously chuckled as he looked at Jill. "Damn, Irma, she says whatever comes to her mind." He hurried out and locked the door before Irma could respond.

They swiftly went downstairs and out through the kitchen.

"That was a lot easier with you than with Irma," Kyle chuckled. "She raided the kitchen on the way out."

Jill giggled.

"Did you notice a doll on the tree?" Kyle asked.

"I didn't see any, did you?"

"No, honey," Kyle replied, pulling his cap down over his ears. "The weather is the same as the other day when Irma and I tried to leave. I've been through Chattanooga quite a bit, but I've never seen snow this heavy."

"It never stops," Jill tugged the zipper on her jacket to the top. "It reminds me of Maine."

"That's the truth. I don't understand it, but what makes sense in this place?"

"There's a lot of things in life that don't if you ask me." Jill gazed into his eyes. "People don't make sense."

Kyle felt as though he was looking into Jennifer's eyes at that moment, and he looked nervously away.

"Did I say something wrong?" Jill asked.

"No, not really," Kyle nodded meekly and smiled. "My ex-wife always said that exact same thing."

Jill bit her lip worriedly and said, "I'm sorry."

When Kyle saw Jill nibble at her lip, his eyes widened as he turned away and thought, *holy shit, not only does Jill look like Jennifer, but she also has the same sayings and habits. How is that possible?*

"Kyle, did you hear me?" Jill asked. "In what direction are we going?"

"Oh, I'm sorry, honey," Kyle nervously grinned. "Let's go straight." Kyle pointed. "We will follow the driveway to the road." He pointed towards the front of the Inn. "The wind is powerful once we get into the clearing, so be prepared."

Jill grabbed Kyle's hand and held it tightly. The Christmas lights lit up the front as they passed the Inn. The wind fiercely howled, and the snow was deep, but they were almost halfway to the tree-lined driveway in a matter of minutes. Kyle was amazed at the difference between Irma and Jill. Irma complained the entire time and could barely keep up with him, and Jill never complained and kept right on his heels.

When they got to the driveway, Kyle turned to Jill and said, "Now the trees will block some of the wind, and it shouldn't be too bad until we get to the road. At least dawn is breaking, and we won't be walking in the dark like Irma and me."

They walked up the driveway, and Kyle stopped and peered into the trees.

"What's wrong?" Jill asked.

"This is where we saw Pat," Kyle turned on his flashlight and pointed it towards the trees.

"Pat?" Jill shrieked.

"Yes, she was right there." Kyle pointed. "Well, not really her, but her ghost. She had the blackest eyes and the most horrific voice. She was terrifying."

"Well, I'm glad that she's not here because I would be too scared to continue." Jill quickly glanced at the other side of the driveway. "I'm surprised that Irma made it this far."

"She didn't want to. Believe me." Kyle looked ahead and could see the road in the distance. "Oh, damn, I can't believe that Irma and I were this close to the road last night." He stuck the flashlight back inside of his pocket. "We're almost out of here. Look, Jill."

"Oh, good," Jill smiled and turned Kyle's hand loose. "Let's keep moving. I'm freezing just standing here in one spot." She crossed her arms against her chest as she tried to warm up.

Kyle felt relieved and never took his eyes off the road as they continued up the driveway. The dull, overcast, gray sky looked bright and sunny through Kyle's eyes, and the strong, icy wind that creaked and moaned through the thick tree line sounded like music to his ears. He knew they would reach the gas station in at least an hour or two if they kept the current pace.

As Kyle stepped from the driveway onto the road, his heart leaped with delight. He looked down the street in the direction of the gas station and pointed. "Look, Jill, Honey, Jamie and Sesailee are only a couple of miles this way," he shouted joyfully. "You'll love them. When we get there, I will buy you a nice hot cup of cocoa and some peanut butter cups." He laughed and turned around, but Jill was nowhere in sight. "Jill, Honey," he shouted as he walked back to the edge of the driveway. "Where are you, doll?"

He turned back towards the road and froze in fear. The old, rusted post mailbox that leaned to the side stood upright, shiny, and new. He crept up and rammed against it with all his might, but it didn't move. Kyle stared in bewilderment at the post when he heard something behind him.

"Jill, you're not going to believe this," Kyle shouted, pointing at the mailbox as he turned around.

"You're not going to believe this," Charlie roared.

"Charlie," Kyle screamed and ran out into

the middle of the road. He looked back, and Charlie was gone. *Did Charlie get Jill? How could that be Charlie? What does he want from me?* Vivid thoughts about his last day with Charlie flew into his mind as he frantically glanced around and noticed that the fallen tree was no longer there. Instead, a heavily snow-covered road that cuts through the thick lining of the forest has taken its place.

"What the hell?" Kyle stared straight ahead at the clearing between the trees. "I must have taken a left at the fork road, and this is the way up the mountain. So, I'm where Brenda and Sesailee told me not to go."

Kyle went back to the end of the driveway and shouted, "Jill, honey, where are you? Jill, please answer me!" He waited for a few minutes and decided to go without her. *Maybe she got scared and went back to the Inn.* He thought as he briskly headed in the direction of the gas station.

Although the deep, powdery snow became hard and icy and made walking difficult, he was determined to keep going as he reflected on all the strange things that had happened since he arrived on the mountain. Then, he felt a renewed energy as he spotted the twenty-foot-tall red rock on the side of the road in the distance.

"Look out, girls," Kyle cheerfully shouted. "Your manther is back!"

The freezing temperature was no longer an issue as he rushed joyfully toward the rock. In his mind, he imagined how Jamie and Sesailee would react when he entered the store. "I can't wait to get the hell out of here," Kyle shouted as he stopped in front of the large rock. Suddenly, his heart dropped as he glanced around in disbelief. "Where in the hell is the gas station?" He briskly went to where the building once stood and slowly circled around. "There's no way in hell a building like that could just disappear in a week." Kyle's face turned red with anger as he clenched his fists, threw his arms in the air, and shouted, "Why are you messing with me?" He fell to his knees and bowed down. "I can't take it anymore. Please, stop," he cried out.

From the road, he heard an engine roar and a horn blast. Kyle thought someone was there to help him and eagerly looked up. He felt as though his soul had left his body at that moment. The blue eighteen-wheeler was stopped right in front of him. The driver laughed as he laid on the horn again.

"Go away," Kyle covered his ears as he pleaded desperately. "I give up! You win! Kill me, and let's get this over with!" Finally, he lowered his head back to the ground.

He wept and waited to die, but to his amazement, he heard the eighteen-wheeler's engine roar as it drove away. Kyle quickly raised his head and got up from the ground. He briskly went to the road and watched as the taillights of the truck faded away.

"I can't believe that even the psycho truck driver felt sorry for me." Kyle looked around but could not find any evidence that the gas station ever existed. "I don't understand any of this. What should I do? Should I go down the road that brought me here in the first place, or should I go back towards the Inn, find the fork in the road, and go right." Kyle weighed out the consequences in his mind and decided to go back in the direction of the Inn.

The fierce, icy wind hammered his body and pierced his face as he headed up the road. He tried to keep an eye on the area around him, but the heavy snowfall blinded him.

"Come on," Kyle shouted as he waved his fist into the air. "Give me a damn break!"

Suddenly, he saw something in the distance on the right side of the road. *What the hell is that? Is that the truck?* Kyle thought as the snow crunched beneath his boots and his feet grew numb. Kyle's terror mounted with every step as he closely watched the object in front of him. As he got closer, he realized that it was a huge sign. His heart dropped as he stared in utter disbelief.

"Opening soon, Cassandra's Country Inn," Kyle smirked as he looked at the arrow that pointed left on the bottom of the sign. "I'm trying to escape the damn place and definitely not trying to find it." He quickly looked towards the right and noticed the clearing between the trees. "This is it! It's the fork in the road that Brenda and Sesailee told me about." He turned back and glanced back in the direction of the gas station. "I don't know what's happening right now, but I know that gas station existed. Brenda, Jamie, and Sesailee were there, and I know it wasn't my imagination, regardless of what I see now."

Kyle turned around and headed down the clearing. He trudged through the heavy snow and thought about all of the horrible things he had done throughout his life. He wondered what his life would have been like if he had been with Cassie rather than Jennifer. Someone in a relationship for love, not the love of money. Every evil thing he did for Jennifer was never enough because she was always hungry for more.

Suddenly, something slammed into the middle of his back, and a woman giggled. He turned around, but no one was there. Then, out of nowhere, a snowball struck him in the head, and he fell to the ground. She burst into laughter again as Kyle grabbed his head and quickly sprang back to his feet. He turned and looked behind him, and fear crept up his spine. The lady stood on the side of the road, dressed in black and wearing a gray scarf that covered half her face.

"Who are you!" Kyle's voice echoed with fear as he stared at the woman and recognized her eyes. "Deniese, is that you?"

The lady laughed.

"Deniese?" Kyle's stomach clenched as Charlie emerged from the woods.

"Well, honey," Charlie chuckled. "Perhaps we should build a fire and sit around and chat about old times.

"I'm sure Kyle would love to make us a hot chocolate," Deniese laughed.

Panic surged through him as he turned quickly around and froze with horror. The man in the red and black plaided shirt was right in front of him. The man swung the bloody ax from his side and raised it high above his head. Kyle felt like his bones had turned into jelly, and he couldn't move. He stared at the ax above the man's head as terror coursed through his veins.

"Look, Deniese," Charlie chuckled from behind him. "The big, bad ole boogeyman is about to slaughter the little chicken!"

"He deserves it, Charlie! Kill him," Deniese shouted.

Fear fueled Kyle's body as he bolted into the woods. He could hear the branches snap and the loud crunch of the man's footsteps in the snow behind him. Kyle's eyes darted from left to right as he tried to find the clearest path to escape. Finally, he found a large fallen tree and hid behind it. He covered his mouth and held his breath as he listened for the man's footsteps to pass him. The man stopped in front of Kyle, and Kyle's heart hammered in his chest. *He knows where I am! Should I run?* Thoughts flooded his mind as he tried not to panic. He exhaled a deep sigh of relief when the man swiftly walked away. Kyle's body felt numb from fear as he laid flat on his back on the ground. *Why is this happening to me?* He got up and went in the opposite direction of the man. Kyle walked for hours and finally spotted a small red house in the distance.

"Please, let someone be home so I can get some help," Kyle pleaded.

He trudged through the snow and never took his eye off the little red brick house. His spirit brightened as he drew closer and saw the smoke emerging from the chimney. As he stepped onto the porch, the place felt strangely familiar. Two white metal chairs sat in front of the large window on the porch, which was the length of the house. There was a large, tarnished brass bell with a long, thin rope hanging from it by the door.

"I've seen this somewhere before?" Kyle muttered as he gently tugged the rope. The bell rang loudly, and he quickly backed away from the door. He waited a few seconds, but no one answered. "Hello! Is anyone at home!" Kyle shouted as he knocked on the door. He lowered his hand to grasp the doorknob when the door opened. "Hello?" His hand shook as he nervously pushed the door open and peered inside. Slowly, he entered the room and glanced around. A small living area was in the front of the house, and the kitchen was in the back. Kyle could see the bedroom through the doorway in the living room. *Why does this place look so familiar?*

"Hello! Is anybody home?" Kyle shouted. "I'm not here to rob or hurt you! I need help!" He heard a noise in the bedroom and waited for someone to answer, but no one came out. "Look, I'm a guest at the Inn up the road, Cassandra's Country Inn, and we need help. I need a ride into Shivered to get the sheriff, so please come out and talk to me."

Kyle crept into the bedroom, but no one was there. So, he went into the kitchen and found a half-eaten muffin and a cup of coffee on the counter. He felt the cup, and it was still warm. *Someone should be back soon, so I'll wait.* Then, he saw a plate full of banana nut muffins by the stove and grabbed one.

As he stood in front of the fireplace and ate the muffin, he looked around the room. Two white chairs sat in front of the fireplace with crocheted throws on the back. A small table with an embroidered rose doily stood between the chairs. In front of that was a basket filled with yarn. *An old lady must live here.* Kyle chuckled to himself as he went into the kitchen and grabbed another muffin.

He went back and stood in front of the fire. *This place is full of antiques, and even the appliances are old. It's a small house, and it's obvious that whoever owns it has money. Look at all the crystal and fine china in the cabinet. So why would someone want to live here in the middle of nowhere?*

Kyle walked around the room. He stopped and admired the ceramic Christmas tree that stood on a small table in the corner.

"Aww, this is so beautiful," he muttered, touching one of the colored lights that protruded from the painted snow-tipped end of the green tree. "This reminds me of the one that Jennifer got when her grandmother died."

"Well, it should," A woman shouted from the bedroom. "It's the same damn tree. You could never keep your grubby little hands off of it."

Kyle's legs felt wobbly with fear as he crept towards the bedroom door.

"You and that whore of a granddaughter I got couldn't wait to get your hands on my belongings."

The ninety-one-year-old lady sat up in the bed as Kyle peered into the room. The color drained from his face as he stared at her thin-frail body, curly gray hair, and leathery face.

"Well, what do you have to say for yourself?" She frowned as her eyes bore into him.

"Mary?" Kyle shuddered.

"What's wrong with you?" Mary angrily asked.

"It can't be you," Kyle shrieked. "You're dead."

"Well, you should know because you're the one that poisoned me," Mary's voice roared.

"This can't be real," Kyle felt dizzy and nervously ran his fingers through his hair.

"Oh, this is very real," Mary chuckled wickedly. "I've been waiting for a very long time for you. Thirty years to this exact date." She raised her eyebrow as she sized him up. "You're still the trembling little coward as you were back then. I was your second victim. Poor Clyde, your own stepdaddy, God rest his evil soul, was your first. Although you did not take anything from him, you and Jennifer couldn't wait to take over my belongings, particularly my bank accounts. Once you got your grubby little hands on them, there was no stopping you."

"That was Jennifer's idea, not mine," Kyle angrily reciprocated. The room started spinning, and he grasped the door frame for support.

"Stop it," Mary shouted. "Stop blaming Jennifer!" She waved her hand into the air and pointed her boney, crooked finger at him. "It's your fault! You're the one that gave me the poison! You're such a coward! You knew that nobody would question the death of a ninety-one-year-old woman. You didn't even have enough balls to just pour it down my throat. So instead, you had to slip it into my hot chocolate," her eyes softened, and she began to chuckle. "You know that he's coming for you."

"Who's coming for me?" Kyle gasped as he closed his eyes and stumbled backward against the wall.

Mary looked at him and laughed.

"Answer me," Kyle cried out as he strained his eyes and tried to focus on Mary.

Mary pointed towards the window. "He's outside waiting for you," She laughed. "What's good for the goose is good for the gander. I hope you enjoyed the muffins, Kyle."

As he fell to the ground, everything became blurred.

"Kyle! Kyle! Can you hear me?" Cassie screamed.

Kyle opened his eyes and looked up at her. "Cassie?" He looked around and realized that he was on the porch. "How did I get here?"

"Hush! Don't talk!" Cassie sprung up and shouted. "Rick, I need a hand!"

Rick rushed out of the door and looked down at Kyle. "What happened?"

"I don't know," Cassie replied worriedly. "As I was going to my office, I noticed something on the porch." She grabbed Kyle's hand. "Help me get him inside."

"Move out of the way. I got him." Rick picked Kyle up and carried him inside. "What the hell was he doing outside?" He smirked as he dropped Kyle on top of the couch.

"Don't be so rough!" Cassie rushed to Kyle and sat beside him on the edge of the couch. "Are you okay? You've been gone all day. What were you doing out there?" She gently brushed the top of his head with her fingers.

"I'm okay," Kyle muttered as he tried to sit up but couldn't.

"What's wrong?" Cassie asked.

"What do you think, Cassie? He was outside in the freezing temperatures for God knows how long." Rick leaned over the back of the couch and grinned at Kyle. "Nice job. I see that you brought back the entire rescue team," Rick sarcastically remarked as he hovered above him.

"Don't make fun of him," Cassie smiled as she patted Kyle's arm. "I'm sure that he was trying to help us."

"I don't feel good," Kyle glanced around the room. "Where's Jill?"

"Jill," Cassie snapped. "Why are you worried about her?"

Rick laughed, and Cassie shot him a dirty look.

"Jill was with me, and then she disappeared," Kyle's voice trembled. "We left early this morning to try to get us some help, but she only made it to the end of the driveway, and she vanished."

"You made it to the road?" Cassie looked bewildered. "I can't believe that you made it that far."

"I went farther than that," Kyle glanced around the room again. "I made it as far as the gas station, but it turned out that there was no gas station. It never existed."

"I told you that," Cassie shook her head.

"So, where's Jill?" Kyle asked.

"Jill never left with you," Cassie scowled. "She's been with us all day."

"You can ask her yourself," Rick pointed towards the stairs. "Hey Jill, come here for a moment!"

As soon as Jill saw Kyle, she ran to his side. "I've been so worried about you today," she smiled. "Did you go out alone?"

"No," Kyle replied, staring at Jill in disbelief. "I went out there with you."

"What are you talking about?" Jill looked surprised. "I know that we were planning to go out together, but Loretta and I decided not to chance it. So, I figured you would get the message if I didn't show up this morning."

"Kyle," Irma happily shouted as she trotted down the stairs. "Where did you go, my ole buddy, ole pal!" She rushed to the back of the couch and leaned over. "I missed you!" She blew him a kiss and snickered as she looked at Cassie.

"Irma! What's wrong with you?" Kyle angrily shouted as he sat up. "I spoke with you this morning before I left." He pointed at Jill. "You heard Jill this morning when she came to our room, right?"

"No, I didn't hear anything," Irma narrowed her eyes as she looked at Jill. "She never came to the room." She leaned over the back of the couch and looked worriedly into Kyle's eyes. "Kyle, last night we argued about going, and you never woke me up this morning, so I thought that you gave up on the idea."

"What the hell is going on?" Kyle shouted.

"I told you that he probably had something to do with LaDonna's disappearance," Rick smugly stated. "Now, do you believe me?"

"What? LaDonna is gone," Kyle shrieked.

"She disappeared at the same time that you decided to take a stroll in the blizzard," Rick puckered his forehead as he glared at Kyle. "That sounds very suspicious to me."

"That's enough," Cassie blurted out. "Look at him!" She pointed at Kyle. "Can't you see that he's not feeling well?"

"Who cares," Rick rolled his eyes. "This freak is behind all of this, and you're worried that the poor baby isn't feeling well."

Kyle lowered his head and laid back down.

"Kyle, we'll stay down here tonight, friend," Irma smiled. "I won't leave your side."

Rick raised his eyebrow and grinned as he looked at Cassie. "Well, there you go. That sounds like a perfect plan," he laughed and walked away.

"That is probably a good idea. He is too weak to climb the stairs, and Rick would probably drop him on purpose." Cassie stood up. "I'll get us some blankets and pillows."

"Get us some blankets," Irma shrieked. "Since when did it turn into the three of us?"

"There are three couches, one for each of us," Cassie said, looking at Irma and batting her lashes as she walked away.

"Well, what do you think about that one?" Irma sat down on the edge of the couch next to Kyle. "She's jealous of our relationship."

Kyle closed his eyes and pretended that he was asleep.

"I did miss you today, you ole shithead," Irma giggled. "Can you hear me?"

Kyle never moved.

"Well, sleep tight," Irma leaned forward and kissed Kyle on the forehead. "I think that I'm falling in love with you." She brushed his hair with her hand and then moved to one of the other couches.

Kyle felt the tension in his body as Irma said the evil word, love. *Why would she say something like that? I have enough problems without Irma trying to jump on the love wagon. So, what the hell is happening to me anyway? I can't tell them anything about today without telling them about my past. If I tell them about my past, they will think I am responsible for all the missing women. So, what the hell am I going to do? The only thing I can do is leave, which is impossible, but I must keep trying. That's the only way out of this nightmare.*

"Okay, here's a blanket and a pillow for you, Irma," Cassie threw the items on Irma's couch and turned to Kyle. "Oh, he's asleep."

"Well, he probably isn't now, with your big mouth," Irma huffed. "So, shut up and let him rest."

Cassie covered Kyle with a blanket and gently picked up his head as she placed the pillow underneath. She smiled and gently brushed his cheek with her fingers.

"Well, damn," Irma shouted angrily. "Do you want me to leave?"

"One could only hope," Cassie grumbled as she laid down and pulled the blanket over her head.

Kyle listened to them argue until they finally fell asleep.

~ 12 ~

DECEMBER 17

"I'm going to kill you," Rick angrily shouted and rushed to Kyle's couch.

Cassie and Irma sprung up and bolted to Kyle's side.

"Move out of the way, Cassie," Rick yelled as he reached behind her and grabbed Kyle by his neck.

"N-o-o-o!" Cassie attempted to block Rick's fist as it flew through the air and exploded against Kyle's face.

Kyle's eyes rolled back in his head as he flopped back down on the couch.

"Kyle! Kyle! Are you okay?" Irma leaned over him in an attempt to prevent any more punches, but Rick shoved her away.

"Stop it, Rick!" Cassie pulled at his arms.

Shannon and Loretta heard the commotion and ran to the couch to help.

Cassie stood in front of Rick while Shannon and Loretta stood behind him. They held onto his arms for dear life and tried to stop him, but he was too strong. He broke through them and charged towards Kyle. When

Irma saw the rage in Rick's eyes, she immediately moved out of the way. He grabbed Kyle like a rag doll and tossed him towards the fireplace.

"Rick! Rick!" Lavivian screamed from the stairs. "Stop!"

Rick turned and looked at his Mom. Cindy, Cynthia, and Jill stood on the steps behind her. Rick held up a gold burlap doll with Cindy Etta written across the chest. "Look, Mom! Look, everybody! Look what he did!"

Everyone in the room gasped at the sight of the doll.

"We're the only ones left." Rick turned toward Kyle and kicked him. "That was my wife."

Cassie rushed and stood between Rick and Kyle. As Kyle struggled to get up from the floor, she reached out her hand to help him.

"Rick, I love Cindy Etta too, but just because she's missing doesn't mean that Kyle had anything to do with it," Lavivian softly spoke as she went to stand next to Rick.

Rick looked down at the doll and threw it into the fireplace. His eyes filled with tears as he quietly watched the doll burn.

"I'm sorry, Rick," Jill gently rubbed Rick's back.

"We are just like sitting ducks," Cynthia cried. "Every day, someone disappears, and we just sit around and wait for our turn."

"How stupid is that?" Cindy shook her head.

"My poor baby," Cynthia cried. "She's gone."

Cindy hugged Cynthia. "We don't know that. Chances are, Candace is somewhere warm and safe." She wiped the tears from Cynthia's cheek. "The weather is terrible, and she might not be able to return until it clears up."

"I don't care what any of you have to say," Rick angrily glared at Kyle. "I think that you're behind this."

"What makes you think that?" Shannon raised her eyebrow and folded her arms across her chest. "Because Cindy Etta is missing?"

"No! I thought that from day one," Rick stated, pointing at Kyle. "Think about it. The day that he showed up, Pat disappeared. He admitted that he had the dolls in the trunk of his car, and ever since Kyle arrived, he's been acting weird."

"Well, we think it's you," Irma shouted. "Kyle and I saw you by the little log cabin."

"What log cabin? What are you talking about?" Rick glared at Irma. "So, you think that I killed my wife?"

"Well, you wouldn't be the first man to kill their wife," Irma smirked.

"Enough," Cassie shouted. "We're done with this little blame game."

"We are also done with searching this place over and over like a bunch of idiots." Shannon looked at Cassie and gave her a dirty look.

"Since you always act like you're in charge," Cassie glared back at Shannon. "What do you suggest that we do?"

"Okay, there's ten of us left. We need to divide up into two groups. The first group will try to leave and get us some help today, and the second group will try tomorrow." Shannon looked at Lavivian's worried face. "Don't worry, Ms. Lavivian. We don't expect you to go out in that weather."

Lavivian looked at Shannon and smiled.

"That sounds like a plan," Loretta grinned. "Much better than waiting around to be rescued and acting as though nothing happened."

"Okay, that sounds good to me. Kyle, do you feel up to it today, or do you want to be in the second group?" Cassie asked.

"No, today is fine," Kyle nodded meekly and smiled.

"Okay, Kyle, Irma, Loretta, Cindy, and I will be the first group." Cassie grabbed Rick's arm. "You, Shannon, Cynthia, and Jill will be the second group. In order for the groups to be equal, I will go out again tomorrow."

"Oh, no," Rick angrily raised his voice, pointing at Kyle. "He's not staying here with my mother. Are you crazy?"

"I will go out with your group tomorrow, and Cassie can stay here," Kyle quickly interrupted.

"Are you sure, Kyle?" Cassie asked.

"Yes, it's no big deal," Kyle grinned. "I would rather be out there than in here doing nothing."

"Okay, everyone that is going out today, get dressed, and we'll meet back here in thirty minutes," Cassie shouted as she headed towards the stairs. "Don't forget and layer your clothes!"

Irma followed Kyle upstairs to his room. He took his phone out of the drawer and checked for any missed calls, but the battery was dead. Irma silently watched him as he plugged the phone into the charger. She could tell that Kyle was worried about something.

"Can you believe that LaDonna and Cindy Etta are gone?" Irma went to the window and looked out. "I wonder who is going to be next?" Kyle didn't respond. She turned around and watched him as he stared at himself in the mirror above the dresser. "Are you okay?"

"Irma, I'm not okay," Kyle turned and looked at her. "We're not okay. Something is very wrong here, something evil. All the strange occurrences, people disappearing, and we can do nothing to stop it."

"Well, I told you that a while back, and you acted like I was being a negative Nancy," Irma smirked.

"Irma, I'm serious," Kyle went and stood beside her. "I swear Jill came to the door yesterday, and you shot off a few of your usual remarks."

"You're buggin me out, man," Irma gasped. "I told you that I never woke up."

"Listen to me," Kyle angrily raised his voice. "Jill and I made it to the road, and suddenly, she disappeared. Remember the gas station where I threw the box of dolls away and met Jamie, Sesailee, and Brenda?"

"Yes, I remember."

"Well, it was gone. The whole damn place just disap- peared. It looked like it never existed," Kyle lowered his head into his hands. "Irma, I feel like I'm losing my mind. They gave me a card and told me about Strittmatter Inn." His eyes sparkled with excitement as he pulled his wallet out of the top drawer.

"What are you looking for?"

"The business card that Jamie gave me," He emptied his wallet, but the card wasn't there. "I must have left it in the car." He stuffed everything back inside and tossed the wallet in the drawer. "Anyway, they told me about the fork in the road and for me to keep right. So that's how I ended up here. I went left instead. I noticed a sign that was not there when I first went through that read, open- ing soon, Cassandra's Country Inn." Kyle slammed his fist on top of the dresser. "I know, without a doubt, that J.H. Pitt Stop existed, just like I heard your little comments or when Jill left with me yesterday morning."

"Kyle, we all feel the same way," Irma sighed. "Ever since I arrived, I never felt comfortable. There is some- thing negative or evil lurking inside this place. I felt it re- ally strong the day that you showed up." She turned and looked out the window. "It's like that log cabin. I know that I'm going to die there."

"Honey, don't say that," Kyle hugged her. "That's not true. I'm not going to let anything happen to you." He gently pushed her away from his chest and looked into her eyes. "I promise."

"I know your words are sincere, but there isn't anything you can do to stop it," Irma's face turned red as she tried to fight back her tears. "I think that you know that too. I told you before that I have the ability to see and communicate with spirits. Some of the things that I see are so evil that I have to turn away. Believe me when I say that we are all trapped here waiting for our turn to die."

"I know," Kyle muttered.

"What are we going to do?"

"We're going to fight," Kyle clenched his fist. "We need to try to leave this godforsaken place. If we fail today, we'll try again tomorrow, and so on, until we finally make it out of here." Kyle looked at Irma and grinned. "I don't know about you, but I don't plan on dying, and I'm not going down easy."

"Me neither," Irma perked up. "You're right. We need to try."

"Well, honey, let's get dressed so we can meet up with Cassie," Kyle grinned. "I'm pretty sure she thinks we've changed our minds."

All eyes were on Kyle and Irma when they came downstairs.

"What's wrong?" Kyle nervously asked as they approached Cassie.

"We thought you might have chickened out," Cassie remarked.

Cindy and Loretta chuckled.

Kyle looked at Irma and smiled. "I told you so."

Cassie opened the front door, and they went outside. An icy gust of wind made all of them stop in their tracks.

"Brrr!" Loretta crossed her arms in front of her chest. "It's freezing out here."

"No shit, Sherlock," Irma shook her head as she rolled her eyes. "What did you expect?"

"Irma, be nice," Cindy scolded as she pulled Irma's scarf up over her mouth and laughed.

"Ladies, we're not off the porch yet, and you're already misbehaving," Cassie grumbled. "Save that energy because you're going to need it." She looked at Kyle. "What's the plan?"

"Oh, my God," Irma shrieked. "While we were inside, you should have made plans. Not freezing on the porch."

"Shhh!" Cindy hissed in front of Irma's face.

"I think we should go down the driveway to the road and keep going." Kyle glanced at Irma. "Are you going to be able to keep up?"

"It was only until we reached the driveway that I had a problem. After that, I was fine, Kyle," Irma huffed. "Why? You don't want me to go now?"

"No, that's not it." Kyle patted Irma on the shoulder. "The road is slick, and even I had a hard time walking on it. If you want to stay here, you can."

"You mean to stay here and die," Irma murmured. "No, thank you. I'll take my chances out here."

"Okay, let's all hold hands so I know that no one is falling behind," Kyle grabbed Cassie's hand.

"That's a good idea." Cindy held on tightly to Cassie and Loretta's hand.

"Well, Irma," Loretta smiled and extended her left hand. "That makes you the caboose."

"So, what else is new," Irma grumbled. "I'm always last."

As they slowly made their way through the deep snow and toward the tree-lined driveway, Kyle thought about Jill and how quickly they had gotten there when it was just the two of them. The cold wind battered against them and helped drown out the complaints and cries that came from Irma. They stopped when they finally made it to the driveway.

"Irma," Kyle shouted. "I told you to stay at the Inn. All you're doing is complaining and slowing us down."

"Despite what you think, you are not my boss, mister," Irma pouted. "Besides, I wasn't the only one complaining." She looked at Loretta.

"I am complaining because you are pulling my arm out of its socket," Loretta shouted. "It's called walking, Irma, not pulling."

"It's too late now for her to turn back," Cassie glared at Irma. "She would never make it back to the Inn by herself."

"Loretta is trippin'," Irma groaned. "I'm cool."

"So, ladies, let us try this again," Cassie rolled her eyes and nodded, waiting for Kyle to proceed.

They continued down the driveway towards the road. Kyle watched closely for the crooked tree where he and

Irma saw Pat. *We should be near the road by now.* Kyle thought as he stopped quickly and looked back towards the Inn. His jaw dropped, and he couldn't believe his eyes. He could still see the Inn and the end of the thick tree line from where he stood.

"What's wrong?" Cassie asked.

"We've been walking for a while and barely moved," Kyle pointed towards the Inn.

Cassie looked back and turned towards Kyle with a confused look on her face. "I don't understand. That doesn't make any sense."

"What's wrong?" Cindy shouted.

"Nothing," Cassie snapped. "Keep going."

Kyle turned and walked at a faster pace. He knew the ladies were getting tired by the way Cassie pulled his hand and started to slow down.

"Stop, Kyle," Loretta shouted. "Irma, are you alright?"

"No," Irma huffed, releasing Loretta's hand. "I feel like I can barely breathe."

"Kyle," Loretta shouted. "Something is wrong with Irma!"

Cindy rushed to Irma's side. "Are you alright? You don't look good."

"I need a minute." Irma placed her hand against her chest. "I'll be okay."

Cassie looked at Kyle and shook her head. "Maybe this wasn't a good idea after all."

"She'll be fine. Just give her a minute." Kyle looked worriedly at Irma.

They huddled together for warmth around Irma and waited for her to recuperate.

"Kyle, how far did you get yesterday?" Loretta asked.

"A couple of miles." Kyle looked into Loretta's light brown eyes, filled with fear.

"Did you see anything?" Loretta asked.

"No, it was nothing around." Kyle immediately thought of the little red house.

"Then why are we doing this, Cassie?" Cindy scowled. "It's pointless if there's nothing around here."

"There's another road that we can try, Cindy," Kyle quickly responded. "That's where the town of Shivered is located."

"Why didn't you go that way yesterday?" Loretta questioned. "Why would you choose to go in a direction where nothing exists?"

"It's a long story," Kyle patted Irma on the back. "Are you okay, honey?"

"Yes, let's go," Irma glanced at Kyle and grinned.

Once again, they held hands and headed down the driveway. Kyle heard Loretta and Cindy complain that their feet hurt and that they regretted leaving the inn.

What's happening now? We've been walking for several hours, and we're nowhere near the road. Kyle thought as he searched for the big, crooked tree.

Cassie stopped and turned back towards the group. "Look, I know that everybody feels like they are freezing to death, but we have to keep going," She shouted. "So, stop complaining! You're just making the situation worse!"

Kyle turned and grinned at Cassie. She smiled back, and they proceeded down the driveway. Then, finally, Kyle spotted the tree and slowed down.

"What's wrong, Kyle?" Cassie whispered into his ear. "What's taking so long? We should be on the road by now."

"I don't know, Cassie," Kyle mumbled. "We should have been there a long time ago."

As they continued, Kyle kept a close eye on the crooked tree. The scenery remained unchanged as their feet moved. They grew tired, and he felt as though they were on a treadmill.

Suddenly, Kyle abruptly stopped and turned around. "I don't know how this is possible or what's happening, but we've been in the same place for several hours." He pointed towards the tree. "See that crooked tree? I've been watching. It's been a while, and we never passed the damn thing."

"What the hell," Irma shrieked. "Look!" She pointed. "Someone is standing by the tree!"

They all turned in a panic and looked in the direction that Irma pointed.

"I don't see anyone," Loretta peered at the thick tree lining.

"Me neither," Cindy huffed. "Is this one of your sick jokes, Irma? The fact that we're tired, cold, and scared is bad enough. Now you're trying to make things worse."

"I did see someone," Irma angrily snapped.

"Who would be out here watching us?" Loretta rolled her eyes as she shook her head.

"Not me," Cindy gave Irma a dirty look.

"Maybe we should turn back," Cassie looked at Kyle.

Kyle remained quiet and stared at the tree.

"Kyle," Cassie shouted. "What are you looking at?"

"Oh, nothing," Kyle nervously grinned.

"We have been out here a long time, and we should have reached the road by now," Cassie stated as she observed Kyle's odd behavior.

"Yes, I think we should go back," Kyle nervously agreed. "Something strange is happening." Kyle turned towards the tree. "It's not letting us leave," he mumbled.

"What did you say?" Cassie asked.

"Nothing," Kyle quickly turned and faced Cassie.

Cassie went up to Irma and grabbed her hand. "I'll lead us back."

Kyle held Cindy's hand as they walked towards the Inn. He turned his head and looked back at Charlie as he stood in front of the crooked tree. *Why can only Irma and I see him?* Kyle thought, and his eyes widened as Deniese appeared by Charlie's side.

"Kyle, are you okay?" Cindy shouted. "You stepped on the back of my boot!"

"What?" Kyle turned and looked at Cindy. "Oh, I'm sorry, honey." He turned back, but Charlie, Deniese, and the crooked tree were gone.

Kyle looked ahead and could see the Inn. He moved up quickly and walked beside Cindy. She smiled at him, and he smiled back. *What is wrong with these people? How can we be back at the Inn so fast? Don't they realize that we've been out for most of the day trying to get out of here, and we're back in a matter of minutes?* Kyle watched in bewilderment as their faces brightened as they trudged through the snow and finally stepped up onto the porch.

Cassie swung open the door. "We're back," she shouted.

"Oh, thank God!" Lavivian rushed up to her. "Did you find anyone to help us?"

"No, I'm sorry," Cassie hugged her. "Maybe Rick will have better luck tomorrow."

"You've been gone almost all day," Shannon shouted as she bolted across the room. "What did you see? How far did you get?"

"A bunch of trees and snow, and we never made it off the property." Loretta kicked off her boots and headed towards the fireplace.

"What the hell?" Shannon threw her hands up into the air and looked at Jill as she entered the room.

"I don't understand it myself," Cindy remarked as she went and stood by Loretta in front of the fire.

"Did you see any signs of Candace or Patricia?" Cynthia asked.

"No, we didn't," Cassie replied.

"What took you so long then if you never left the premises?" Jill asked.

"I don't know," Loretta replied, pointing at Kyle. "We followed him."

"Well, hell," Rick shouted from the bottom of the stairs. "That explains that. That Duffus probably led you guys around in a circle." He walked up to Kyle and glared into his face. "After all, he's behind all of this. So, why is he going to try to get us rescued when he wants to kill us?"

"Okay, Rick, that's enough," Cassie angrily raised her voice and stood in front of Kyle. "Maybe you can do better tomorrow."

"It wouldn't take much," Rick snarled.

"I made a pot of chicken noodle soup." Lavivian smiled meekly. "Just go into the kitchen and help yourself."

"You didn't have to do that," Cassie said, going over to Lavivian and hugging her.

"I know," Lavivian sighed. "When I'm upset, I like to cook." She looked at Rick. "I'm going up to my room to rest for a while. I can't believe that Cindy Etta is gone."

"Me neither, Mom." Rick helped his Mom up the stairs.

"Hey, you guys," Loretta shouted from the dining room. "Come have a seat, and I'll get you a bowl of soup."

"I hope Lavivian made her delicious rolls, too, because I'm starving!" Irma ran to the dining room.

"I don't understand how on earth you would enjoy being around her," Cassie grumbled.

"She's not that bad," Kyle looked at Cassie. "She's just delusional, like the rest of us, who think we can leave this place."

As Kyle sat at the table and ate his bowl of soup, he wondered why the ladies reacted the way that they did. First, he looked at Cassie and Cindy as they bickered about something that had happened when they were young girls. Then, Irma tricked Loretta into looking away while she stole crackers from the side of Loretta's bowl. *It's just like life is normal. It doesn't bother them that their friends are missing, and even when they are upset, they recover quickly. I think they would be really upset by what happened today, and they are not even discussing it.*

"Well, you sure are quiet, Kyle." Loretta smiled.

"Yeah, he looks deep in thought." Cassie giggled. "What are you thinking about?"

"Nothing important." Kyle grinned.

"Look, Kyle," Irma shouted. "Look! There's someone behind you!"

"No, you're not stealing my crackers," Kyle chuckled.

All the ladies laughed.

After dinner, they gathered in front of the fireplace and decided to stay together that night. Cassie and Cindy slept on one couch, Loretta and Irma on another, and Kyle had one by himself. Nobody discussed what happened earlier when they tried to leave or mentioned anything about the missing women. Instead, they argued over who would get the last candy bar and how they wished Lavivian would make them some hot chocolate.

~ 13 ~

DECEMBER 18

"Kyle! Kyle," Cindy screamed. "Wake up!"

Irma ran to the couch where Kyle slept and grabbed his arm. "Get up," she shouted.

Cassie, Irma, and Cindy hovered above him as Kyle opened his eyes. "What's wrong?" He asked.

"Look!" Cindy pointed to his chest.

Kyle spotted a bright gold burlap doll as he looked down on top of the blanket. He quickly grabbed it from the top of the blanket and sprung up. His hands trembled as he held the doll in front of him and read the name Loretta embroidered in dark green across the chest.

"Oh, my goodness," Kyle's eyes filled with tears as he looked at the couch next to his. "She was right there."

"I don't know what you are blubbering about," Irma shrieked. "I'm the one that was sleeping by her. It could have been me."

"Irma, please," Cassie smirked and rolled her eyes.

"That's not nice, Cassie," Irma glared into Cassie's eyes. "I know what you're thinking."

"I doubt that, Irma." Cassie took the doll from Kyle and held it in front of her. "I was wondering, why was the doll by you rather than on the tree?"

Kyle looked at Cassie in disbelief. "Why would you ask me something like that? How should I know?"

Cassie stopped when she heard Shannon, Jill, and Cynthia on the stairs. As they descended the stairway, the three ladies joined Cassie in front of the fireplace.

"Who's missing?" Jill asked.

"Loretta," Cindy sighed.

"Why is this happening?" Cynthia buried her face in her hands.

Kyle's eyes widened when he caught a glimpse of a silver bar bracelet around Cynthia's wrist.

"What are you looking at, Kyle?" Cynthia frowned.

"At his next victim," Rick shouted as he entered the room with Lavivian.

"Behave, Rick," Lavivian nudged him and stared at the doll in Cassie's hand. "Oh, my, is Loretta missing?"

"Yes, Ms. Lavivian. It was her turn today." Shannon turned towards the group. "I don't know why everyone acts so shocked." She threw her hands up into the air. "If we don't find someone to help us today, we will all have our turn with the stupid doll bandit."

"That's the truth," Cindy agreed.

"Everybody that's going out today, get dressed, and we will leave in thirty minutes." Rick went up to Kyle. "You're still going, right?"

"Yes, I am," Kyle replied nervously.

"Better," Rick smirked as he walked away.

Kyle, Jill, Cynthia, and Shannon went to their rooms to get ready before meeting back downstairs. Kyle was the first to return to the lobby.

"Do you want me to go with you, Kyle?" Irma asked. "As we all know, you and Rick do not get along."

"No, honey," Kyle smiled. "I'll be okay. I appreciate the offer, though."

"Yes, Kyle, be careful out there." Cassie hugged him.

"I will," Kyle grinned.

Jill, Shannon, and Cynthia sat in front of the fireplace while they drank their coffee and waited for Rick to arrive.

"I made you a thermos of coffee to take with you, Kyle, to help keep you warm," Lavivian smiled as he handed him the thermos. "I made everyone else hot chocolate, but I know you hate it."

"Thank you, Ms. Lavivian," Kyle grinned. "I appreciate that."

Lavivian went to the fireplace and gave Jill, Shannon, and Cynthia each a thermos.

"Okay, let's go," Rick shouted as he trotted down the stairs.

"Here you go, Rick," Lavivian handed him a thermos. "I made you some hot chocolate." She hugged him. "Be careful out there."

"I will, Mom," Rick grinned.

They gathered by the door while Cindy, Irma, and Cassie wished them luck.

"Okay," Rick opened the door. "Let's go!"

"Be careful," Cassie shouted as she closed the door behind them.

"Okay, we're going down the driveway." Rick paused and looked at Kyle. "You've been out here before, so why don't you tell us the plan."

"We'll go down the driveway to the road and turn left. About a mile up the road, we will come to a fork. I have been to the right, but there is nothing there. Therefore, we will go to the left. The town of Shivered is a mile away from the fork."

"Okay, you heard the boss man," Rick smirked. "Everyone, keep up, and if you fall too far behind, just shout."

"Yesterday, we held hands so nobody would fall behind." Kyle looked at Jill. "What do you think?"

"Yesterday, you didn't get far," Rick sneered. "Probably because you were too busy holding hands with the girls." Rick darted off the porch and motioned for everyone to follow.

Kyle watched as Shannon and Cynthia briskly followed Rick.

"Let's go, Kyle," Jill grabbed Kyle's hand and smiled. "I think that was an excellent idea."

Kyle and Jill quickly caught up with them as they trudged through the deep snow in the clearing in front of the Inn. The wind howled loudly and felt stronger than yesterday.

"Stop," Cynthia shouted. "Wait!"

Jill quickly grabbed Cynthia's hand and pulled her behind. Everyone kept their heads down until they got to the safety of the tree-lined driveway.

"What the hell was that?" Rick shouted as he pulled his scarf away from his face. "Was it like that yesterday?"

"The wind is a lot stronger today." Kyle pointed down the driveway. "The trees will protect us until we get to the road."

"I thought I was going to blow away," Cynthia shrieked. "I never experienced anything like that before."

"Then you better go back," Rick pointed towards the Inn. "It's only going to get worse."

"No, I'm staying," Cynthia gripped Jill's hand tightly.

"Okay, but don't be slowing us down!" Rick turned and headed down the driveway.

"Come on, everybody," Shannon motioned for them to follow. "Don't pay any attention to him. He's not our boss."

Kyle, Jill, and Cynthia held hands as they followed Shannon down the driveway. Rick walked so quickly that he moved way ahead of the group.

"Rick! Slow down," Shannon shouted. "Rick! Stop!" She stared down the driveway at him as the distance grew greater until suddenly, he disappeared. "What the hell! Why did he do that?"

"Who knows," Cynthia stopped and released Jill's hand. "I need to rest a minute."

"Are you okay?" Jill released Kyle's hand and stood by Cynthia.

Kyle walked away from them and joined Shannon farther down the driveway.

"I can't believe that he did that," Shannon shouted angrily. "All that crap that he talks about you, and look at him. He ran off and left us."

"That's okay," Kyle grinned. "We're probably better off without him. At least I know that I am."

"Yes, you definitely are better without him," Shannon giggled as she turned around. "Where's Jill and Cynthia?"

Kyle turned quickly to where Jill and Cynthia were standing, and they were gone.

"What happened to them?" Shannon darted to the side of the driveway and searched for any footprints in the snow. "Take a look around where they were standing, Kyle, and find out which direction they went."

Kyle went to the location where he had last seen them. "Shannon, look," He shouted as he pointed toward the ground.

Shannon rushed to his side and looked down. She couldn't believe her eyes. The only boot prints in the snow were where they last stood. It was just two sets of footprints facing each other, with no tracks leading up to or away.

"That's impossible!" Kyle stared down at them. "It's like they appeared and disappeared into thin air."

"That's freaky," Shannon looked at him.

"Yes, it is," Kyle glanced towards the tree line on each side of the driveway. "I wonder what happened to them?"

"I have no idea. I hope that Jill and Cynthia are okay," Shannon sighed. "Should we continue or go back to the Inn?"

"I don't know," Kyle looked worriedly into Shannon's eyes. "Yesterday, we tried and barely made it this far." He glanced down the side of the driveway and saw the crooked tree. "See that tree up ahead?" He pointed.

"Yes."

"Well, that's as far as we got." Kyle turned back towards Shannon. "Jill and Cynthia probably went back to the Inn. I think the snow and the strong wind were too much for Cynthia to handle. Besides, what else could have happened? People just don't disappear like that."

"You're right," Shannon chuckled. "There has to be a logical explanation for all of this. So, I say that we continue, and maybe we can catch up to Rick."

Kyle thought about how Jill and Cynthia had just disappeared into thin air as they continued down the driveway. *There was no way Jill and Cynthia could have decided to turn back and disappeared out of sight so quickly, just like Rick. So, how did he get that far ahead of them?* In his mind, he relived yesterday as he remembered all the complaints about the strong wind and snow. *I noticed that the snow buried their feet as I talked to them, but did they leave any footprints?*

Shannon suddenly stopped.

"What's wrong?" Kyle asked.

"I need to catch my breath," Shannon said, placing her hands on her hips and taking a deep breath.

Kyle looked on the side of the road at the crooked tree. When he turned back towards Shannon, she was gone. Looking up the driveway, Kyle only saw one set of tracks. He dropped down to his knees.

"Why," Kyle cried. "Why me?"

"Why you?" A man laughed.

Kyle recognized the laugh and turned quickly towards him. "Dondi?"

"Ching! Ching!" Dondi shouted. "Don't you mean sugar daddy? Or maybe you prefer ole money bags." He walked closer to Kyle.

Kyle jumped to his feet. "You're dead!"

"DEAD?" Dondi chuckled. "Do I look dead to you?"

"No, but I know you are," Kyle's voice trembled.

"And how do you know this?" Dondi crossed his arms across his chest, glaring at Kyle's eyes.

Kyle's heart pounded as his body shook with fear.

"I'll tell you!" Dondi's eyes flashed red with anger as he charged up to Kyle. "You murdered me!"

"No-o-o!" Kyle screamed.

"You wanted my money, my truck, and anything of value. I worked hard for my possessions, and you took them like it was nothing. I still had a lot of life to live ahead of me, and you poisoned me," Dondi shouted. "Now you have the audacity to ask why!"

"You better grow a pair, boy," A man shouted from behind him while a lady laughed.

"David and Trish Rios?" Kyle stuttered.

"He'll never grow any because he's a snake!" Trish scrunched up her face and bared her teeth. "H-s-s-s!"

"Look at the little chicken, Deniese," Charlie laughed as he appeared on the other side of Kyle. "He's shaking just like that day with the boogeyman."

Deniese laughed as Kyle turned towards them. His eyes widened with fear as his Mom appeared behind Charlie.

She held out a cup in front of her towards Kyle. "Drink up, you stupid boy," she shouted. "We don't have all damn night!"

Kyle screamed and darted up the driveway towards the Inn. As he looked back, everyone had vanished. His skin became cold and clammy, and his legs felt wobbly as he fell to the ground.

"Kyle, wake up!"

Kyle immediately opened his eyes and saw Jill's face.

"You had a bad dream," she said with a smile.

"Jill, honey, I'm so happy to see you," Kyle smiled as she wiped his head with a cool, damp cloth.

"Jill?" she gruffed. "Who in the hell is Jill?"

He glanced around and realized that he was inside of his old house. The house that he once shared with Jennifer.

Kyle looked into her big blue eyes. "Jennifer? What's going on?" Kyle sat up and glanced around the room. "How did I get here?"

"What do you mean? How did you get here? You live here! You laid down to take a nap and started screaming," Jennifer snapped angrily. "Now, who in the hell is Jill?"

"I live here?" Kyle glanced around the room once more and spotted a photo of him and Jennifer on the mantel of the fireplace.

"That might be up for debate," Jennifer snarled. "Well, who's Jill?"

"I don't know a Jill," Kyle nervously rubbed his head. "That was one hell of a nightmare." His eyes widened when he noticed the wedding ring on Jennifer's hand. "Why are you wearing the wedding ring that I bought you?"

"Because we're married at the moment, but if you keep dreaming about other women, you won't have to worry about it much longer!" Jennifer stood up and slapped him across the arm with the damp towel. "Get up and come eat dinner. It's ready."

Kyle followed her to the dining room and sat down. *What the hell is happening now? The house looks the same as twenty years ago.* Jennifer walked into the room with a platter of fried chicken and sat down next to him.

"I made your favorite," Jennifer grinned and grabbed a chicken breast off the platter. "So, Kyle, what were you dreaming about?"

"Where's Tim?"

"Who's Tim?" Jennifer lifted her eyebrow as she studied him. "Are you okay? Your behavior hasn't been right since the moment you awoke."

Kyle got up from the table and went to the window. He slowly pulled back the curtain and peered outside.

"What are you looking for?" Jennifer asked.

Kyle stared at the black pickup truck in the driveway. *That's the same truck that I owned for years until I went to work for Charlie and Deniese Hanks.*

"Where's my red Corvette?" Kyle asked.

"What red Corvette?" Jennifer laughed until she cried. "You crack me up!" She wiped the tears from her cheeks. "Red Corvette! You've never scored that high before," She chuckled. "I wish that you could find some patients with money."

Kyle went back to the table and sat down.

"Kyle, you're starting to worry me," Jennifer said, feeling his forehead and rubbing his cheek.

"I'm sorry, Jennifer," Kyle grinned. "I'm confused, but I'll be okay."

"Well, I hope so," Jennifer smiled. "Because we are going to put up the Christmas tree tonight, and you know what that means." She grinned and stood up. "I'll be right back. I made your favorite dessert."

Kyle watched her as she smiled and exited the room. *What the hell is happening? Have I been here the whole time, and Cassandra's Country Inn never existed? Maybe it was a bad dream, and I never went to work for Charlie.* Kyle glanced around the room. *I do miss this. The time I spent with Jennifer was the happiest days of my life.* He watched as she entered the room with a large cherry cheesecake and placed it on the table in front of him. He looked into her heavenly blue eyes and smiled. *I don't know why this is happening but screw it! I'm going to savor every moment of this while I can.*

Kyle's face brightened as he grabbed a couple of pieces of fried chicken and gobbled it down.

"I forgot what a great cook you are, doll," Kyle grinned and got a large helping of mashed potatoes and gravy.

"I can tell," Jennifer chuckled as she watched him shovel the food into his mouth. "I'm just happy that I got my old Kyle back."

After dinner, Kyle went to the basement and brought out all the Christmas decorations. Jennifer made eggnog, and they listened to their favorite Christmas Carols while they decorated the house.

"Kyle, I bought a Christmas tree earlier, and it's in the back of your truck. Do you mind getting it?" Jennifer asked as she unpacked the garland.

"No problem, doll, I'll get it." Kyle hurried out the front door and to the truck.

"Hi, Kyle," The neighbor shouted. "I see that you're getting ready for Christmas!"

Kyle looked up and was shocked to see his old neighbor, Roy. He leaned the tree against the front of the truck and walked over to his neighbor's house. His eyes filled up with tears as he looked at the frail old man.

"Roy?" Kyle's voice cracked.

"What's wrong, Kyle?" Roy asked. "Why are you so sad?" He lowered his head and pouted. "You and the Mrs. arguing again?"

"No, we're not arguing," Kyle chuckled. "I'm just happy to see you."

"Well, it's too cold out here for these old bones," Roy grumbled. "Do you want to come inside?"

"No, I can't," Kyle smiled. "Jennifer is waiting for me."

"Okay, then. Come by in the morning and have coffee with me." Roy opened the front door.

"Wait, Roy," Kyle blurted.

Roy stopped and turned towards Kyle.

"Roy, I never had a chance to tell you this, but I want to thank you for everything." Kyle smiled. "You were always my best friend and always there for me." He stepped up onto the porch and hugged Roy. "I wanted you to know that you were the dad that I never had, and I love you."

"I love you too, son," Roy patted Kyle on the back and pulled away to look into Kyle's eyes. "Hell, you are acting like I died or something." He chuckled. "Did that busybody who works for my doctor call you about my test results? As soon as the doctor ordered the x-ray for my lungs, she had me diagnosed with cancer because I smoke too much." He shook his head and walked inside. "I'll see you in the morning, son. I need to warm my bones."

Tears ran down Kyle's face as he watched Roy close the door. "You hard-headed old man, that's what killed you," he muttered as he walked back to his house.

Kyle picked up the tree and went inside. He placed the tree by the fireplace in its usual spot. As he inhaled a deep breath, the fresh pine aroma reminded him of Cassandra's Country Inn. Kyle thought about Cassie and the bond that formed between them.

"It felt so real," Kyle muttered as he gently brushed the ends of the pine branches with the tips of his fingers.

"What felt so real?" Jennifer asked.

Kyle grinned with delight when he turned and saw Jennifer in her sexy red lingerie. "I forgot about this."

"How can you forget?" Jennifer giggled. "It's a tradition for us to spend the first night in front of the fireplace after we decorate the tree." She handed him a camera. "Here, take my picture."

Jennifer hurried and sat in front of the Christmas tree. She tossed her long blonde hair towards the front and posed while Kyle snapped the picture. He grinned and set the camera down as he moved next to her. She embraced him tightly as he kissed her.

"Okay, Kyle, stop!" Jennifer laughed. "Keep that up, and you'll make us break our tradition."

"The hell with tradition!" Kyle held her in his arms as they gently fell to the floor.

~ 14 ~

DECEMBER 19

Kyle woke up that morning with Jennifer in his arms. He hugged her tightly and kissed her on the forehead.

"I can't believe that I'm still here," Kyle muttered.

"I'm glad that you are," Jennifer giggled as she opened her eyes and smiled at him. "Well, I think I like our new tradition better than our old one."

"Me too, baby," Kyle grinned.

"As soon as I take a shower, I will begin preparing breakfast for us." Jennifer got up and wrapped the cover around her.

"Okay," Kyle smiled. "I'll get the coffee started."

Jennifer blew him a kiss as she walked up the stairs. Kyle stood up and gathered up his clothes. A Gucci crocodile wallet fell to the ground as he pulled up his jeans.

"What the hell is this?" Kyle quickly picked up the wallet and opened it. He pulled out one of the credit cards. "Charlie Hanks," he muttered as he dug through the wallet frantically and found Charlie's driver's license. "I did work for Charlie."

Kyle ran to the window and looked outside for the red Corvette. *The night with Jennifer cannot be real if Charlie is real.* He glanced around the living room. *Our neighbor Roy died ten years ago, and after I left, Jennifer bought all new furniture.* He opened the door next to the fireplace, which used to be his office. In front of the large window stood his old oak desk and brown leather chair. *The day after she threw me out, she gave everything away, so how could it possibly be here?* Kyle sat down on the couch and buried his face in his hands. *Why is this happening to me?*

"Why? Why?" Kyle groaned, closing his eyes and clenching his fist. "Why did you have to reopen the old wounds between Jennifer and me? I was finally happy."

"Oh, you're happy now?" A deep voice chuckled.

As soon as Kyle opened his eyes, he became overwhelmed with fear. The moment he glanced around the room, he suddenly realized that he had entered the living room of his stepfather, Clyde.

"I'm so happy that you're happy," a sly grin appeared on Clyde's face as he entered the room.

Kyle trembled as Clyde walked across the room and sat down in his favorite chair. Clyde's bald head glistened from the glow of the fireplace. His face appeared battered from too much alcohol and working years of construction out in the hot weather. Clyde married Kyle's Mom when Kyle was six years old, and the marriage lasted for ten years. It was the worst ten years of Kyle's life. In addition to being an alcoholic, Clyde also physically abused his mother, which caused her to become distant and bitter.

"So, are you just going to sit there and stare at me all day?" Clyde's blue, bloodshot eyes glowed as he glared at Kyle. "Now that you're so happy, get your ass up and get me a beer."

Kyle was shocked to find Clyde ordering him to bring him a can of beer. *What year does he think it is? It's not nineteen eighty, and I'm not ten years old!*

Suddenly, Clyde flew across the room and slapped Kyle across the forehead. Kyle grabbed his head as he slipped onto the couch and fell to the floor.

"When I tell you to do something, boy, I expect you to run with it!" Clyde angrily stomped towards the kitchen.

Kyle sat up slowly and sat back down on the couch. His forehead was sore and felt tender to the touch. *What the hell?*

"Where's your whore of a mother?" Clyde barked as he sat back down in his chair.

Kyle remained quiet as he stared at the fire in the fireplace.

"Do you need another one, boy?" Clyde yelled. "I asked you a damn question!"

"How should I know?" Kyle muttered.

"Turn the TV on, boy," Clyde ordered, snapping his fingers. "My football game is on."

Kyle stood, turned on the television, and sat down again.

"Look at those sexy-ass cheerleaders," Clyde grinned. "That makes the old tent pole stiff because your old crone of a mother sure can't." He looked at Kyle and laughed. "Look at who I am talking to!"

As Kyle absorbed himself in his thoughts, he watched Clyde scream at the television. *The day that I poisoned you was the best day of my life. That's when I discovered how easy it is to take someone's life and get away with it. You deserved it! Just thinking about all of the abuse that you gave my Mom and me makes me sick. You turned my mother from a kind, beautiful woman into a bitter, hateful woman in the end. So why am I just sitting here like I'm ten years old? I'm a grown-ass man that can whip your ass now.* Kyle stood up and glared at Clyde. "I hate you," He shouted as he smoldered with resentment.

"What did you say, boy?" The rage in Clyde's eyes seared through him as he looked at Kyle.

"I said that I hate you," Kyle shouted angrily.

Clyde looked at him and laughed. "Well, boy, you decided to grow some big cojones!" He stood up and darted towards Kyle.

Clyde grabbed a handful of Kyle's hair in one hand and grabbed Kyle's crotch with his other hand. Then, he placed his shoulder into Kyle's chest and lifted him off the ground.

"I don't care if you hate me because I hate you," he shouted as he slammed Kyle down on the floor and got on top of him. Clyde wrapped his hands around Kyle's throat and choked him. "I hate you and your Mom, and now you're going to die!"

Kyle clawed at Clyde's hands in vain, using his last breath to scream for help until he slowly fell unconscious.

"Please let my friend be okay," Irma cried, holding a cool, damp towel on Kyle's forehead.

Kyle opened his eyes and glanced around the room.

"Cassie! Cassie! Come quick!" Irma joyfully shouted. "He opened his eyes!"

"Irma," Kyle gasped. "Oh no! I'm back in this place!"

"With an attitude like that, Rick probably should have left you on the driveway, mister," Irma nastily replied.

Cassie bolted to the couch and kneeled beside Kyle. "Are you okay?" She smiled. "I've been so worried about you?"

"We've been worried," Irma huffed. "Like you're the one that's been sitting by his side all night." Irma gave Cassie a dirty look.

"What happened?" Kyle asked.

"Rick found you face down in the driveway. Apparently, you slipped and fell and knocked yourself unconscious," Cassie said, gently touching his forehead. "You have a large goose egg on your head as a result of your fall."

"How long was I out?" Kyle rubbed his forehead and scrunched up his face in pain.

"For a day," Irma blurted. "I've been by your side all night."

"What happened to Jill and Cynthia?" Kyle asked as he glanced around the room.

"They're okay," Cassie smiled. "Cynthia thought she was slowing you down, so she and Jill returned."

"What happened to Shannon?" Kyle asked.

"She came back shortly after Jill and Cynthia," Cassie looked worriedly at Irma.

"Why are you looking at Irma like that?" Kyle sat up and noticed Cynthia, Cindy, and Jill standing by the Christmas tree. "Where's Shannon?"

Cassie pulled a purple and hot pink burlap doll out of her pocket and held it in front of her.

"Oh, no," Kyle shrieked, grabbing the doll from Cassie's hand and holding it tightly. "I'm so tired of this. I thought that I was finally free of this place."

"What does that mean?" Cynthia rushed to Kyle's side. "Did you find someone to help us?"

"How on earth could he find help when he only made it halfway down the driveway," Rick shouted as he entered the room and sat next to Kyle. "What happened out there?"

"I don't know," Kyle sighed. "The last thing I remember is that Shannon disappeared."

"Well, she's really gone now," Rick smirked as he stood up. "Thanks to you, old buddy."

"I really can't explain what happened." Kyle looked at Rick. "How far did you make it?"

"I went left at the fork, just like you said, and I walked for at least two or three miles."

"You did?" Kyle gasped. "Did you find someone to help us?"

"How stupid are you?" Rick scowled. "If I found help, do you think I would still be here?"

Irma laughed and looked at Kyle.

"There was no town," Rick shouted angrily. "Not a single building! Nothing!" He pointed his finger against Kyle's chest. "Just more of your lies!"

"Rick, stop," Jill shouted. "At least he's trying to help."

"Yes, he is," Cassie agreed.

"Of course, you two would defend him," Rick smirked. "From the moment he arrived, he flirted with both of you. Honey, doll, winking and singing love songs. Then, Cassie, he ran after you as though you were in heat."

"That's enough!" Kyle stood and glared at Rick. "You can disrespect me all you want, but you're not going to disrespect Cassie or Jill. I like Cassie, Jill, Irma, Cynthia, and Cindy. In fact, I liked all of the women. They're always friendly, understanding, and nice. Unlike you."

"I don't care if you don't like me," Rick got up in his face. "I don't like you, and I think that you're behind all of this. I should have left your sorry ass on the driveway."

"Richard Hagan," Lavivian shouted as she entered the room. "Leave the man alone. You don't know who's responsible for all of this." She stood next to Rick. "Whoever it is, one day they will have to answer for their actions."

"Yes, they will," Cindy agreed.

Lavivian smiled at Cindy and grabbed Rick's hand. "Now, son, come with me. I need your help in the kitchen."

Rick looked back and gave Kyle a dirty look as they walked out of the room.

"Wow," Cassie smiled. "Thank you for defending me."

"No problem," Kyle grinned.

"He really doesn't like you, Kyle," Cindy chuckled.

"We all know that, Cindy," Irma rolled her eyes. "Rick even said that he did not like him." She wrapped her arm around Kyle. "I'm going to make us some sandwiches, and we can spend the evening up in your room." She winked. "Just like old times."

"You know what, Irma," Kyle grinned and winked back at her. "That sounds good to me."

Irma stuck her tongue out at Cassie and skipped away to the kitchen.

"Are you really going to spend the evening in your room with that troll?" Cassie frowned. "Wouldn't you rather stay down here with all of us?"

"I think I owe her that much," Kyle smiled. "After all, she did stay by my side all night."

"Yes, she did, but she was snoring away," Cassie snickered.

"Kyle, I think you had a good dream last night," Jill grinned. "You had a big smile on your face."

"He was dreaming about me," Cassie laughed.

"I hate to ruin the party," Cynthia blurted out. "However, aren't you people concerned about who will be the next? Only eight people are left, and I think it would be better if we all stayed together."

"So do I," Cindy agreed. "We all know what happened to Shannon last night when she returned to her room."

"Loretta was down here on the couch with three other people, and look what happened to her," Cassie quickly commented, patting Cindy's back. "It doesn't matter where you are or who is with you. If it's your time, it's your time."

"What?" Cindy shrieked.

"It's a fact," Cassie stated. "There's no way out of here. Kyle tried numerous times to leave, and each attempt was unsuccessful."

"That's the truth," Kyle muttered.

"So, we're going to die," Cynthia pouted as she glared at Cassie.

"I think so," Jill sighed.

"Okay, Kyle," Irma shouted as she walked into the room with a tray of sandwiches. "We're out of here."

"Geez, Irma," Cassie groaned as she stared at the overloaded tray. "Do you think that you have enough food?"

"We like to snack during the night, but I don't want to creep around the kitchen at night." Irma hurried to the stairs. "Well, are you coming?"

"Well, ladies, I will see you in the morning." Kyle grinned. "Thank you for taking care of me last night, Cassie."

"You're welcome," Cassie smiled. "If you get tired of hanging out with the troll, Cindy and I are sleeping down here on the couches tonight."

"I got a troll for you," Irma grumbled as she went up the stairs.

They went upstairs and into Kyle's room.

"Honey, we're home," Irma shouted and placed the tray of sandwiches on top of the dresser.

Irma watched Kyle as he unplugged his phone from the charger and checked for any missed calls or messages.

"That thing is worthless," Irma chuckled. "You might as well just throw it away."

"Irma, any other time, I would probably argue with you over that, but I agree with you right now. It is worthless," Kyle grumbled, tossing the phone inside the drawer. "The one time that I need help, and it doesn't work."

They sat on the floor in front of the fireplace and ate. Kyle told her what had happened, including the night he had spent with Jennifer and seeing his old neighbor Roy. Then he told her about Clyde, his stepfather, and how that evil man ruined his life.

"Well, Kyle," Irma gazed into the fire. "I gave up trying to figure out this place. I know I am going to die here, and I have accepted that fact. My life hasn't been the same since I dated John."

"My life has been pretty messed up, too," Kyle sighed. "Occasionally, I regret my actions, but for the most part, I am not sorry. I learned at an early age that you have to take care of yourself because no one else cares. Death is a part of life, and you might as well enjoy it to the fullest while you can." He looked at Irma's gloomy face and held her hand. "Cheer up, doll. I promised you that I would not allow anything to happen to you, and I intend to keep my word."

"I know you do," Irma said, smiling at Kyle. "You may not be able to protect me from this place, but I will follow your advice. I'm here with my handsome friend, whom I like very much, and I'm going to stop feeling sorry for myself. We're going to find a way out of here."

Kyle got up and went to the window. *I don't have the heart to tell her what really happened to Clyde and that I was responsible for his death. If she knew that I murdered over a hundred people, she wouldn't feel so safe and secure, some for their money and possessions and others to cover up my crime. She would think I'm behind the disappearances around this place, and I'm not. Perhaps she assumes that I am experiencing all of my hallucinations and ghostly encounters because I have cared for those individuals at one time. Little does she know that it is not a matter of caring for them. It is more about karma. That night we played truth or dare, Irma was right about an evil presence around me, but did she pick up on the ghost or me?*

"What are you thinking about?" Irma went and stood next to Kyle at the window. "Look, Kyle!" She pointed towards the log cabin. "The light is on."

"Irma, do you see that?" Kyle pointed directly below the window at the man with the red and black plaided shirt.

"Yes," Irma whispered.

Silently, they watched as the man trudged through the snow towards the cabin with a large black bag on his back.

"What would you expect to find in a bag that size?" Irma muttered.

"A body," Kyle murmured.

They watched as the man went inside the cabin and closed the door. Then, in the window, his dark shadowy figure appeared and disappeared.

"What is he doing?" Irma gasped.

"Whatever it is, it isn't good," Kyle muttered.

"Who is that?" Irma shrieked and pointed towards the side of the cabin.

The color drained from Kyle's face as they watched the couple walk closer to the Inn. From the Christmas lights that hung from the edge of the roof, the young woman's dirty blonde hair shimmered. Kyle's heart pounded as the couple stopped right below his window.

"What are they doing?" Irma's voice trembled.

The brown-haired young man looked up, and Kyle screamed as he backed away from the window.

"Get away from the window," Kyle shouted, but Irma didn't move. So, he grabbed Irma's arm and pulled her towards him.

"Look, Kyle," Irma screamed as she wrapped her arms around his waist. "They're floating!"

Kyle looked at the couple as they floated outside his third-floor window. When he looked into the young man's hazel eyes, he realized that he looked familiar.

Then Kyle quickly glanced into the young woman's big blue eyes and froze in shock. *That's Jimmy and Denise Hill from Vidor, Texas.* Fear flooded through his body as he stared at the couple as they slowly came through the glass into his room.

"Kyle! Get Down!" Irma pushed Kyle to the floor and laid on top of him. When she turned back to look at the couple, they had disappeared. "Are you okay?" She stood up and held out her hand towards Kyle.

"Yes, doll," Kyle replied as he grabbed Irma's hand, and she helped him to his feet. "Are you?"

"They weren't here for me," Irma remarked, returning to the window and looking out. "Now, the cabin light is off."

"I had enough of that damn window for tonight." Kyle sat down on the bed. "Irma, what did you mean when you said they are not here for you?"

"I told you that I can see ghosts." Irma sat down next to him. "They're after you. Who were they? They had to be in their twenties."

Just two shy people that got in my way, he thought as he looked at Irma and shrugged his shoulders. "I have no clue."

"Well, they obviously knew you." Irma stood up. "The fireplace is calling my name, so do you want to join me?"

"Yes, I do."

They spread a blanket and the pillows on the floor and sat on top. Irma wrapped her arm around Kyle and held him close.

"I don't know who's behind the missing women, and I never believed in ghosts." Kyle laid down and pulled Irma next to him, gazing at the ceiling. "It has always seemed to me that you live and then you die, and that's it. I never really bought the whole heaven and hell thing, but this place got me second-guessing myself."

"I always believed," Irma looked at Kyle's troubled face. "Don't worry. We'll get through this together."

"Irma," Kyle smiled. "I'm glad you're here because I wouldn't know what I would do without you."

"Me neither, Kyle, me neither," Irma grinned as she closed her eyes.

~ 15 ~

DECEMBER 20

Kyle awoke to find Irma gone. "Irma! Oh no!" Kyle sat up and glanced around the room. "Not Irma." Kyle jumped to his feet and ran to the window.

"Hey, dude," Irma shouted as she entered the room. "The leftover sandwiches are on the dresser if you're hungry."

"Damn, Irma!" Kyle grabbed his chest and took a deep breath. "I thought that you were gone."

"You're not that lucky," Irma chuckled. "I couldn't sleep, so I got up and took a hot bath, hoping that would help me relax, but it didn't." She grabbed a sandwich from off the tray and sat down in the chair by the fireplace. "So, I've been up for a while waiting on you."

"I wonder who disappeared last night?" Kyle sighed and looked out of the window at the log cabin. "That was probably the next victim inside the bag."

"Oh, geez," Irma gasped. "I hope not." She got up and stood next to Kyle at the window. "Seriously, what do you think happens in there?" She muttered as she stared at the log cabin.

"Well, he has to cover up the crime, so he is destroying the bodies in some manner." Kyle looked at Irma. "What do you think?"

"I saw myself in the pond that day, so maybe he's throwing the bodies in there."

"I don't think so," Kyle raised his eyebrow and tilted his head. "That would be too easy, plus it's solid ice."

"I do know one thing," Irma looked into Kyle's eyes. "I don't want to find out. Let's try to leave this place again." She saw the hesitation in Kyle's face. "I know that you've tried several times and were unsuccessful, but if we stay, we're going to die."

"I was thinking the same thing, Irma," Kyle shook his head and looked back at the cabin. "After we go downstairs and find out what's happening, we'll break away from the others, come back, layer our clothes, and sneak out. I don't think we should tell anyone, not even Cassie."

"I agree," Irma grinned. "Well, let's go downstairs and check it out." Irma dashed to the door.

As Kyle and Irma exited the stairs, Cassie, Cindy, and Cynthia stood in front of the fireplace. Cassie held a bright, rainbow-colored burlap doll in her hand.

"Oh, no," Kyle glanced around the room as he bolted towards Cassie. "Where's Jill?"

Cassie held it up in front of her and turned the name towards Kyle. The doll brought tears to his eyes as he looked at it.

"I can't believe that she slept next to me last night," Cindy cried. "Poor Jill."

As Cynthia hugged Cindy, Kyle noticed the silver bar bracelet protruding from under the sleeve of Cynthia's sweater again. Cassie threw the doll into the fire and watched in silence as the flames devoured the doll. Irma nudged Kyle's side and pointed at Cassie.

"Cassie, are you okay, honey?" Kyle asked.

"All four of us slept down here last night, and I don't understand why we can't catch the person," Cassie scowled.

"I don't think he will ever get caught," Cynthia gave Cassie a dirty look. "It's too late for my daughter and my sister. At least you still have yours," she grumbled and stomped out of the room.

"What's wrong with her?" Cassie gasped.

"Like the rest of us, she is probably stressed and scared," Cindy patted Cassie on the shoulder. "She certainly didn't mean it to sound that way."

"Well, I think she did," Cassie snapped.

"I'll go talk with her and make sure she's okay." Kyle darted out of the room after Cynthia.

As he made his way into the kitchen, he found Cynthia sitting at the counter, weeping as she gazed out the window.

"Honey, are you okay?" Kyle rushed to her side. "What's wrong?"

"I can't believe that I'm here," Cynthia sobbed. "I should have listened to my gut instinct and turned this stupid job down."

"I think that we all feel that way, doll," Kyle hugged her. "I regret not staying at the gas station that night."

"Now, my sister and daughter are gone because of me." Cynthia raised her hand and wiped her tears. Kyle's eyes widened at the sight of the silver bar bracelet. "What are you looking at?" She sniffled.

"I couldn't help but notice your bracelet."

"That old thing," Cynthia pulled up her sweater sleeve and grasped the bar between her fingers.

"What's written on it?" Kyle asked.

"My Honeybee, why?" Cynthia pulled her sweater back over the bracelet as she glared at Kyle.

"What," Kyle gasped. "Who gave you the bracelet?"

"You know what! All you care about is who gave it to me and what's written on my stupid bracelet, and I'm upset," Cynthia shouted as she headed toward the door. "Don't follow me, and don't talk to me anymore! I'm done," she yelled and slammed the door.

As Kyle turned to run after her, something struck him in the head, knocking him out. When he awoke, he found himself inside of a narrow wooden box. *What the hell?* Kyle attempted to open the lid, but it would not budge. He then pushed and kicked at the top of the box, acting in a state of panic.

"Help me," Kyle screamed. "Somebody, please help me!"

Kyle's heart pounded in his chest as he glanced about in the darkness and waited quietly for a few seconds for someone to respond, but no one did. He then noticed a small glimmer of light coming from a hole in the side of the box. He raised his head slightly as he stuck his eye up to the small opening and peered out. *I'm in the kitchen.* His feet were suddenly in the air as one end of the box lifted.

"Help me! Please," Kyle screamed. The kitchen door opened, and he felt the box being dragged down the stairs outside. "Where are you taking me? Who are you?"

He looked out of the hole and saw nothing but snow. *Why is this happening to me?* Suddenly, he heard the same eerie whistling tune that he had heard in the hallway. Kyle was mute with horror when he sensed the box crossing another set of stairs. He listened to the creak of the door as it opened. *Where am I?* He waited until the box had stopped before peering out of the small opening.

A long butcher's table stood in the center of the small room. Shelves on both sides of a fireplace lined the walls, filled with bottles and plastic storage containers. Then, Kyle watched as the man with the red and black plaided shirt placed a large black bag on the table. The blood in his veins froze when he saw the slender arm of a woman drop and dangle from the edge of the table. The man lifted the arm and placed it back next to the person. For a couple of minutes, he stood motionless. *What the hell is he doing?* Kyle watched as the man walked in and out of his sight. *I wish he would turn towards me so I could see his face.* The man then returned, picked up the lady's arm, and removed something from her hand or wrist. His hand swiftly grasped her long blonde hair as it cascaded from the table, and he quickly placed it back on the table.

"Jill," Kyle screamed. "Jill, get up! Please, get up!"

The man ignored Kyle's screams and picked up an ax from the side of the table.

"No," Kyle cried. "Jill, get up! He's going to kill you!"

The man raised the ax above his head as Kyle screamed. Blood sprayed everywhere as he dropped the ax with lightning speed to the table.

"Jill," Kyle cried and lowered his head back down.

Kyle's face was smeared with tears as he struggled to mute the continuous whacks against the table.

"You're a monster," Kyle cried. "My poor Jill. I will always be grateful for our friendship. I love you, my friend."

In reality, it was probably only a matter of thirty minutes before the chopping ended, but it seemed to take an eternity. Kyle felt too frightened to lift his head and look out of the hole, so he remained quiet and motionless inside the box. His stomach clenched, and fear fluttered through Kyle's body as the image of Jill lying helpless on the table could not be erased from his mind. *Am I next? Is he going to chop me up into pieces?* His nausea worsened as the sudden pungent bleach odor filled the small space. Then, just as Kyle raised his head and looked out, a mop flew past the opening of the box.

Most of the blood was gone, and a large black plastic garbage bag sat on top of the table. *Is that how the killer does it? He chops them up like they're nothing and throws their remains in a garbage sack.* The man started to whistle his usual eerie tune as he grabbed the bag from the table and tossed it against the wall. As Kyle watched, the man placed another bag on the table and pulled out another female body. The killer immediately raised the ax above his head. Kyle abruptly closed his eyes and lowered his head back down. Again, the ghastly sounds of blood splatter and bones severed into pieces filled the small room. As Kyle lay trapped in the wooden box, the killer continued his gruesome act, picking up bag after bag. His terror mounted with each second that passed. Finally, the room was quiet. Kyle raised his head and peered out through the small opening around the room. The killer cleaned up the blood and was nowhere in sight.

Kyle laid his head back down and inhaled a deep breath. *Where did he go? What is he waiting on? Just kill me and put me out of my misery.*

"Why is this happening to me?" Kyle shouted and closed his eyes.

One end of the box suddenly lifted into the air, and it started to move.

"Where are you taking me?" Kyle screamed. "Why are you doing this?"

The door creaked open as Kyle felt the box strike the steps of the stairs as it plunged downward. He could hear the sound of the snow crunching under the killer's boots. The sound of tree limbs snapping along with the rough terrain made Kyle realize he was not heading in the direction of the Inn. *We must be in the forest, but why?*

After some time, they finally came to a stop. Kyle raised his head and peered out of the hole once again. As he looked at the pile of black bags in front of him, his eyes widened in alarm. Once he realized where the killer had taken him, his heart hammered, and panic gripped him. *We are on the very edge of a mountain.*

Suddenly, he heard the man whistle as he appeared in front of the box. *I wish he would show me his face.* Kyle watched in horror as the man threw one bag after another over the edge of the cliff before disappearing into thin air. Kyle hit and pushed the top of the box as he panicked and tried to free himself.

"Help me," Kyle screamed. "Somebody, please, help!"

An unexpected force pushed the box over on its side.

"Hey, I'm in here," Kyle shouted. "I can't get out! Help me!"

The box tumbled again, and Kyle was faced down.

"Hey, man! What the hell are you doing?" Kyle shouted. "Get me out of here!"

Then the box flipped back onto its side as Kyle screamed.

"What the hell?" Kyle shouted. "Let me out!"

Suddenly, something hit the side of the box, and it began to slide. Then, the box crashed into something, and all at once, the lid broke off. Kyle flew out of the box and into the deep snow. When he saw the tree that stopped his fall, Kyle realized he was just four feet away from losing his life. His eyes darted from left to right as he searched the forest for the killer. Finally, he got up and bolted into the woods.

Kyle walked through the forest for hours before he reached the back of the Inn. Then, as he gazed back at the woods, he exhaled a sigh of relief.

"I can't believe I made it back here." Kyle looked at the Inn. "I wonder why the killer left and didn't watch the box fall over the edge?"

Kyle glanced back at the woods and quickly headed towards the Inn. As he walked through the parking lot, he discovered that the snow had completely covered his red Corvette.

"That's just great!" Kyle glared at the large pile of snow.

The door swung open as Kyle approached the front of the Inn. Irma ran out to greet him on the porch.

"What happened to you?" Irma shouted. "I've been looking all over the place for you!"

Kyle walked up the steps and hugged her. "Irma, doll, where's Cassie?"

"She's inside in front of the fireplace." Irma looked at Kyle's worried face. "What's wrong?"

"It's bad, Irma," Kyle muttered, wrapping his arm around her and leading her inside.

"Kyle," Cassie shouted. "You had everyone worried to death."

Kyle went and sat by Cassie on the couch.

"Where have you been all day, Kyle?" Cindy asked.

"I think that I know what's happening to everyone," Kyle replied solemnly.

"Really, what?" Cindy asked.

"They are being butchered and then thrown over a cliff on the other side of the forest." Kyle's eyes welled with tears as he looked at Irma. "I'm sorry that I had to tell you this, doll."

"How could you possibly know that?" Cassie shouted.

"The last time I saw you, you were in the kitchen with me," Cynthia glared at Kyle.

"When you left the kitchen, someone struck me on the head and knocked me out." Kyle got quiet when he saw Rick and Lavivian enter the room.

"Well, well," Rick smirked. "Look who's back."

"Kyle was just telling us that someone knocked him out in the kitchen earlier today," Cynthia stated, rolling her eyes.

"Well, you better not say it was me because I've been with my Mom all day," Rick sneered as he shoved Irma out of his way and sat down next to Kyle.

"So, how do you know about the cliff?" Cassie asked.

"The killer placed me in a wooden box and dragged me to a location where he chopped the bodies up with an ax and threw them into a bag. Afterward, he walked through the forest to a cliff and threw the bags over the edge."

"Are you kidding me?" Rick laughed. "If that really happened, why would he let you go?"

"He attempted to push the box off of the cliff, but the box impacted a tree, and it burst open. I got out and searched for him, but he was gone." Kyle glared at Rick. "Believe me! He wanted to kill me, too!"

"Bullshit," Rick snapped, frowning. "Do you honestly expect us to believe that crap? Why would he go through all that trouble? Why wouldn't he just come in here and shoot us?"

"Because he enjoys his kill and likes using an ax," Cynthia mumbled.

Cindy looked worriedly at Cassie. "What do you think?"

"Right now, I am not sure what to think." Cassie glared at Kyle. "I don't understand why you saw those things and lived for one, and I don't understand the meaning of those stupid dolls."

"I know what I saw," Kyle shouted as tears filled his eyes. "I saw Jill on that table and had to look away. When I saw what he had done, I could not look at the others."

"You saw Jill?" Irma gasped.

Kyle lowered his head and cried.

"I believe him," Rick patted Kyle on the back. "From this point forward, we should all stay together."

"I believe him too." Cynthia looked at Kyle. "God knows I don't like you, but I don't think that you would lie about seeing Jill."

"Oh, my," Lavivian sighed. "I can't imagine what those poor women went through."

"Me neither." Tears ran down Cindy's cheeks as she stared at Cassie.

Cassie saw the terror in her sister's eyes. "Why are you staring at me? What's wrong?" Cassie asked.

"Nothing," Cindy responded quickly.

"If you have something on your mind, just say it," Cassie remarked. "That or stop staring at me!"

"Well, girls, let's not argue," Lavivian said as she stood up. "Everyone's nerves are on edge, so Rick, go with me to the kitchen, and I'll make us all a hot cup of cocoa." Lavivian smiled at Kyle. "I'll make you a coffee."

"Hot chocolate will be fine," Kyle smiled.

"Oh, well, hot chocolate it is," Lavivian grinned.

"I'll get the pillows and blankets." Cassie stood up. "Cynthia, can you give me a hand?"

"Sure." Cynthia got up and followed Cassie out of the room.

"Kyle, I can't believe you saw Jill," Irma said, grabbing Kyle's hand. "I'm sorry you had to witness that because I know you liked her."

"Yes, that must have been terrible," Cindy's voice trembled.

"It was terrible," Kyle looked at the worried expression on Cindy's face.

"Are you okay, Cindy?" Kyle asked. "Your hands are shaking."

Cindy quickly shoved her hands under her legs and looked at Kyle. "Did you see the face of the killer?"

"No, he kept his back turned towards me," Kyle replied. "Why?"

"Why what?" Cassie asked as she entered the room and tossed a couple of blankets and pillows on Kyle's couch.

"Nothing," Cindy snapped. "I wanted to know why he changed his mind about drinking hot chocolate."

"That is a good question," Cassie grabbed one of the blankets and a pillow and sat down next to Kyle.

Cynthia gave Cindy a blanket and pillow and threw the others on the empty couch.

"Cynthia, stay here next to me," Cindy pulled the blanket across her lap as Cynthia sat down by her.

"Here comes the cocoa," Irma shouted.

"Irma," Lavivian smiled and held the tray out in front of her. "It doesn't take much to make you happy."

Irma chuckled as she took a cup from the tray.

As they sipped their hot cocoa, they covered themselves with blankets and stared worriedly at the fireplace. A warm glow from the fire illuminated their troubled faces as Kyle's horrific story about the killer weighed heavily on their minds. Yet, there were no words spoken. Only the crackle and pop of the fire filled the room.

~ 16 ~

DECEMBER 21

"Where's Cindy?" Cynthia shouted as she jumped up from the couch.

"What?" Cassie glanced around the room. "Where's my sister?" Her eyes widened as she sprang from the couch and ran upstairs.

"Oh, no," Lavivian cried. "How is that possible? All of us stayed together."

"Look," Irma shouted as she stood and pointed at the Christmas tree.

"I can't believe this," Kyle sighed.

Upon exiting the stairs, Cassie noticed everyone had their eyes fixed on the tree. As she looked up, she saw the lavender burlap doll and yanked it from the tree branch.

"I can't believe the killer was here in the room with us," Cynthia cried.

"That's what I don't understand," Rick said, looking at Kyle. "If the story about the ax is true, why didn't he just kill us all while he had the chance? Hell, we were all here!"

"How should I know," Kyle snapped.

"The story is true, Rick," Irma said, sitting down next to Kyle. "Kyle does not tell lies."

"Yeah, right," Rick smirked.

"I think that we should all try and leave today," Cynthia remarked as she sat down between Rick and Lavivian.

"Leave," Rick chuckled. "Leave and go where?"

"Anywhere," Cynthia replied. "If we stay here, we're going to die."

"Well, I have some news for you," Rick shook his head in disbelief. "There is no way out of this, so you better make peace with your creator. I walked for miles that day, and there's nothing out there. So, I'm not going out." Rick leaned forward and slapped Kyle on the knee. "However, I'm sure that he would love to try again."

"Would you, Kyle?" Cynthia asked.

"No, doll," Kyle lowered his head. "After what I experienced yesterday, I think that I've had enough."

Cynthia and Irma started to cry.

"I'm sorry, dolls," Kyle sighed. "I just can't."

"I don't want to die," Irma cried.

Lavivian watched Cassie as she stared at the doll clutched in her hand as she stood in front of the fireplace. "My dear, why don't you sit down next to me."

Cassie stood motionless and didn't answer.

Kyle raised his head and looked puzzled at Cassie. He had expected to see tears in her eyes, but instead, he saw rage.

"Cassie, dear," Lavivian said, slightly raising her voice. "Come sit down."

Suddenly, Cassie threw the doll into the fire. "You're just stupid," she muttered as she sat beside Lavivian.

"Honey, it's not Cindy's fault that the killer got her." Lavivian gently grabbed Cassie's hand. "We did everything we could. As long as we were together, you would think he would keep away from us, but that wasn't the case."

Cassie rolled her eyes as she stared at the doll burning in the fireplace.

"This is so depressing," Irma cried. "It is bad enough to know that there is no way out of here, but to sit around all day waiting for your turn is even worse."

"Well, I should have turned this job down," Cynthia sneered at Cassie. "Right now, I would have been in Miami, Florida, with my daughter and my sister. We planned on taking the Carnival Cruise Ship for seven days and six nights. Patricia and I have taken many cruises together, but this would have been the first trip for Candace."

"I was supposed to be in Atlanta, Georgia," Kyle sighed. "Donald and Catrina McSpadden hired me to care for his eighty-year-old mother." Kyle shook his head. "I really needed that job."

"I would have been home in Indiana with my husband, Don." Lavivian eyes filled up with tears. "I was planning to cook a big Christmas dinner."

"You still are, Mom," Rick smiled. "I will get you home in time." He lowered his head. "I cannot believe Cindy Etta is no longer with us. We should have kept the Inn on Virginia Beach. She loved it there."

"Well, I had no place to go," Irma whined. "So that's why the invitation to come here seemed so inviting."

"I'm going to make some coffee for us." Lavivian stood up and headed towards the kitchen.

"I'll go with you, Mom." Rick got up and followed her.

"I can't believe that everybody is gone," Cynthia sighed.

Kyle looked at Cassie and wondered why she was not showing any emotion. *Geez, that was her sister that disappeared, and she looks mad, not sad. Cynthia still cries and looks upset. I wonder why Cindy changed the subject last night when Cassie entered the room. She seemed upset and wanted to know if I saw the killer's face, so why would she tell Cassie it was about me drinking hot cocoa? Did she know something about the killer?*

"Oh, my God," Irma shouted. "Somebody is looking through the window!" She hit Kyle on the arm. "Look," she yelled, pointing towards the window by the door.

Kyle jumped up and looked. Then, after wiping the glass repeatedly with her red glove, the lady pressed her face against the surface.

"It's Brenda," Kyle joyfully shouted as he ran to the door. "It's Brenda Menifee from the gas station! I told you that gas station existed!"

Cynthia and Irma ran to the window. Brenda stared inside, and it appeared as though she looked right through them.

"Something is wrong with the door," Kyle hurried to the window and knocked on the glass in front of Brenda's face. "Brenda, it's me, Kyle," He shouted.

Brenda looked puzzled and walked off the porch. Kyle tried to open the door and run after her, but the door wouldn't open. Irma and Cynthia screamed at the top of their lungs for help, but Brenda kept walking away. Finally, Rick ran into the living room, and Irma pointed out of the window at Brenda.

"Move out of the way," Rick pushed Kyle aside and grabbed the doorknob. He jerked and twisted the knob frantically, but the door would not budge. "What the hell is wrong with the door?" He shouted and ran back to the window. "Hey, lady!" He pounded on the glass, and Brenda looked back. "Help us!"

"She heard you, Rick," Irma shouted with joy as Brenda stopped in front of the Inn.

Rick went back to the door. He twisted the doorknob and kicked at the door. "What's wrong with this stupid door?"

"I don't know!" Kyle ran and grabbed a vase and threw it against the glass. The vase shattered into pieces, but the glass remained intact. "What the hell?"

"We need help," Irma screamed as Brenda held her hand above her eyes and glared at the Inn.

Rick rushed to the window and looked out. "The lady in red is gone," He shouted. "Why didn't you break the window?"

"I tried," Kyle stared at the glass. "Why was she constantly wiping the glass like it was dirty when it is spotless?"

"Move out of the way," Rick shouted at Kyle as he raised his arm over his head. "I'm going to throw this paperweight and break that damn window."

"No, you're not!" Cassie snatched it out of Rick's hand. "Did everybody lose their damn mind? Brenda, or the lady in red, had to have seen you. Right?"

"I don't know because she didn't acknowledge me," Kyle replied.

"Well, I know that she heard all the screaming," Cassie said as she looked at Irma and Cynthia. "You guys probably scared her, and she left to bring back some help." Cassie went and placed the paperweight back on the counter. "In the meantime, I don't need you two destroying my Inn. That vase cost me over a thousand dollars." She went to the door and opened it. "Why couldn't you just open the door and go after her?"

"That door was jammed," Rick shouted as he walked to the door. "That's impossible."

"Everything about this place is impossible," Kyle muttered.

"Do you believe that she left in order to return with help?" Cynthia asked.

"Yes, because she turned back and looked at us." Irma looked at Kyle. "What do you think?"

"That's possible." Kyle looked out of the window. "In fact, Brenda looked back several times as she walked away, so perhaps she got scared, and that's why she was in such a hurry."

"Do you really think so?" Cynthia's face lit up with excitement.

Kyle looked into Cynthia's joyful eyes and didn't have the heart to say what he thought, so he nodded, "Yes, I think so."

Irma hugged Cynthia and jumped up and down. "We're going to be rescued!"

"What?" Lavivian's eyes lit up as she carried the tray of coffee into the room.

"Yes, Mom!" Rick ran up to her and took the tray. "Kyle's friend just left, and I am sure she will return with some assistance."

"Oh, thank goodness," Lavivian sighed. "My heart is so happy to hear that."

"Well, everyone," Cassie shouted. "Take a seat, and let's enjoy our coffee."

"It's just a matter of time now." Cynthia rushed to the couch and hugged Lavivian. "I just wished that Patricia and Candace were still here."

"I miss all of them." Irma's face glowed as their memories flooded her mind. "Pat, with her flaming red hair and her fiery personality. She was always picking on Cathy. Callie and Shannon always kept everyone upbeat with their singing. Patricia and Candace were the two you could always rely on, and they were always willing to help. Brenda and Cindy Etta for their delicious desserts. Loretta, Cindy, and Jill felt like the sisters I never had, and who could forget LaDonna? The queen of green," Irma chuckled. "Whatever happened to Lucky, the frog?"

"They sure brought life to this place," Cynthia smiled. "Irma, I don't know what happened to Lucky."

"I have Lucky in my room," Lavivian grinned. "I found him on the mantel one morning. Kyle, would you mind getting him? My room is unlocked."

"No, I don't mind," Kyle smiled. "I need to stop by my room for a few minutes."

"I'll go with you!" Irma sprang to her feet.

"No, I'll be okay, Irma." Kyle stood up. "Stay down here and enjoy your coffee."

Irma sat back down, and Kyle headed upstairs. He went inside his room and pulled out his wallet. He glanced around the messy room and the dirty fireplace piled high with ashes as he sat down on the purple chair.

He opened up the wallet and took out the credit cards. He found a picture of Jennifer in front of the Christmas tree between the cards. His eyes filled with tears as he gazed at the picture and realized that she had the same red lingerie on as she had the other night. He flipped the photo over.

"I love you more than life, Jennifer, December 17, 2001," Kyle shrieked. "How in the hell is that possible to go back in time?"

He turned the picture back over and stared into Jennifer's blue eyes. *I can't believe that Jill and Jennifer look so much alike.*

"Poor Jill," He sobbed. "I can't believe what happened to you."

He placed the picture back between the cards, stuffed them into the wallet, and then shoved it inside his pocket.

"Why couldn't I have stayed with Jennifer instead of returning to this stupid Inn?" Kyle grumbled as he went to the dresser and pulled out his phone.

"Another missed call from Tim," Kyle glared angrily at his phone and threw it back inside the drawer. "I wish you would track me down so I can get the hell out of here."

Kyle left his room and went back down the hallway to Lavivian's room, which was located by the stairs. He opened the door and saw Lucky on top of the dresser. He went inside and grabbed the frog.

"Well, Mr. Lucky," Kyle held the frog out in front of him and smiled. "You and LaDonna made a lot of friends."

Suddenly, the door slammed shut, and Kyle turned immediately around.

"Now what?" Dondi laughed as he sat in the recliner in front of the television. "Is that little frog your new best friend?"

"You're not real," Kyle huffed as he briskly walked to the door.

"Of course, I'm real," Dondi shouted. "I'm as real as this football game on TV. Don't bother with the door because it's not going to open."

Kyle's face turned red as he jiggled the doorknob and pulled.

"I told you so," Dondi said as he stood up. "You and I have some unfinished business to discuss."

As Kyle turned to face Dondi, the recliner and television disappeared.

"I want to know why you did it!" Dondi glared at Kyle. "What did I have that you so desperately wanted that you had to kill me?"

"What are you talking about, Dondi?" Kyle's voice trembled as he tried to hide his fear. "We were friends."

"Friends!" Dondi flew up to Kyle's face. "You took everything that I owned! Is that a friend?"

"Look, it wasn't me," Kyle stuttered. "It was Jennifer. She made me do it. She threatened to contact the police and tell them about my past. I told her to wait until the next job, but she refused. So, I had no choice but to poison you." Kyle lowered his head and looked down at the ground. "I'm sorry, man. I really did like you. You were my friend, not my patient." Tears ran down Kyle's face as he cried. "Please forgive me."

When Kyle finally looked up, Dondi was gone. He glanced around the room as he dried his eyes with his hand and held Lucky tightly with the other.

"Is that what they want from me?" Kyle muttered. "A damn apology."

In a split second, the door flew open, and Kyle jumped.

"What's taking you so long, man," Irma shouted. "Lavivian made sandwiches, and we are waiting for you to come down so we can eat."

"I should have known that it would take food for you to come to look for me," Kyle snickered.

Irma laughed.

"Irma, I have something to tell you, so I am glad that you came up here." Kyle pulled her inside the room and closed the door.

"What is it?" Irma asked.

"Yesterday, I noticed a bracelet on Cynthia's wrist." Kyle grabbed Irma's hand and looked at the bracelet. "It was the same as yours."

"That's not unusual," Irma chuckled. "It is a common item at the moment because it is fashionable."

"Fashionable?" Kyle laughed. "What year is this? Those things haven't been popular for a while now." He looked at Irma and snickered as he shook his head. "Anyway, that's not important. What is important is that the same thing, My Honeybee, was inscribed on hers too."

"What?" Irma shrieked. "Are you serious? Do you think that she dated John?"

"Well, you said that he had a lot of girlfriends," Kyle raised his eyebrows as he looked at Irma. "It's strange that two of his girlfriends would be in the same place at the same time, especially here."

"What did she say about the bracelet?" Irma asked.

"Since she was upset at the time, she became angry with me when I asked her," Kyle replied. "So, maybe you can question her."

"Yes, I will." Irma walked towards the door. "I don't think that she likes you very much."

"What makes you think that?" Kyle smirked.

Irma laughed as they headed downstairs. After they reached the bottom of the stairs, they spotted Cassie in front of the Christmas tree. As Kyle watched her stare at the top of the tree, he noticed the empty look on her face.

"Here, Irma," Kyle handed Lucky to her. "Give this to Lavivian. I want to talk to Cassie for a minute."

"Okay," Irma rolled her eyes and grabbed Lucky as she watched Kyle rush to Cassie's side.

"Are you okay, honey?" Kyle hugged her.

"No, not really," Cassie huffed.

"I'm so sorry about Cindy," Kyle held her tightly in his arms and thought it strange that she became so tense after hearing him speak. He pulled quickly away from her and looked into her eyes. "Did I say something wrong?"

"No," Cassie turned away and looked back at the Christmas tree. "I just have a lot on my mind."

"I can only imagine," Kyle nervously slipped his hands into the pocket of his hoodie.

"What do you mean by that?" Cassie snapped.

"Well, nothing really," Kyle stuttered. "You invited all these women to stay here, and now they're missing."

"So, do you think that I'm responsible for that?" Cassie angrily raised her voice.

"No, I don't think you're responsible for any of the disappearances," Kyle nervously chattered and awaited her response, but she never responded. Instead, she just stared at the Christmas tree. He put his arm around her waist and stood silently by her side.

After a while, Irma shouted from the couch. "What are you guys doing? My sandwich would be much better if I could eat it before the bread becomes stale!"

"Cassie, are you ready to join the others?" Kyle looked at Irma and smiled.

"I wonder who is hanging those stupid dolls from the tree?" Cassie muttered.

"What did you say?" Kyle asked.

"It's nothing," Cassie walked away from Kyle and sat down on the couch next to Cynthia.

He felt foolish as he stood alone by the tree for a few seconds, then sat beside Irma. *Why is she acting like that?* Kyle thought as he stared at Cassie. *She doesn't look sad at all that her sister is gone.*

"Cynthia isn't wearing the bracelet, so I didn't say anything," Irma whispered in Kyle's ear.

Kyle glanced at Cynthia's wrist, and the bracelet was gone. *That's strange.*

"I do not know why the lady has not returned yet," Cynthia grumbled, grabbing a sandwich off the tray and looking at Kyle. "Is she getting help for us, do you think?"

"I know she is," Rick grinned. "The lady looked straight at me. Because of the weather, it's probably taking longer for her to return. I walked for miles, and there was nothing around, so who knows how far she has to travel to find us some help."

"If it's not today, for sure she will return tomorrow," Irma replied with a mouth full of food. "So stop worrying and eat!"

Everybody stayed in front of the fireplace for the rest of the evening. They shared stories about their missing loved ones and friends as Lucky the frog sat on the coffee table beside the sandwich tray. Each person looked hopeful, with the exception of Cassie and Kyle. Their faces appeared troubled, as if they were aware of what fate had in store for them.

~ 17 ~

DECEMBER 22

"Oh, no," Irma shouted and woke everyone up.

"What happened?" Rick jumped to his feet and glanced around the room. When he saw the yellow and green doll hanging from the top of the tree, he immediately looked to see who was missing. "Where's Cynthia?"

A panicked Cassie rushed to the tree and yanked the doll from its branch. "It's Cynthia." She lowered her head and stared at the yellow burlap doll.

"Oh, gosh," Lavivian cried. "Poor Cynthia."

"You mean poor us," Irma shrieked as she nervously paced back and forth in front of the fireplace.

"What happened to the lady yesterday?" Lavivian looked at Kyle. "Why didn't she come back?"

"The snow is deep out, and most of the roads are probably closed still, Mom," Rick looked at her and smiled. "Don't worry. She should return either today or tomorrow."

"Well, I hope so," Irma grumbled.

"Me too," Kyle sighed.

Cassie went to the fireplace and threw the doll into the fire.

"There are only five of us left, so hopefully, it will be today because one of us will not be around tomorrow," Irma remarked as she watched the doll burn.

Tears filled Lavivian's eyes. "That's the truth."

They sat quietly and stared at the fire. Then, suddenly, they heard a loud crash coming from upstairs.

"What the hell was that?" Cassie shrieked.

"I'll go check it out," Kyle said as he got up and headed for the stairs.

"Wait," Irma shouted. "I will go with you!" She looked quickly at Cassie. "Don't get jealous, but I think that you should stay here with Rick and Lavivian." Seeing Cassie roll her eyes, Irma smirked and ran up the stairs to catch up with Kyle.

Kyle and Irma checked the second floor, and everything looked in order. An overwhelming, musty smell filled the air as they approached the third floor.

"What is that smell?" Irma gagged as she crinkled up her nose.

When Kyle got to the last step, he stopped.

"What's wrong? It's freezing up here," Irma shrieked, pushing him to the side and walking past him. "What happened?" She gasped.

The walls were no longer white but dirty and stained, with large holes. Pieces of the broken chandeliers lay scattered across the once deep purple shag carpet that now appeared worn and matted.

"This is what it looked like that night when I saw Dondi," Kyle muttered as he slowly went to Lavivian's room and opened the door.

A rancid odor filled the air as soon as they entered the room.

"Look, Kyle," Irma shrieked as she pointed at the dirty, bare mattresses in the center of the room. "What happened to everything?"

Immediately, Kyle pulled the neck of his hoodie over his nose as he entered the room. The walls and carpet looked the same as in the hallway, and the furniture looked soiled and damaged. Irma followed him out of the room and back into the hallway.

"Kyle, I'm scared," Irma muttered.

"Don't be afraid, honey. I swear on my life that I will not let anything harm you," Kyle smiled and grabbed her hand. "Let's go check out my room."

Irma held tightly onto Kyle's hand as he led the way. Kyle slowly opened the door, and they went inside.

"Oh, no," Irma shouted as she glanced around the room. "Look at the window!" She pointed. "The glass is busted out."

Kyle rushed to the dirty dresser and looked inside. All of his clothes were still neatly folded inside. The large mirror over the dresser was cracked and dingy.

"The room looks abandoned, Irma, but my clothes are still clean and neatly folded inside the drawers." Kyle closed the drawer and went in front of the fireplace. "Look at this chair. The material is torn and filthy. Same as the bed." He glanced around the room with a look of confusion on his face.

"At least it doesn't smell like something died in here." Irma went and stood in front of the window.

"I'm going to look in Cassie's room." Kyle walked to the door. "Do you want to come with me or stay here?"

"I'll stay. At least I have a window to jump out," Irma muttered.

Kyle went into Cassie's room, and it was the same as his. Everything was dirty and broken. He opened the dresser drawer, and her clothes were still inside but dirty and had a musty odor.

"That's odd," Kyle muttered as he closed the drawer.

"So, you think that's odd!"

Kyle looked around quickly, and there stood Charlie and Deniese. He attempted to walk past them, but Charlie refused to let him.

"You're not going anywhere, so you might as well have a seat," Charlie yelled.

"Look," Kyle chuckled. "It's clear you're here for an apology, so let's get it out of the way. Please accept my apologies for what I have done to you and Deniese." The shocked expression on Charlie's face caught Kyle's attention. "I worked for you for two years, and even though you did not like me, I believe we built a relationship that you trusted. I also apologize for taking your money, personal belongings, and especially your red Corvette. Jennifer, my ex-wife, made me do it. If she did not receive the money by Christmas, she would contact the police.

I'm so sorry. I enjoyed working for you, especially you, Deniese."

Charlie and Deniese burst into laughter as they looked at each other.

"Why are you laughing?" Kyle shouted.

"So, you're sorry, and that makes everything okay?" Charlie looked at Deniese as he mimicked Kyle. "I'm sorry for stealing your money! I'm sorry for taking your car!"

"I'm sorry that I poisoned you," Deniese mimicked Kyle's mannerisms as she ran her fingers through her hair and combed it over to the side.

"Now, that was a good one, Deniese," Charlie laughed.

"If you do not want an apology, what do you want from me?" Kyle cried.

"Revenge," Charlie yelled as he pushed Kyle away from him. "Now, go sit down in that chair."

Deniese stood beside the chair and tapped the seat as Kyle glanced across the room at her.

"What are you staring at?" Charlie shouted. "Go!"

"What are you going to do to me?" Kyle nervously asked as he walked towards the chair.

"Sit down," Charlie ordered, pushing him down in the chair.

"What do you want?" Kyle whimpered.

"Did you make Kyle a special cup of hot chocolate, Deniese?" Charlie grinned.

"I sure did." Then, as Denise smiled, a cup filled with hot cocoa appeared out of nowhere.

Charlie grabbed the cup and handed it to Kyle. "Here you go."

"Drink up," Deniese chuckled.

"Are you kidding me?" Kyle shrieked. "You're going to poison me?"

"No, not poison," Charlie laughed. "I like to call it a cup of karma."

"What in the hell does that mean?" Kyle glanced around the room. "Are you responsible for all of this? Is that why I'm here? Are you behind the missing women?"

"No, I'm not," Charlie angrily remarked. "I'm not like you! I'm not a killer, but you are!"

"Then, if you're not the reason I'm here, what is?" Kyle looked at Deniese. "Dondi just wanted an apology! What do you want?"

"Charlie told you," Deniese raised her voice and pointed at the cup of cocoa. "Fate led you here, not us."

"Stop all of the chitter-chatter and drink up," Charlie shouted.

Suddenly, he heard Irma shouting from the other room.

"Blondie, are you coming back?" Irma screamed. "We need help! There's a serial killer around here! Please be careful! Can you hear me? Are you coming back?" Irma cheered. "Thank you! Come back with help as fast as you can!"

Irma dashed into Cassie's room, and Charlie, Deniese, and the cup of cocoa disappeared. "What are you doing?"

She grabbed Kyle's hand and pulled him up. "There are two women outside!"

Kyle and Irma rushed into his room and to the window.

"That's Jamie and Sesailee," Kyle shouted. "Hey, Jaime! Sesailee! It's me, Kyle!" He screamed.

Jamie and Sesailee looked back towards the Inn.

"It's manther! Help me, please," he yelled at the top of his lungs.

Jamie pointed towards him and turned away.

"Did she hear me? Why are they leaving?" Kyle cried as they walked away.

"Don't worry," Irma joyfully chirped. "She's coming back. She heard me and waved her arm in the air."

"She did?" Kyle grinned.

"Yes, they both looked at me, and blondie waved. When I told her that there was a serial killer in the area, she probably left to get the sheriff."

"I'm glad you told Jamie because I don't want anything to happen to her or Sesailee. Brenda must have told them that I am here." Kyle stared out of the window. "At least the snow has stopped, but there is still a strong wind."

Irma looked at Kyle and grinned, "A manther, huh?"

"It's a long story behind that," Kyle chuckled. "I can't believe that she heard you. I am so relieved."

"Me too," Irma sighed, glancing around the room. "But this scares me, and I'm ready to go back downstairs."

"It scares me too, Irma," Kyle hugged her. "Since I arrived here, I have been frightened."

"Me too," Irma looked into Kyle's eyes. "Why were you sitting in Cassie's room in a chair?"

"You didn't see anybody?"

"No, just you with that stupid look on your face sitting there," Irma chuckled.

"It was nothing," Kyle raised his hand and nervously ran his fingers through his hair. "I don't think I can take much more of this place."

"It won't be too much longer, and we'll be out of here."

"Let's go tell the others," Kyle grabbed Irma's hand, and they headed downstairs.

"What took you so long?" Cassie shouted as she stood in front of the fireplace. "I have been worried about you."

Kyle and Irma rushed to Cassie's side.

"We're going to be rescued," Irma said with a smile.

"How do you know that?" Cassie asked.

"The two ladies from the gas station, Jamie and Sesailee, were here." Kyle grinned. "Brenda must have informed them that we needed assistance."

"What was the cause of the noise we heard upstairs?" Rick asked.

"I am not sure how to describe what we saw," Kyle looked at Irma.

"I do," Irma blurted. "The third floor appears to have been abandoned for quite some time. But, of course, this is impossible since we all stay on the third floor. Once, beautiful, luxurious, and clean." She threw her hands up into the air. "Shazam! It's dirty, moldy, stripped-down, with holes in the walls and broken-out windows."

"What?" Cassie shouted and ran up the stairs.

"How did that happen?" Lavivian asked.

"I don't know," Kyle sighed. "But I don't think that it is safe to go up there."

"So, where were the two ladies?" Rick asked.

"Outside of Kyle's window," Irma grinned. "I know that they heard me because she waved at me."

"I can't believe it," Lavivian sighed. "Do you think that they will be back today?"

"I hope so," Kyle muttered. "I don't know how much more of this I can take."

After a while, Cassie looked bewildered as she exited the stairs and stood in front of the Christmas tree.

"Cassie," Lavivian shouted. "Are you okay?"

"I can't believe it," Cassie grumbled. "The entire third floor is a total disaster."

"It's awful," Kyle sighed. "When I first arrived, the place was absolutely gorgeous."

"I'm sorry, Cassie," Lavivian shook her head sadly. "I know that this place meant the world to you."

"It's everything," Cassie replied brokenly.

"Well, I don't think that I would be too depressed," Irma snickered. "It is unlikely that you would attract any business after everyone learns about all the missing women. Besides, stay here and die, or leave this place and live." She chuckled. "If I were you, I would sell everything and start over again."

"Well, you're not me," Cassie snarled.

"I'm glad," Irma smirked. "There is no way I would want to be you. Because, once the families of those who are missing learn of the tragedy, you will have lawsuits, and you will be in a world of trouble."

Cassie glared at Irma as she walked to the couch and sat next to Kyle.

"I wouldn't worry about that right now, doll," Kyle patted Cassie's knee. "Let's get through this first, and if you need help, I'll help you."

"Do you believe that the person hanging the dolls on the tree is responsible for the damage to the third floor?" Cassie asked Kyle.

"No, I don't," Kyle replied. "There is no way anyone could cause that much damage in an hour or two. I can't explain it, but it appears to have deteriorated for many years up there."

"Is it that bad?" Lavivian gasped.

"Yes," Cassie lowered her head.

"If I were Cassie, I would burn this place down to the ground," Irma smirked as Cassie gave her a dirty look.

Kyle grabbed and patted Cassie's hand. "That's enough, Irma," He grumbled. "Poor Cassie has enough to deal with without you provoking an argument."

Irma looked at Cassie and stuck out her tongue.

"So, Irma," Rick leaned forward on the couch in a relaxed manner. "Are you certain that the two ladies saw you?"

"Yes, I am positive they saw me," Irma smiled. "They came from the front and walked to the side of the Inn." She glanced at Cassie and grinned. "Since Kyle's window is busted out, I leaned out of the opening and waved. The two ladies headed in the direction of the log cabin, and that's when I warned them that there was a serial killer in the area. I knew then that they could hear me because they looked at me and headed back to the front. They looked scared, especially the burgundy-haired lady."

"That's Sesailee," Kyle grinned. "I bet that did scare them."

"My deepest hope is finally coming true that someone will come and rescue us. However, I can't help but feel bad for the others," Lavivian sighed. "Poor Cindy Etta."

Irma picked up Lucky, the frog, from the coffee table and held it in front of Cassie. "This is the reason why you are going to be in trouble. When LaDonna's family and friends find out about her disappearance, don't you think they will try to find her?" Irma chuckled. "Even Rick! Do you think he's going to forget about his wife?"

Cassie jumped to her feet. "Okay, Irma! I had enough," She shouted. "If you know what's good for you, you will sit down and shut your big mouth. You better pray that those two women get back here soon with some help before you turn up missing!"

Irma looked into Cassie's eyes and sat down next to Lavivian. Everyone sat around the fireplace and remained silent while nervously waiting to be rescued.

~ 18 ~

DECEMBER 23

The sound of an explosion that reverberated through-out the lobby woke Kyle. He opened his eyes and glanced around the room. *What the hell was that?* He thought as he sat up and looked over at Cassie, who was sound asleep next to him. *How did she manage to sleep through that loud noise?* Then, he quickly looked at Rick and Lavivian, asleep on the other couch. *Where's Irma?* His eyes scanned the room as he jumped up. Kyle's heart raced as he slowly approached the Christmas tree and searched for a doll. Kyle exhaled a sigh of relief when he realized there wasn't one.

"Kyle, come up here," A faint voice echoed upstairs.

"Irma?" Kyle muttered.

As Kyle raced up the stairs, he stopped in terror at the sight of the second floor. It was a complete disaster in the same way as the third floor.

"Kyle, I'm down here," The soft voice echoed down the hall.

"Irma?" Kyle slowly made his way down the dark, musty corridor.

Kyle heard a noise coming from inside the room as he neared the end of the hallway and opened the door.

A brown leather couch with cow print pillows was in front of a large red brick fireplace. The sweet aroma of honeysuckles filled the air. Kyle walked inside and glanced around the room. He immediately recognized the firefly Tiffany lamp in the corner of the room. *Is this Jennifer's house?*

"Well, do you have my money?" Jennifer huffed as she entered the room.

When I last saw her, she was wearing the same outfit. Kyle thought in disbelief as he stared at her.

"Well?" Jennifer grumbled as she grabbed her glass of iced tea and sat down on the sofa. "Are you going to stare at me all day?"

Oh no, this is our last day together. The thought occurred to him as he began to tremble.

"Kyle," Jennifer shouted. "I mean it! I'm not in the mood for your stupid games. I want my money. Do you want me to make that phone call and turn you in?"

Kyle went to the couch and sat down. He stared at the fireplace as he contemplated what to say to her. *Should I reenact that day or change the conversation and hopefully have a different outcome?*

"You don't have my money, do you?" Jennifer smirked.

"Yes, I got it," Kyle smiled. "It's in the car."

"Well, that's stupid," Jennifer slammed her glass of tea down on the end table. "Why would you leave that much money sitting around in your car?"

"Where's Tim?"

"How should I know?" Jennifer chuckled. "Ask me if I care."

While Kyle nervously ran his fingers through his hair, Jennifer quickly grabbed his hand and pulled it towards her. Jennifer's eyes widened as she removed the watch from under his sleeve.

"Damn, Kyle," Jennifer gasped. "You got a Rolex. How much money did you get?"

"This belonged to Charlie, so I took it."

"What kind of car did you take?" Jennifer asked.

"Charlie had a red Corvette," Kyle watched as Jennifer's face turned red with anger. *This is the exact conversation that we had. I wonder if the bracelet is in my pocket like it was that day.* Kyle thought as he leaned back and reached his hand into his pocket. "But don't worry, I got something for you, too," he grinned.

"You did?"

Kyle held the diamond tennis bracelet in front of Jennifer. Her eyes sparkled, and her face lit up with joy.

"Do you like it?" Kyle asked.

"Are you kidding me?" Jennifer slid down the couch next to him and kissed him. "I have never received a better present than this." She chuckled. "Except for the money, of course."

It is possible that if I apologize to her, all this will disappear, and I will be able to continue my search for Irma.

"Hello," Jennifer shouted. "I just asked you a question."

"Oh, honey, I'm sorry," Kyle grinned. "What did you say?"

"I asked if you brought me anything else?"

No, and that damn bracelet wasn't for you. Kyle thought as he watched as she went to the lamp and examined the diamonds underneath the light.

"Are these cubic zirconia's?"

"No," Kyle angrily raised his voice. "That's a five-thousand-dollar bracelet."

"Don't raise your voice at me," Jennifer snapped. "What else did you get me?"

"No, I'm sorry." Kyle went and stood by her. "Jennifer, I'm sorry for everything that happened between us, and I'm also sorry that I wasn't the husband that you wanted. I loved you from the moment I first saw you, and I will love you until the day that I die. I wish things had turned out differently for us, and I could have provided you with everything you ever wanted."

"Aww, that's sweet," Jennifer wrapped her arms around him. "Why don't you spend the night with me?" She smiled. "I can go with you to Atlanta and drop you off."

"Drop me off?" Kyle chuckled. "I got my Corvette."

"If you truly wanted me to forgive you, you would give me the car."

"Are you kidding me?" Kyle pushed her away from him. "You a greedy ass bitch!"

"What did you call me?" Jennifer screamed.

"I can't believe you asked me for my car," Kyle's face turned red with anger. "You made a fool out of me, Jennifer. First, you carried on with Tim behind my back for years. You then had the audacity to throw me out of a house I bought with only the clothes on my back." Kyle ripped the bracelet off her wrist. "I'm not giving you a damn thing!"

"Oh, really," Jennifer shouted. "You're going to pay for this, Kyle Parks!" She went to the fireplace and grabbed her cell phone off the mantel. "I'm calling the police!" She looked down at the phone.

Kyle rushed up to her and pushed her down against the corner of the fireplace's bricks. Jennifer fell to the floor. Blood gushed from a deep laceration on the side of her head as she rolled on her back. She looked up at Kyle and cried. He grabbed a large marble horse statue off the mantle and raised it above his head.

"Please! No," Jennifer begged as she raised her hands in front of her.

Kyle swung the statue at Jennifer's head exactly where the first wound appeared, using all of his strength. He stared into her eyes as he watched her soul leave her lifeless body. Then, suddenly, Jennifer disappeared, and the room faded to black.

"What the hell," Kyle shrieked. "I can't see a thing."

"What did you say, boy?" A voice yelled from behind him.

As Kyle turned, the room suddenly became illuminated by a golden light from the old floor lamp that sat in the corner. A gold upholstered rocking chair sat beside an oak ashtray stand underneath the light. On the chair, with her legs covered with a tulip-quilted patchwork throw, sat his mother. Her head was engulfed in smoke as she puffed on her cigarette and glared at Kyle.

"You've been a naughty boy," She cackled.

"Mama," Kyle shrieked.

"Come here, boy," She squinted as she waved her hand up in the air and fanned the smoke away from her eyes. "My eyesight ain't what it used to be."

Kyle trembled as he slowly walked closer to her.

"I always knew that there was something about you that seemed a little off. Hell, I blamed your piece of shit daddy, and thought that maybe you inherited some of his bad genes, but you make him look like a saint." She snuffed out her cigarette in the ashtray and lit up another one. "So, Clyde was your first kill," She chuckled. "I can't really blame you for that one. He was an evil old bastard. Though I considered killing him myself, I was afraid of getting caught." She glared at Kyle. "You hid behind your nursing career and found victims. Elderly people, people with illnesses, or without families, because you knew no one would question their deaths. Even your own mama, boy," She shouted. "What do you have to say for yourself?"

Kyle lowered his head and cried.

"It's a little too late for that crying nonsense," She yelled. "Be a man for once and say what you did."

Kyle covered his eyes and sobbed.

"Poor little fool, Jennifer," She smirked. "She thought she had a real man." She laughed. "It is no wonder she rekindled her romance with her old college flame."

Kyle dried his tears and lowered his hands as he stared at her.

"Oh, that got a rise out of you," She chuckled. "Jennifer was the only friend you had during your entire life, and tragically, she was the only one to die a violent death." She raised her left eyebrow as she scowled. "Why did you do it, boy?"

"She was going to turn me in," Kyle gruffed.

"Are you that stupid?" She scoffed. "If she had turned you in, she would have gone to jail too." She straightened the throw as she pulled it higher up her torso. "Well, boy, I think I'm ready for a cup of your delicious hot chocolate." She pointed to the other side of the room. "Go get it for me, boy!"

Kyle turned around and saw his mother's gold mug on top of the tea cart against the wall.

"Well, just don't stand there, you stupid boy," She grumbled. "We don't have all night!"

Kyle slowly walked to the tea cart and picked up the mug.

"Chop! Chop!" She yelled. "Run with it!"

Kyle walked quickly to her side and handed her the mug.

She held the mug in front of her and stared into Kyle's eyes. "Why did you do it, Boy?" Her eyes filled up with tears. "Why did you poison me? I had no money and nothing for you to gain. It does not make sense to me how you could do something so cruel to someone who loved you dearly. Throughout my life, I have always put your needs before my own."

"You became a different person after Clyde's death," Kyle whimpered.

"Different," She shrieked. "What was different about me?"

"You became bitter and cruel," Kyle lowered his head. "The way you treated me was cold and distant."

"I became distant and cold towards you because I was afraid of you," She cackled. "What a stupid boy!" She peered at him above the mug. "What happened to my brother? What did you do to your Uncle Don?"

"I didn't do anything to him," Kyle angrily raised his voice.

"Bullcrap," She shouted. "It is rather odd that he died in a recliner with a coffee cup on the ground next to him."

"I didn't have anything to do with it," Kyle shouted. "I liked Uncle Don! Why don't you ever believe me?"

"Oh," She chuckled. "The old temper seems to be coming to the surface now."

Kyle's face turned red with anger as he stared silently at his mother.

"I wonder what the ladies at Betsy's Beauty Shop would have thought about me if they had known the truth about you." She tightened her jaw, and her eyes became filled with disgust. "Every Friday, I would sit in that place for hours and brag about you. Kyle bought a new house. Kyle makes so much money. Kyle bought this fur coat for me," She jeered. "Hell, I raised nothing but a thief and a serial killer!"

Kyle angrily lunged for her throat.

"That's my boy!" She laughed as she disappeared into thin air.

The room went dark once again, and Kyle fell to the ground. "Why?" He shouted. "Whatever you're going to do to me, just do it," He cried. "I can't take any more!"

"Kyle," Cassie shouted as she opened the door and pointed the flashlight directly at his face. "What on earth are you doing in there?"

"Cassie," Kyle squinted as he quickly stood and raised his hand over his eyes. "Is that really you?"

"Of course, it's me," Cassie responded loudly and opened the door wider. "Get out of there."

Kyle briskly went to the door and hugged Cassie.

"What are you doing up here?" Cassie asked.

"There was a loud crash, and then I thought I heard Irma calling out to me."

"Was it a crash like the one we heard yesterday?" Cassie asked as she opened the door directly across the hallway.

"Yes, exactly like that." Kyle looked over Cassie's shoulder as she pointed the flashlight around the room.

"I don't understand what is happening to my Inn," Cassie grumbled. "This never happened before."

"Before?" Kyle blurted out. "You just opened less than three weeks ago."

"Uh?" Cassie nervously grinned. "I know that. I did not experience anything of this kind when renovating the building."

"Well, it's not safe up here, so let's try to find Irma and go back downstairs." Kyle grabbed Cassie's hand. "I'm sorry about the Inn. I know that you have invested a lot of your time and money in this place. It was beautiful, and we can make it that way again if you wish."

"What are you saying, Kyle?" Cassie pointed the light into Kyle's eyes and tucked her hair behind her ears.

Kyle moved away from the light. "Cassie, I would do anything in the world for you. I believe that we were on the right track for a relationship before the women began disappearing, and when all this is finally over, I hope to resume our relationship where we left off."

"Me too, Kyle," Cassie smiled.

"If you want to renovate this place again and make this Inn look like it once did, or even better, I would be happy to invest my money in this place," Kyle grinned. "I would never stay here again, but if this place makes you happy, I will do my best to make you happy."

"Oh, thank you, Kyle," Cassie hugged him tightly. "Nobody ever offered to help me."

"What happened here isn't your fault, so don't listen to Irma," Kyle grinned. "I would love for you to leave this Inn and start a new life with me. We could live wherever you choose and perhaps open a bed and breakfast somewhere else. But I know that you love this place, and that's all that matters."

Cassie gazed into Kyle's eyes and gently caressed his face. "At one time, I did love this place. But, while I would love nothing more than to walk away from here and start my life over, it is too late. So I have no choice but to stay."

"You always have a choice," Kyle held her hand and kissed it softly.

"Soon, you will understand," Cassie nervously grinned as she pulled her hand away.

"So let's find Irma and go back downstairs." Kyle turned away and headed down the hallway.

"Kyle, wait," Cassie shouted.

"What's wrong?" Kyle asked as he stopped and turned around.

"Irma is gone," Cassie pulled a red and green burlap doll out of her pocket.

Kyle rushed over to her and yanked the doll out of Cassie's hand. He rubbed his fingers over Irma's name and cried.

"I promised her that I would protect her," Kyle shouted. "I cannot believe I am so stupid!"

"It's not your fault," Cassie rubbed her hand across Kyle's back. "Let's go downstairs."

"Where did you go?" Rick yelled as Cassie and Kyle exited the stairs and entered the lobby.

He sat down next to the place where he last saw Irma and held the doll tightly in his hand.

"Did you hide the body upstairs?" Rick smirked. "I would feel bad, but she was a little annoying at times."

"Rick," Lavivian shouted as she slapped his leg. "That's not nice."

"Well, there's only four of us left, and you've been with me the entire time. So, it's not me, and it's definitely not you," Rick pointed at Lavivian. "Since Cassie could not lift some of the bodies, it cannot be her." He glared at Kyle. "So that leaves you."

"What?" Kyle shrieked. "It's not me! I would never hurt any of these women." His face became red with anger as he stared at Rick.

"Okay," Cassie shouted. "We need to stick together. Not turn against each other."

"Cassie's right. We need to stop accusing each other and stick together." Lavivian stood up. "It has to be someone from the outside." She pointed at Kyle. "You can see how heartbroken he is over Irma."

Rick tugged at his mother's hand for her to sit back down. "Well, all I have to say," he looked at Kyle. "You better hope that I'm the next victim because if my Mom disappears before me, I will kill you."

"Okay," Lavivian waved her hand into the air. "That's enough!" She glanced at Rick and Kyle. "We were all happy yesterday, hoping for our rescue, and just look at us today." She nervously smiled at Cassie. "Do you think that they're still coming?"

"I hope so," Cassie mumbled.

There was total silence around the fireplace as they waited in horror for their rescue or to find out who would be the next victim.

~ 19 ~

DECEMBER 24

"Wake up," Cassie shouted.

Kyle opened his eyes and looked into Cassie's terrified face. "What's wrong?"

"We got to go now," Cassie grabbed his arm.

Fear fluttered in Kyle's stomach as he glanced around the room. As with the other two floors, the lobby now appeared old, dirty, and abandoned.

"Come on, Kyle," Cassie frantically pulled at his arm.

"I can't believe this," Kyle gasped as he stood up. "Why is this happening?"

"I don't know, but we don't have time to worry about it now." Cassie's hands trembled as she pulled a pink burlap doll from her pocket. "Lavivian has gone missing, and I removed this doll from the tree before Rick found it. He went upstairs to look for her, and now we have to leave before he returns." She looked worriedly into Kyle's eyes. "He believes that you are behind all of this."

"I was right here with you, Rick, and Lavivian, so why is he blaming me?"

"Who knows, but he's going to kill you if he finds you," Cassie said, cramming the doll back inside her pocket, grabbing Kyle's hand, and pulling him behind her as she hurriedly headed towards the kitchen.

"Where are we going?" Kyle asked.

"We are going to the log cabin." Cassie tossed Kyle an army coat that hung from an old coat rack near the kitchen door.

"What?" Kyle shrieked. "I'm not going nowhere near that cabin."

"It is not your choice," Cassie blurted out as she grabbed a black coat from the rack and quickly slipped it on. "There is no way I will leave you here for Rick to kill you."

Putting his arm in the sleeve, Kyle noticed the initials JC written on the jacket's collar. Cassie swung the door open and waited for Kyle to walk out first.

"Are you sure about this?" Kyle's voice nervously cracked. "I'm scared of that place."

"We don't have a choice," Cassie motioned for him to go.

While trudging through the deep snow, Kyle trembled from fear, not from the cold itself, but from what he had seen inside the cabin. He glanced around, hoping Brenda, Jamie, or Sesailee would appear and save him. His terror mounted with every step, and his heart felt uneasy as they got closer to the cabin. Kyle felt something inside of him telling him that he was going to die.

Cassie opened the door and walked inside. "Come on in, Kyle," she chuckled. "You're going to let in all the cold air."

Kyle nervously walked inside, and his eyes widened.

"What's wrong with you?" Cassie asked as she looked at the expression on Kyle's face.

"This isn't the same place," Kyle muttered as he looked around.

The cabin was one large room with no furniture. A small kitchenette was in one corner, and a huge fireplace with a blue shag rug in front filled the opposite wall. The polished, light-colored wood floor shimmered. The little cabin was clean and cozy.

"What did you expect to find here?" Cassie went to the kitchenette and placed a kettle on the stovetop.

"I thought the killer brought me here, but I was mistaken," Kyle said, glancing around the room. "In the place where I went, shelves lined the walls, and a large table was in the center."

"Oh, well, it wasn't here," Cassie chuckled. "Why don't you get a fire started?" She looked at Kyle and smiled.

Kyle started the fire and sat down on top of the blue shag rug.

"I am aware that you are not fond of hot chocolate, but it is all I have," Cassie handed Kyle a mug and sat next to him on the rug. "It will help keep us warm."

"Oh, I don't mind," Kyle grinned as he took a sip of cocoa. "As a matter of fact, it is delicious."

"Good, I'm glad," Cassie smiled.

"Cindy told me that this was your ex-husband's workshop." Kyle ran his hand over the smooth wood floor. "It does not look like the floor of a workshop."

"Cindy doesn't know what she's talking about," Cassie said, her face turning red and irritated. "Years went by, and I didn't even see my sister. So, let's talk about something else. You have always been eager to learn about my past, and I am interested in learning more about yours. So, since we're stuck here, this is the ideal time for us to get to know one another better." Cassie smiled as she watched Kyle sip on his hot chocolate. "You're always talking about yours, but I got a feeling you haven't been completely honest with me."

Kyle's face became pale. He removed his jacket, wiped his forehead with it, and then placed it beside him.

"Are you okay?" Cassie asked. "You don't look so good."

"Not really." Kyle took another sip of his cocoa. "Maybe it's just nerves finally catching up with me. We've been through so much. Lately, it's been overwhelming."

"Yes, I know." Cassie rubbed his forehead and grinned. "So, do you want to go first, or shall I?"

"Man, what's wrong with me?" Kyle held his head.

"Finish your cocoa, and I will make you another." Cassie caressed his face with her hands. "Poor thing, it has to be nerves," she chuckled. "I know that I would be a bundle of nerves too if crazy Rick were looking for me."

Kyle finished up his cocoa and handed Cassie the mug.

Kyle stared into the fire while Cassie made him another hot chocolate. Then, finally, she sat down beside him and handed him the mug.

"I need to tell you something, Cassie." Kyle looked into her eyes. "First of all, I want you to know that I really care for you and would never do anything to hurt you."

"Yes, I know that," Cassie smiled.

"I hope that everything will work out between us, but I am afraid that what I have to say might cause you to think differently about me." Kyle lowered his head.

"I think the world of you, Kyle." Cassie gently ran her fingers through his hair. "Nothing you can say will ever change that."

"I'm afraid that this will," Kyle's voice cracked. "I'm not a very good person."

"Who is," Cassie laughed.

"Seriously, doll," Kyle's eyes filled with tears as he raised his head and looked at Cassie. "I'm a murderer."

"You!" Cassie laughed. "Your scaredy-cat nature would never allow you to do anything like that."

"Cassie, I'm telling you the truth." Kyle rubbed his eyes and shook his head. "What's wrong with me?"

"Okay, so how many people have you killed?" Cassie smirked.

"Over a hundred, at least," Kyle muttered.

"What?" Cassie shrieked. "I'm in shock! How did you do it?"

"Poison," Kyle muttered, looking at Cassie. "Those who are elderly, sick, or without family would be my picks. I would take their money, car, jewelry, and anything else of value." Kyle lowered his head. "Jennifer knew, and after the divorce, she used it as a blackmail tactic."

"So, that's why you never got caught," Cassie smirked. "That was pretty brilliant of you. Did you tell Irma about your past, or did she figure it out using her so-called psychic abilities?"

"She didn't figure it out, and I certainly wouldn't tell her," Kyle grinned. "She wouldn't have been able to handle it."

"Probably not," Cassie chuckled as she stood up and reached for Kyle's empty mug. "I'll make us one more hot chocolate, and then I'll tell you my story."

What the hell is wrong with me? Kyle thought as he tried to focus on the fire. Finally, he pulled his knees up to his chest and rested his head on the top of his arms. A short while later, Cassie sat back down beside him and handed him another cup of hot cocoa.

"Are you okay?" Cassie held her hand against Kyle's forehead. "You feel cold."

"I'm freezing," Kyle groaned, wrapping his hands around the hot mug.

Cassie stood back up and placed a couple more logs on the fire. She then pulled out a blanket from the cabinet and draped it across Kyle's back.

"That should warm you up," Cassie smiled and sat back down. "I think someone was fibbing about not liking hot chocolate," She chuckled as he sat down the empty mug.

"I wonder why Jamie, Sesailee, and Brenda never came back." Kyle laid down on the rug and rested his head on the jacket. "I hope you do not mind, but I am extremely dizzy." He rubbed his hands over his face. "I don't know what is wrong with me."

"No, I don't mind. In fact, I am about to tell you something you may want to take lying down anyway," Cassie chuckled.

"It can't be that bad." Kyle grinned. "It could not possibly be worse than mine."

"I wouldn't be too sure about that!" Cassie tucked her hair behind her ears and gazed at the fireplace.

As Kyle looked into Cassie's beautiful espresso-colored eyes, he knew she was deep in thought.

"Don't be afraid." Kyle reached out and rubbed Cassie's arm. "I promise not to judge you, just as you did not judge me."

"Okay, if you're sure," Cassie looked at Kyle.

"I can't wait to hear it," Kyle grinned.

"Here's my story. I'm from Ohio and was married before. I met him through my sister, Cindy. We were so excited to get married and move to Tennessee. We lived in a small house in Chattanooga, and I worked in a restaurant close to home. He bought this property without telling me, but he knew I wanted my own bed and breakfast. At the time, I thought he was trying to make me happy, but he really wanted to keep me busy."

Kyle watched Cassie's face turn bitter as she talked about purchasing the Inn.

"The first time we drove up here, I thought he had purchased the entire mountain. The only thing visible was a dirt road. Then, finally, he drove up the tree-lined graveled driveway to an old rundown Victorian house. I can still recall his exact words, so here is your dream, honey." Cassie's eyes burned with anger. "Kyle, this place was hideous."

Kyle rubbed his eyes and tried to focus while he smiled.

"Within six months, he had this log cabin built. Next, my husband and I hired a man that we met while living in Chattanooga to help renovate the Inn. His name was Tony. As part of my daily routine, I met Tony and his crew next door and worked throughout the day. The plan was for my husband to retire and assist me with the Inn once the business had become established. Everything was coming together until he had to ruin it," She angrily looked at Kyle. "Are you listening to me?"

"Yes, doll," Kyle opened his eyes and grabbed his chest. "I'm having a hard time breathing."

"Oh," Cassie felt Kyle's chest. "You'll be fine."

"What happened with your husband?" Kyle muttered.

"I discovered that he was cheating on me since the day we were married," Cassie grumbled. "Can you imagine how I felt learning that my entire marriage was a lie?"

"No, I can't," Kyle murmured as he gasped for air and closed his eyes.

"Kyle," Cassie shouted. "Pay attention! I need you to listen to me!"

Kyle opened his eyes and looked at Cassie.

"My husband stayed away from home months at a time. This particular time, he was gone for almost six months. By the time he returned, Tony and his crew had completed most of the work on the Inn. Since they spent sixteen hours a day at the Inn, they each took a room on the third floor. Everything was perfect and ahead of schedule until my husband came home." Cassie patted Kyle's chest and looked into his eyes. "Are you still with me?"

"Yes," Kyle murmured.

"When he went inside the log cabin, I found his book full of phone numbers hidden inside of his truck. I confronted him with it, and he became irate. We argued for hours, and he accused me of having an affair with Tony. I finally had enough and went back to the Inn. He sat in front of this very fireplace and drank whiskey the rest of the day."

Cassie stood up, went to the cabinet, and pulled out a large black bag. Kyle noticed the bag and slowly sat up.

"What is that?" Kyle stared at Cassie in confusion as she approached him.

"In this bag, my piece of shit husband stuffed Tony's body," Cassie replied calmly.

"What," Kyle shrieked.

"That night, in a drunken rage, he went inside the Inn and murdered Tony." Cassie's temper sparked as she threw the bag towards Kyle. "The black bag you saw out in the snow when I was in your room that day. The one that you were too scared to mention. Well, that's the bag." Cassie squatted down before him. "My husband's name was John. He drove a blue eighteen-wheeler, and he's the one that led you here."

"What?" Kyle muttered. "I don't understand."

"John stabbed Tony and stuffed his body inside of that bag. I can still hear that stupid song he whistled as he walked down the hallway and carried Tony's lifeless body to this log cabin. John placed Tony on the floor and chopped him into pieces with an ax. In fact, John's old hunting jacket, the one I let you wear, lies in the same spot where he butchered him."

"Where is he?" Kyle scooted away from Cassie and trembled with fear.

"Oh, you don't have to worry about him," Cassie chuckled. "That night, John passed out in front of the fireplace, and I did the same to him as he did Tony."

"How can that be?" Kyle cried and pointed towards the door. "He was there that night! I saw him!"

"You thought it was Rick! Why are you acting like a sniffling coward after all of the things you have done?" Cassie angrily shouted. "Your patients didn't deserve to die. You killed for greed. John deserved what he got." She stood up and went in front of the fireplace. "Tony was a true friend, and John took him away from me." She glared into the fire. "The next day, the workers inquired about Tony's disappearance, and I pretended that I did not know what happened to him. They agreed to stay and finish the work. Finally, the moment I had waited for arrived. The grand opening of my beautiful Inn." She grabbed something from the top of the mantel and threw it to Kyle.

Kyle picked up the object, and his eyes widened as he held the silver bracelet in his hand.

"I carefully selected the guests from John's little black book and invited them to stay here for a week at my expense. I even placed a couple of them on my payroll." Cassie pointed at the bracelet. "There was a page in John's book that contained only his favorites to which he gave a bracelet. He gave them a cheap little sterling silver bracelet with *My Honeybee* engraved on the bar. Just like the one your little best friend Irma wore," Cassie shouted angrily. "The only thing that I didn't plan was for a couple of them to invite their sister, daughter, husband, and mother-in-law!" She grabbed a burlap doll from off the mantel and threw it at Kyle. "But I didn't let that stop me!"

Kyle trembled when he read Rick's name embroidered on the green burlap doll's chest. He felt frightened and knew he had to leave. Kyle attempted to stand but became dizzy and lost his balance. He fell back to the ground.

"I don't think you're going anywhere," Cassie laughed as she pulled the pink burlap doll out of her pocket and threw it into the fire. "The only thing that I don't understand is the meaning of those stupid dolls and who kept hanging them on the tree." As Kyle gasped for breath lying on his back, she turned and walked to the cabinet. "Well, I guess that doesn't matter anymore."

Cassie went back and stood at Kyle's side.

"Open your eyes, Kyle," Cassie shouted and tossed a magazine on top of his chest.

Kyle was mute with horror as he opened his eyes and looked up at Cassie. She wore a red and black plaided shirt with her long brunette hair tucked inside a black cap on her head. He picked up the magazine and held it in front of him.

Cassie knelt beside him and had an ax by her side. "Kyle, I knew what you did from the very first day that you arrived. I'm the one that went through your bags, and I found the poison that you used to kill your patients."

Kyle recognized the cover of Loretta's magazine, and tears ran down his face as he read the date. "How is that possible? Why, Cassie?" He muttered as he closed his eyes.

Cassie gently ran her fingers through Kyle's hair. "The way it occurs does not make sense to me, but I know why it occurs. You're a bad man, Kyle Parks! To put it another way, it wasn't a wrong turn, and you did not end up here by accident. Fate led you here! Fate and a blue eighteen-wheeler," She chuckled. "So I thought it would be appropriate for you to die in the same manner as your patients."

Tears ran down Kyle's face as he struggled to breathe.

Cassie lovingly kissed his forehead. "I am sorry because I really liked you. Maybe we can be together in your next life."

Kyle opened his eyes and looked at Cassie as he drew his last breath.

Cassie brushed her hand over Kyle's eyes to close them. Then, she picked up the green burlap doll and threw it into the fire. As she opened the door, Cassie turned and took one last look at Kyle.

"What remains of my heart has been broken by you, Kyle Parks." A tear ran down Cassie's cheek as she walked out and closed the door.

"Well, look at this, Deniese," Charlie chuckled as he stood at Kyle's feet.

"Oh, I brought him something!" Deniese placed a black burlap doll on top of Kyle's chest.

"That's the perfect touch," Charlie smirked.

"It's the color of his heart," Deniese grinned.

"I knew those dolls would be good for something one day." Charlie looked at Deniese and smiled.

"They're perfect," Deniese giggled as she looked at Kyle.

"Well, Deniese, it looks like karma can be a real bitch!"

"It sure does, Charlie!" Deniese looked at Kyle as they laughed. "It sure does!"

~ 20 ~

CHRISTMAS DAY

Brenda sat inside her red Lexus, her eyes fixed on the Inn in front of her as she waited for everyone to arrive. She watched as the broken oval sign hanging from the tattered green post struggled to remain upright. Reading the letters on the sign was impossible because it was so faded.

As Brenda continued to gaze upon the dilapidated sign, she noticed the boarded-up windows and door on the large three-story Victorian house. The once grand structure now appeared abandoned and forgotten, and the years of neglect had taken its toll, leaving only a shell of its former self.

"What in the hell were you doing here, Kyle?" She murmured, staring at the porch window that she looked in between the boards the other day. "Where were you?"

She glanced at the forest surrounding the property and noticed the log cabin. "That's odd." Then, suddenly, Brenda saw something in the window. "Oh, my God," She shrieked. "Is that Kyle?"

Brenda jumped up in the seat and screamed when she heard a horn behind her. She quickly looked into her rearview mirror and saw Jamie and Sesailee.

Brenda got out of the car and chuckled. "You scared the hell out of me," She shouted as they opened the car doors.

"I know," Jamie laughed. "What were you looking at?"

"At that log cabin," Brenda pointed. "I thought I saw someone standing in the window."

Sesailee stared at the cabin for a few seconds and then looked at Brenda. "I don't see anything."

A large white pickup truck quickly pulled up behind Jamie's car. It was the sheriff of Shivered, RD Blevins.

"Hello, ladies," RD shouted as he exited the truck and walked towards them. RD was a good-looking man with a grayish goatee and always wore a white cowboy hat.

"I'm sorry that we had to bother you on Christmas Day, Sheriff," Brenda apologized as she shook his hand.

"It's no bother," RD smiled.

"A little more than two weeks ago, I met this man at Jamie's gas station, Kyle Parks. The man acted strangely, but he seemed to be a nice man." Brenda looked at Jamie and Sesailee. "Don't you think so?"

"Well, if you call a man with stolen credit cards nice," Jamie laughed.

"What?" Brenda shrieked.

"We'll get to that in a minute," RD quickly interrupted. "What made you look for him?"

"Kyle and I had agreed to meet at Strittmatter Inn, but he never showed up."

"He acted very nervous and said that he had to be in Atlanta," Sesailee remarked.

"Yes, we were both going there, and that's why I thought it was odd when he never showed up at the Inn," Brenda explained.

"Yesterday, Jamie and I decided to look for him, so we drove up the mountain as far as we could. On the way back, we stopped here, and spotted Kyle's car parked behind the house. It was getting dark, and we were scared to search the property by ourselves. It felt like someone was watching us," Sesailee said, looking at Jamie. "Didn't it?"

"It sure did," Jamie replied.

"That's when I called you." Brenda nervously looked down. "I feel terrible because I have been here previously but have never driven to the back."

"I wouldn't feel too bad," RD patted Brenda on the back. "Kyle Parks is a wanted man. He murdered his ex-wife Jennifer right before he disappeared."

"Oh, my God," Brenda shrieked.

"I told you something didn't add up," Jamie shook her head with disgust. "The red Corvette and his credit cards had the name Charlie Hanks on them."

"I'm sure he has a lot of secrets," Sesailee frowned. "Just think, we wasted our time worried about a murderer."

"I wouldn't consider it a waste of time," RD grinned at Sesailee. "You're helping a lot of people, especially Jennifer's husband, Tim."

Sesailee smiled.

"Let's go to the back and look at the car." RD looked worriedly at the log cabin as they walked behind the Inn.

"See," Jamie pointed at the license plates. "Charlie."

RD opened the driver's door and looked inside. An unopened bag of almonds and a bottle of frappuccino were in a white plastic bag located on the front seat. He also found the business card that Jamie gave Kyle for Strittmatter Inn. He then went to the back of the vehicle and discovered that the trunk was empty.

RD glared towards the Inn. "He might be in there."

"Why would he go inside?" Brenda asked. "Obviously, this Inn had been abandoned for some time."

RD looked worriedly at the three women. "Let's go back to the front."

"Are we going to check the rest of the property?" Brenda asked as they walked past the porch.

"Yes, but for now, I would prefer everyone remain by the vehicles while I search the building alone." RD motioned for them to go to the back of the car. "Stay together, please, and don't leave this area. I'll explain when I get back."

They watched as RD busted one of the nailed boards across the entrance, kicked the door open, and stepped inside.

"Do you think that he's in there?" Sesailee asked.

"He might be," Brenda nervously folded her arms across her chest. "Kyle seemed like a nice guy. I can't believe that he's a murderer."

"It's good that he didn't go to Strittmatter Inn that night," Jamie hugged Brenda. "You could have been one of his victims."

After a while, RD came out of the Inn. As he approached the three women, he had a troubled expression on his face.

"What's wrong?" Sesailee asked.

"On the third floor, I found his clothes inside an old dresser that he unpacked from his bags." RD turned away from the women and looked towards the Inn. "Why on earth would he do that?"

"That's weird," Jamie remarked. "If he was on the run, why wouldn't he leave the next day after the storm? That doesn't make any sense. The roads remained open throughout the storm, and it was not as bad as predicted."

"The snow barely covered the ground," Sesailee quickly added. "Even the phone service was restored that morning."

"So, where is he?" Brenda nervously glanced towards the Inn. "Are you sure that he wasn't hiding somewhere inside?"

"No, he's definitely not in there," RD replied, turning back and facing the women. "I searched every room."

"He never would have left his Corvette behind," Jamie commented. "The old manther was proud of that car." She looked at Sesailee and grinned.

"Yes, he was," Sesailee giggled.

"Let's go take a look in there," RD pointed towards the log cabin.

"I thought I saw someone inside earlier," Brenda said, pointing toward the cabin. "It looked like someone was standing in front of the window."

"If it was him, he's gone by now," RD stated.

Brenda, Jamie, and Sesailee followed closely behind RD as he headed toward the cabin.

"That's an odd place for a pond," Brenda muttered as something sparkled beside the water and caught her eye. Brenda reached down and picked it up.

"What is it?" Sesailee asked.

"It's a silver bracelet with the words, My Honeybee, engraved on it," Brenda chuckled. "That looks like a bracelet that I had years ago."

RD opened the door to the cabin, and they went inside. A long butcher's table stood in the center of the small room. Shelves on both sides of a fireplace lined the walls, filled with bottles and plastic storage containers.

"Oh, Jesus," Brenda shrieked. "This place stinks!"

RD walked slowly around the room while the three ladies waited by the door.

"What is that?" Jamie pointed towards the table.

"What the hell?" RD picked up the item and walked over to them. He held up a black burlap doll with Kyle's name embroidered across the chest in dark gray.

"What is that?" Brenda shrieked.

"That looks like the dolls he threw away by the gas pumps that night," Jamie gasped.

"Ladies, I think we should leave now." RD glanced around the room as he shoved the doll into his pocket. "I need to make a few calls and get some people out here to help investigate this," he said. They walked out, and RD closed the door behind him. "I need to tell you something about this place."

"What is it?" Jamie asked.

"Do you know the story behind this Inn?" RD looked at Brenda. "I'm sure that you have heard the rumor around town."

"Oh, my God," Brenda shrieked. "Is this the place?"

"Yes," RD replied, pointing towards the Inn. "That was Cassandra's Country Inn. Cassie Cooper owned this place with her husband, John. Cassie murdered all of her guests in that log cabin with an ax. The investigation only led to the discovery of one body in the pond, and her name was Irma Rios. Unfortunately, they could not locate the bodies of the other individuals, but they did find their personal belongings that they left inside the Inn. Cassie also saved a piece of their jewelry that the investigators believed John gave them. I think it was a bracelet of some sort."

Brenda's stomach turned as she clutched the bracelet tightly in her hand.

"The circumstances around John and Cassie's disappearances are still unknown. Now, that's the facts of this case." RD pointed at the log cabin. "Rumor has it that Cassie caught her husband cheating and killed him with an ax. She then invited all the women he had an affair with and butchered them. Nobody knows what happened to Cassie, but some believe that she still roams this place looking for her next victim. They say if you come here at night, you can still see her shadow swinging the ax in the window of the log cabin."

"Oh, that's it," Jamie shrieked. "We're out of here!" Grabbing Sesailee by the arm, she hurried towards her car.

"Wait for me," Brenda shouted, walking briskly behind them.

"Don't get scared," RD chuckled as he rushed over to them. "The story is just a rumor, and it is rather absurd when you think about it."

"That's okay! Absurd or not! I'm never coming back to this place!" Jamie yelled as she got into her car.

"Oh, my God," Sesailee shrieked as she jumped into the passenger seat. "Let's go, Jamie!"

Brenda opened the car door and stopped, looking at RD, and asked, "When did the murders take place?"

"The grand opening of the Inn and the murders took place in the same year as the big snowstorm. 1976," RD said as he climbed into his truck.

"1976," Brenda shrieked, opening her hand and looking at the bracelet. "Oh, hell no!" She threw it towards the Inn. "Jamie, Sesailee, I'm following you!" Brenda hopped into her car, and they drove away.

~ 21 ~

ONE YEAR LATER

One year later, it was less than three weeks until Christmas, and the news predicted a heavy snowstorm for the area that evening. A thin layer of snow covered the ground as Gail Norris Terry drove through Chattanooga, Tennessee.

Gail's cell phone rang, and she quickly picked it up.

"Hello," Gail chirped.

"Where are you?"

"I'm in Chattanooga," Gail grinned. "Are you anxious to see me?"

"Of course, baby," the man replied. "My bed is getting cold without you."

"I should be in Tampa with you tomorrow night. Unfortunately, it's getting late, and I'll have to find someplace to spend the night," Gail sighed.

"Did you get the money?"

"We'll never have to worry about money again in our life," Gail giggled.

"Okay, then, I'll see you tomorrow," he made a couple of kissing sounds. "Bye, baby. I love you."

Gail smiled as she hung up the phone and looked into the rearview mirror. "Girl, of course, he loves you. You just embezzled millions." She grabbed her lipstick from the center console and retouched her lips. She gazed at herself in the mirror and smiled. "Who wouldn't love you? You're gorgeous!"

A loud horn startled Gail, and she quickly looked away from the mirror. Her heart raced when she saw a blue eighteen-wheeler directly in front of her. She jerked the steering wheel towards the right and swerved back into her lane. Her black Porsche Carrera Cabriolet slid across the slick pavement from side to side until she finally regained control. The driver of the eighteen-wheeler blasted the horn as he drove past.

"Asshole," Gail angrily shouted and rubbed her chest. "It's okay. Calm down." She looked across the guardrail and down the mountainside's steep slope. Then, suddenly, the temperature plummeted, and the snow fell heavily. "Where in the hell am I?"

A sudden gust of wind caused the car to swerve out of the lane. She gripped the steering wheel tightly and reduced her speed to a crawl. "This can't be happening?" Gail panicked as she stared out of the foggy windshield at the narrow road ahead that twisted up the mountain. An icy shiver ran down her spine. "Damn, it's freezing in here," she grumbled, turning up the heat and nervously lighting a cigarette. The heavy snow quickly blanketed the ground. Then, in the distance, a bright glow captured her attention. "Please, let that be a gas station," she muttered as she slowly drove towards it. Large, bold red letters appeared on the lighted sign: J.H. Pitt Stop.

"Oh, thank God," Gail exclaimed with relief as she approached the gas station. As she drew nearer, she saw a large red boulder situated by the road, positioned between two posts. Intrigued, Gail looked up and noticed the sign above her. It read: Brenda's Red Rock Café.

Gail smiled and looked into the rearview mirror. "You're going to be just fine, you gorgeous girl," she muttered, winking at herself and tucking her long red hair behind her ear as she pulled up to the gas pumps.

~ 22 ~

FROM THE AUTHOR

Dear Reader,

If you've made it to this page, then you've braved the storm, and felt the icy grip of *Shivered*.

This story was born from a fascination with fate—the idea that no matter how far we run, our past always finds us. Wrapped in the chilling embrace of a relentless winter storm, *Shivered Spirits* explores the ghosts we create, the sins we try to forget, and the consequences we can't escape.

Thank you for stepping into the snow-drenched nightmare of *Shivered*. I hope it left you breathless, unsettled, and glancing a little longer into your own rearview mirror.

Want more? Let's stay connected!

Follow me on Facebook:

Author Carol A Campbell - Ghost Stories

Stay warm. And maybe—just maybe—think twice before your next cup of cocoa.

Until next time,

Carol A Campbell